I0562838

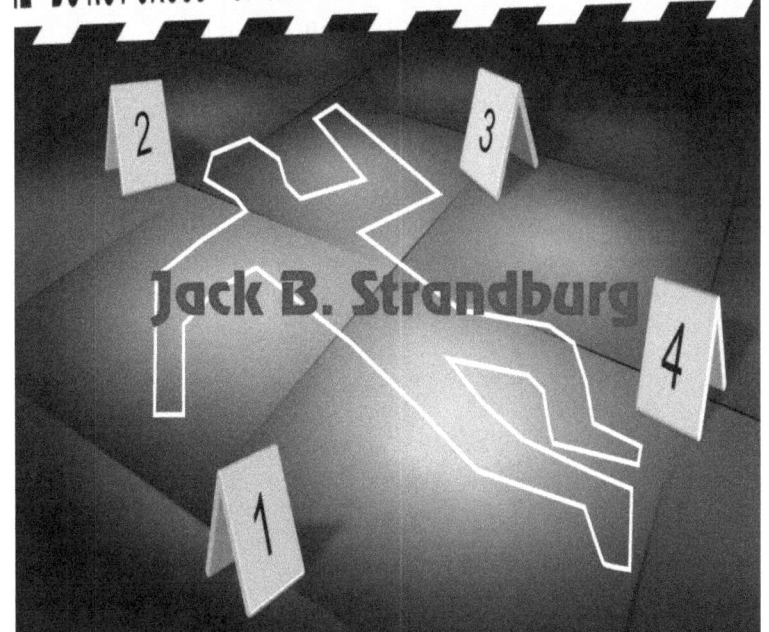

A Head
in the Game

CRIME SCENE - DO NOT CROSS · CRIME SCENE - DO NOT CROSS · CRIME SCENE - DO

Jack B. Strandburg

ALL RIGHTS RESERVED

No part of this book may be reproduced or
transmitted in any form or by any means, electronic or
mechanical, including photocopying, recording, or by any
information storage and retrieval system, without
permission in writing from the author, except in the case of
brief quotations embodied in reviews.

Publisher's Note:

This is a work of fiction. All names, characters,
places, and events are the work of the author's imagination.

Any resemblance to real persons, places, or events
is coincidental.

Solstice Publishing - www.solsticepublishing.com

Copyright 2017 Jack Strandburg

A Head In The Game
Jack B. Strandburg

Chapter One

August 16, 2005

When Chicago Homicide Inspector Aaron Randall arrived at the Tremont Inn at Lazy Willow and Delmont Avenue in Harwood Heights, Illinois, in response to a homicide, memories of his childhood flooded like a tidal wave. Three blocks away, he had attended Union Ridge Elementary. Two miles in the opposite direction was the modest two-story home where he lived until he was ten years old. The events compelling his family to relocate were something he would rather forget.

He was seven the first time their home was burglarized. Thankfully, his parents were working while he was in school. Less than a year later, he sat in a hospital emergency room with his mother, while his father was treated for injuries suffered during a home invasion by three men acting out an initiation from a gang, infiltrating a neighborhood once considered safe.

His father cooperated with the intruders, but they seemed more interested in inflicting harm on an innocent man than with the small amount of cash and jewelry they stole from the house. It required fifteen stitches to close the cuts on his head and face.

The Tremont Inn, a one-story, twenty-eight-room motel, showed the effects of the deterioration of the neighborhood, and was now a place where couples searched for love "in all the wrong places." The walls bled yellow with age and neglect, suggesting the motel's days were numbered.

Today, the neighborhood was on the list of places to avoid when visiting Chicagoland. It was tragic to see how years of hard work and community cooperation took relatively little time to destroy.

Gang activity was evident throughout the streets. One block west, the sign above the door to Angelo's Pizza, once a popular hangout with teenagers on weekends, was missing the 'e' and 's' in Angelo's and the 'a' in Pizza, and now read 'Anglo Pizz.'

Aaron shook his head to clear his mind of sadder times, got out of his car, and retrieved his jacket from the passenger seat. He closed the door and flexed his shoulders to free the sweat-soaked shirt from his back. Brushing the back of his hand across his forehead to wipe away the perspiration, he wrinkled his nose. The air smelled like a neglected public toilet.

Chicago was in the midst of a drought, with no precipitation in the ten-day forecast. Both the temperature and humidity topped ninety degrees. Hard winters were normal in Chicago, but summers can often be equally unbearable.

Aaron reluctantly donned his jacket and walked across the parking lot.

Yellow tape labeled, "CRIME SCENE DO NOT CROSS," stretched across a wooden blockade to designate the outer perimeter. Two uniformed officers stood like sentries, preventing a few curious bystanders from invading the crime scene. Two squad cars, a CSI van, and the coroner's wagon were parked in front of the motel, next to a gold, 2005 Mercedes CLK55 AMG Cabriolet.

Sergeant Sam Richards, a colleague and close friend whom Aaron worked with on scores of cases over the years, stood on the sidewalk outside Room #25, studying a notepad.

Sam stood five-feet seven, with bushy eyebrows and black hair. He blamed the few extra pounds he carried around his middle on his wife's cooking. He wore a cream-colored sport jacket and dark green pants. His light brown shirt was buttoned to the top, with a dark green tie drawn into a perfect knot. A straw hat with a tan and black-checkered band, his trademark apparel, sat atop his head. Despite a heat-index exceeding one-hundred, he appeared cooler than an old man sitting in a bathtub of ice.

Aaron walked up to Sam and lightly slapped him on the shoulder.

Sam raised his head then glanced at his watch. "Running a little late, aren't we? How was your evening?"

"Fell asleep on the recliner watching a movie, thanks for asking," Aaron said. "I knew you'd have things under control here, and as for being late, since when does this job follow a nine-to-five schedule? Besides, dead is dead."

"Not another rerun I hope," Sam said. Aaron's proclivity to watch a movie multiple times was public knowledge at the precinct. "What was it, *French Connection, Seven-Ups*, or the *Sound of Music*?"

"*Sound of Music*? Sorry, not my genre of choice. It was *Jaws*. The last thing I remember, Roy Scheider was shoveling bait into the water when the shark poked its head out to say hello. The next thing I knew, a ringing phone interrupted my sleep."

"Did the shark eat Roy this time?"

"I didn't make it that far, and I watch television to be entertained, not to play detective. I get enough of that on the job."

"Yeah, the nine-to-five that's never nine-to-five," Sam said with a nod.

"Right. What time did you get here, Sam?"

"About an hour ago. Ident's already photographed and sketched the crime scene. The coroner got here fifteen minutes ago." He waved his hand in a circle. "Not exactly a prime spot for a vacation, is it? I bet it's hard to believe you grew up in this neighborhood."

"It does look a lot different," Aaron agreed. "It would be nice if crime took a vacation, at least until it cooled off."

"Now, what would you do with all that free time?"

"I don't know, visit a Caribbean island, sit on the beach, watch the waves, and drink tequila. My second option is to sit on my apartment balcony with a case of Miller Lite."

"It would take you six months to finish a case of beer, Aaron."

"With the right motivation, I'd be willing to adjust my consumption. So, what do we have here?"

"The victim is inside room twenty-five. His name is Jared Prescott. Looks like a gunshot wound to the chest. So far, what we know is…"

"Jared Prescott?" Aaron interrupted, unable to keep the surprise out of his voice.

"Right, do you know him?"

"Not personally, but a Jared Prescott was an All-American running back for Northwestern in the nineties. Most considered him a lock to win the Heisman, and he probably would have if raw talent was the only criteria, but his character came in question. Apparently, he liked the nightlife and had a drinking problem. Personally, I think the media blew it out of proportion, but that's nothing new with sports. You know how they are when they get hold of something juicy, especially if they see a chance to tarnish someone's reputation. Despite the baggage, experts still predicted him to be drafted number one after his senior year, but he blew out his knee in the National Championship game against Stanford."

"Hell of a way to start a New Year," Sam said.

"That's for sure. Anyway, the team owners were willing to deal with the character issues, but after the injury, nobody would touch him. After he recovered, he started drinking and wrecked his car. He finally got professional help and cleaned up his act. If this is the same guy, I wasn't aware he still lived in the area."

Sam thumbed through his notebook. "According to his driver's license he was thirty-seven, so the timeline fits." He pointed to the room. "Want to take a look?"

"Let's go," Aaron said, following Sam into Room twenty-five.

A queen-size bed sat to the left, with a nightstand and green table lamp on the opposite side of the door. A thirty-six-inch Samsung TV rested on a stand next to a three-drawer mahogany dresser, flanked by a shelf and rods to hang clothing. A small landscape painting hung crooked on the wall above the TV. The bathroom, hidden from view, was on the opposite end of the room. The bedspread sat crumpled on the floor; the sheets piled at the foot of the bed. A member of the CSI team was dusting for fingerprints. The victim lay prone on the floor in the middle of the room, covered with a white sheet.

"Pretty bare bones room," Aaron observed.

"For sure," Sam replied. "Not even a Bible in the nightstand."

"I thought those were standard in motel rooms."

Sam laughed. "Maybe the killer felt guilty and took it with him when he left."

"Maybe. Any traces of bodily fluid on the sheets?" Aaron asked.

"We'll pack them up and send to the lab," Sam replied. There's no indication of a struggle or any defensive wounds on the victim.

"Anything in the drawers?"

"Empty."

Aaron looked around the room. "The victim and whoever was with him couldn't choose a more out-of-the-way place to meet," he said, pausing when he noticed a hole in the wall just inside the door. "What's that?"

"We figured the shooter either missed the target or fired a warning shot. The slug was pulled and bagged for ballistics," Sam said.

"Good, let's take a look at the victim."

Aaron donned a pair of plastic white gloves, squatted over the body, and drew back the sheet. The victim lay on his back with his head tilted to the left. A red spot saturated the white shirt.

"Yeah, this looks like the Prescott I knew." He put two fingers on the victim's chin and rotated the head to the right, exposing a gash on the neck. "What do you make of this, Sam?"

Sam squatted and examined the wound. "I don't know. I expect the hole in his chest did the job. Could be a signature of some kind."

"Maybe," Aaron agreed. He dragged the sheet to the victim's waist. A charcoal gray suit jacket lay open, exposing an Armani label.

"Nice suit," Aaron said. *I could probably buy five suits and twenty ties for what this cost.* He covered the body and stood.

"They found four hundred dollars and an American Express card in his wallet," Sam said. "Other than his driver's license, he had a membership card to Park Valley Country Club and an ID tag inside his suit jacket. He was Vice President for ChemPhen Pharmaceuticals. We bagged and tagged his personal possessions, which included his cellphone and Rolex watch."

"Rolex, four hundred dollars, credit card—so much for robbery as a motive," Aaron said.

"ChemPhen is in the news a lot, and I understand Park Valley is pretty exclusive," Sam said.

"I wouldn't know," Aaron said. "It's stuffy in here. Let's go outside."

Outside, Sam gestured to the Mercedes. "This is the victim's car. The inside is spotless. Except for the absence of a new car smell, it could have come straight from the showroom. How much do you think it set him back?"

"Beats me," Aaron replied. "More than I can ever afford, that's for sure."

"Armani suit, Rolex watch, a new Mercedes, ChemPhen must pay their executives quite well," Sam said.

"No question," Aaron agreed, "but flaunting wealth is sometimes like waving a red flag, asking for trouble."

"It does look like this was personal, that's for sure," Sam said, and then indicated a deep scratch on the car running from the middle of the driver's door to the gas tank. "Case in point."

"Talk about adding insult to injury," Aaron said. "Someone was either pissed off, or this and the mark on the victim's neck would support the signature theory." He opened the driver door of the Mercedes.

A walnut console with a 5-speed automatic with a manual mode separated the driver and passenger seats. A car phone sat in a cradle below the controls for air, heat, radio, and CD player, with a state-of-the-art dashboard, equipped with a GPS and monitor.

"Mapquest at the touch of a button," Aaron said.

"A ride like this would be a big temptation to steal," Sam said.

"Except it's too easy to spot, let alone having to read the user's manual on how to start the thing. Did fingerprinting dust yet?"

"Yeah. The garage is sending a tow truck to haul it downtown."

Aaron shut the car door and peeled off the plastic gloves. "Before long, these luxury cars will drive themselves. I know a few people who would be comfortable living in this car. Did anyone question the guests?"

"Yes, three other rooms were occupied, all on this side. Everyone claimed to be in their rooms all night, didn't hear a thing."

"Big surprise. Who found the body?"

"The maid, Lucia Ramirez, found him during her morning rounds and notified the manager, Pat Montgomery, who called 911. He said the key to the room is missing. We took her statement and sent her home."

"Was Montgomery working last night?"

"No, but I asked him to call in the night clerk. I figured you'd want to talk to him as soon as possible."

"You know me well, Sam."

Aaron believed time fogged the memory, especially for people working nights. Potentially critical details can quickly fade, and second-hand information was usually unreliable at best.

Sam pointed behind Aaron. "This might be him."

Aaron turned to see a young man approaching with an officer.

"Inspector, this is Jimmy Evans," the officer said. "He works the night shift."

"Thank you," Aaron said. "Mr. Evans, I'm Inspector Randall, this is Sergeant Richards. Is there somewhere we can talk in private?"

Evans jerked a thumb over his shoulder. "There's a room in the office."

Aaron and Sam followed Evans into a vacant office behind the counter in the motel lobby. Sam closed the door and remained standing. Evans sat on a sofa. Aaron grabbed a chair, put his left foot on the seat, and rested his left forearm on his knee.

Jimmy Evans was thin with a freckled face and curly red hair, and didn't look older than a high school sophomore. A circular earring rested in his left ear lobe, and his wrinkled tank top was decorated with a multicolored dragon design. His small eyes blinked rapidly as he squirmed in the chair.

"Mr. Evans, we know you probably haven't slept much, so we'll make this as quick as possible."

Evans shrugged. "It's okay. I never go right to bed after work anyway."

"Good. Why don't you tell us about last night? Who did you see, who rented rooms, anything unusual, in short, don't leave out any details regardless of how trivial you might think they are."

"Yeah, okay... I mean yes, sir," Evans said, his Adams apple bobbing in his throat.

"Relax, take your time."

Evans forced a smile and exhaled. "Okay, I had only one customer last night, a woman. She came in at eight-thirty. She had on a red, white, and blue scarf, and wore huge sunglasses, like she was a celebrity. She was... well... you know, hot."

"Sure," Aaron said. "How certain are you of the time?"

"Positive. A rerun of Fresh Prince was just coming on TV. It's my favorite show."

Aaron glanced at Sam and suppressed a smile.

"She filled out the form with her name and address, and asked for room twenty-five."

"Did she say why she wanted that specific room?"

"No, and I didn't ask. Sorry."

"That's all right, please continue," Aaron said.

A knock on the door interrupted the conversation. Sam opened the door, and a heavyset bald man handed him a sheet of paper. "Here's the room contract."

Sam took the paper and shut the door. "That was Montgomery, the motel manager," he said, handing Aaron the paper.

"Excuse me for a moment," Aaron said to Evans, and then scanned the document.

"Nancy Edmunds, two twenty-one Pleasant Creek Drive, Chicago, Illinois. I see she didn't write down vehicle information or a license number."

"No, sir," Evans said. "She said a friend dropped her off and would be back in the morning to pick her up. She paid cash for the room." His face turned a shade of red. "Actually, the fact she asked for one night and had no car or bags made me think she was… well… a hooker."

"I see. How long have you worked here, Mr. Evans?" Aaron asked.

"About six months."

"Have you ever seen this woman before?"

"No, sir."

"Did you see her after she checked in?"

"No, sir. After I gave her the key, she left the office, and I didn't see her after that. I left when Mr. Montgomery arrived at six-thirty, and she hadn't checked out yet."

"So, it was slow last night," Aaron said.

"Yes, sir, but that's not unusual."

"You must get bored just sitting in the office."

"It isn't bad. I watch TV or listen to music when it's not busy. It's not the greatest job in the world, but I make enough to get by."

"Not something you'd want to make a career of, I suspect."

Evans laughed. "No, sir, not a chance. I plan to go to college, maybe law school."

Aaron looked at Evans' t-shirt and earrings. He didn't impress him as the lawyer type. "So you sat here for eight hours watching TV and listening to music?"

"Yes, sir."

"And you heard nothing out of the ordinary, like… say… a gunshot?"

Evans's mouth fell open. "Absolutely not, sir. I would have called the police."

Aaron studied Evans' face for a few moments, and then put his foot on the floor. "Okay, that's all for now. We'll contact you if we have any more questions."

Evans left the room, and after Sam closed the door, he turned to Aaron. "What was that all about?"

"A guy his age with nothing to do but watch reruns and thought the woman was a hooker. I think he might be tempted to check things out."

"So, you think he knows more than he told us?"

"It's hard to say, but my guess is if he did see anything, he'd be on his way to the morgue with Prescott. In any case, we'll check out the name and address. My guess is we won't find this Nancy Edmunds."

Aaron and Sam went back outside. An officer holding plastic bags in both hands approached.

"What did you find?" Aaron asked.

The officer extended his right arm. "Marlboro cigarette butt. We found it in the ashtray," he said, and then handed the bag from his left hand to Aaron. It contained a white powder.

"Cocaine or heroin, perhaps," Aaron said. "The lab can tell us after they process it." He turned to Sam. "So, a hooker meets a client, he or she smokes, and one or both do drugs. Money is always part of the equation, but there's no indication of a robbery. Even if Prescott, our *client* in this case, paid Ms. Edmunds for her services, why would she kill him and not take his money, watch, or credit cards?"

"You think it's a drug deal gone bad?" Sam asked.

"That, or they both got high and things spiraled out of control. The toxicology report will tell us whether Prescott had drugs in his system." Aaron ran a hand through his hair. "What else did you find?"

"We'll request the motel phone records for any calls made last night, as well as any from the victim's cell and car phone. We should have those in a day or two."

"Did someone notify the next of kin?" Aaron asked.

"Yes, the victim's wife is Jennifer. They had no children. One of our units drove a priest to the Prescott home."

"Good, anyone else? Parents? Siblings?"

"Parents are deceased, no brothers or sisters," Sam said then added, "The Prescott's home is in Lake Forest."

Aaron whistled. "That's exclusive living."

"That it is," Sam agreed.

An assistant from the coroner's office approached. "Excuse me, Inspector. We need your approval to transport the body."

"Go ahead."

The assistant and another man entered the room, and emerged two minutes later with Jared Prescott's body on a gurney inside a black vinyl bag. They wheeled the gurney to the coroner's station wagon, put the body inside, shut the door, and left the parking lot.

Aaron watched the wagon until it left his sight.

"Sam, why don't you call the M.E. and ask him to let us know when he schedules the autopsy?"

"Got it. Anything else?"

"I think we're done here," Aaron said, then glanced at his watch. "I better get to the office and clock in before the boss sends out a search party."

Chapter Two

The next morning, Aaron received an unexpected phone call at ten minutes after nine.

"Aaron, this is Wes. I called to tell you Jared Prescott's autopsy is scheduled for ten this morning." Dr. Wes Taylor was the Chief Medical Examiner for Cook County.

"Not that I'm complaining, but why so soon? Did you Fed Ex half your workload to Cleveland?"

"Unfortunately not," Taylor said with a chuckle. "No, my boss insists Mr. Prescott's autopsy needs to be our top priority. Obviously, he's feeling pressure. I'm handling it myself."

"Pressure? From whom?"

"To be honest, it's more of a mandate, and he didn't provide details. Jared Prescott was a V.P. at one of the city's largest companies, which automatically makes it a high profile case."

"Yes, but the day after is a little unusual, isn't it?" Aaron asked.

"It's rare, but has happened before. A few years ago, it was a Congressman. I suspect I'm not telling you anything new when it involves these big shots. They get the red carpet treatment even after they're gone. This one has somebody's attention in a big way."

"The living should be so lucky. Sam and I will be down there at two o'clock."

"What's wrong, Aaron, you don't want to watch me carve this turkey?"

Aaron laughed. Dr. Taylor once told him only a morbid sense of humor allowed him to cope with the emotional stress of his job.

"Very funny, Wes, but Thanksgiving is more than three months away, and I'm a bottom-line guy interested in results. How you get those results is your business. That's why we make such a good team."

"I'll leave that one alone," Taylor said.

"Listen, Wes, we found drugs at the scene, so we'll need a toxicology analysis."

"Don't worry, we've been instructed to go the whole nine yards on this one. Full internal, full external, and dissection, but you know tox results will take a couple of weeks."

"We appreciate anything you can do to expedite the process."

"I will. Mr. Prescott must be *somebody*. I'll see you and Sam at two."

"Goodbye, Wes."

Aaron walked to Sam's desk to give him the news. Having the autopsy results this quickly didn't hurt the case, but he didn't agree with one person commanding attention over another because of who they are. Or *were*.

Sam's feet were propped up on his desk, his nose buried in the Sports page. A half-eaten chocolate covered crème-filled doughnut rested on a napkin on top of the desk next to a Styrofoam cup of black coffee. A spot of cream had oozed onto the napkin.

Aaron sat on the edge of the desk and folded his arms. "Looks good, Sam," he said, nodding at the doughnut. "You make a stop on the way into work?"

Sam lowered the newspaper. "Rose from Dispatch stopped at Firecakes. There are two boxes in the coffee room."

"What's the occasion?"

"I think her sister had a baby or something. I don't concern myself with the details, just don't want good food to go to waste."

"I admire your initiative to accept that responsibility."

"A responsibility I take very seriously," Sam said with a wink. "Better get one quick. You know how cops are with doughnuts."

"That I do, but I'll pass," Aaron said. "Personally, I think a new baby warrants breakfast tacos."

"Passing up a doughnut? How did you ever become a cop?" Sam asked.

"I lied on my application. Besides, we have something more important to discuss."

"Don't we always? What's up?"

"Wes called. Prescott's autopsy is scheduled for this morning."

Sam lowered his feet to the floor and sat forward. "That was quick."

"I thought so, too. Somebody with influence wants it expedited. Jared Prescott may be more than a wealthy executive caught in the wrong place at the wrong time. The last thing we need is someone in position getting in the way of the investigation."

Sam gazed at the doughnut for a moment, and then looked up at Aaron. "We're not going to the real deal are we?"

"I told Wes we'd be at the morgue at two o'clock."

"That's good to hear. I'd rather not taste this doughnut more than once."

"It's nice to see the sugar hasn't affected your sick sense of humor, Sam."

Aaron went to the break room, poured a cup of coffee, and chatted with two officers. Before returning to his desk, he took out a glazed doughnut, figuring he needed to eat something, even if it consisted of empty calories. He sat down, bit into the doughnut, and sipped the coffee.

He took out a pen and opened a full-sized notebook. He wasn't averse to using the computer, but putting pen to notebook allowed more freedom and creativity to make notes, draw arrows, diagrams, and sketch in free form. Typing on the keyboard encouraged a tendency to rush and not give sufficient thought to an idea. The computer file could wait until later.

He loosened his tie and jotted notes on the paper. Who was Jared Prescott? Why the urgency to expedite the autopsy, and who was applying the pressure? Would it help or hinder the investigation? He made a list of people to interview, knowing those more powerful and wealthy usually meant a bigger network, more people to interview, and a more tangled investigation. That usually translated to less cooperation, sometimes resistance.

First on the list was the victim's widow, followed by his boss, co-workers, business associates, social network, usually a long list when one belonged to a country club, and God knew who else. After writing for several minutes, he tossed the pen on the desk, picked up the coffee cup, and leaned back in the chair.

"Christ, this job is getting old," he said aloud.

An officer walking by, stopped, and asked, "What's that, Inspector?"

"Nothing. Just thinking out loud."

Aaron needed to distance himself from the noise and conversation in the bullpen style office on the second floor of Area 4 Police Headquarters, Chicago Homicide Division. He picked up his coffee cup and walked outside.

He stood under the shade of trees on W. Harrison Street in front of the building, sipping coffee while watching pedestrian and vehicle traffic. Leaving the office and staring into space was sometimes therapeutic. He didn't have the luxury of his own office where he could close the door and minimize the noise, at least not until he made captain, something he wasn't sure would ever happen; not sure he wanted the position.

The bus stop across the street reminded him he was able to avoid the masses of people choosing public transportation in the form of bus or El train, not to mention free parking.

A man wearing a dark brown suit sat on the bench. Slung over his left shoulder was what appeared to be a laptop computer case. A briefcase sat on the bench next to him; a cell phone was attached to his right ear.

Aaron reflected on the days before cell phones, when business could wait until one arrived at the office. Then again, maybe he was talking to his wife who wanted to know what time he would be home for dinner, or chatting with his girlfriend to kill time. In any case, Aaron didn't need to lug baggage around town, so the job did have its advantages.

Maybe the man was a financial advisor, checking on the most recent fluctuation in the Dow Jones Industrial Average.

Aaron didn't fully understand what influenced the Dow Jones, why it rose, why it fell, or what the points signified, nor did he ever bother to learn. Five years ago, he hired a financial advisor to do what he didn't have the time or patience for—manage his portfolio, if he could even call it a portfolio. Stay patient during the down times, stick it out for the long run, don't panic, you'll do fine. He wondered what someone in Jared Prescott's position did with his money. How much was enough? It seemed unfair, the more money one had, the more they made, while most of the world strained to live from paycheck to paycheck.

The market had not recovered from its fall in 2001 due to 9/11, continued terrorism threats, unemployment, and whatever other factors contributed to market declines.

Aaron sometimes wondered what he would be doing if he was still married. Probably what he did now, eating fast food and washing down pizza with beer on Friday nights.

Aaron met Brenda Wheeler at Ohio State and they married in 1983, two years after they graduated. They divorced less than two years later. If the adage of opposites attract carried any truth, he and Brenda were the poster couple for the perfect marriage.

She worked in real estate, was ambitious and anxious to make her mark on society. She relished rubbing shoulders with the rich and influential, while Aaron's idea of leisure was relaxing in a reclining chair in front of the TV with a beverage and a bowl of Fritos. Often she pleaded with him to accompany her and "hob-knob" with the upper crust of society. He declined, usually using the job as an excuse.

On nights when he arrived home at a decent hour, which wasn't often, Brenda would be out entertaining prospective clients, or celebrating her latest real estate deal.

He once felt guilty his job and unpredictable schedule was the main reason for their divorce, but it was as much her career as his. They'd never discussed children, and although he would love a son, in the end it was best. A single parent raising a child was a recipe for disaster, particularly given his profession.

The last he heard, she married a high profile corporate attorney and lived in Los Angeles.

Truly, a match made in heaven.

They didn't discuss alimony or a settlement, because she would probably earn more money in 10 years than he would over his entire career.

Since the divorce, he dated occasionally, but hadn't met anyone he felt serious enough with to pursue a relationship. At forty-five years old, he had accepted life as a bachelor. The truth was, his job didn't allow him time to consider a serious relationship, let alone marriage. There seemed some truth to the adage, 'cops and marriage go together like ketchup and hot dogs.'

He broke from his reverie when the man across the street boarded a bus. He finished his coffee and returned to his desk.

***

Aaron and Sam arrived at the Cook County morgue on W. Harrison Street at five minutes to two.

"Summer in the Midwest, isn't it wonderful?" Aaron said, wiping his brow.

Sam gestured to the building. "It's a lot cooler in there."

"You can stay in the car and listen to music," Aaron quipped, poking Sam with an elbow.

"Too damn hot, besides, you don't like autopsies any more than I do."

"Never gets any easier does it? Just think, Wes sees this every day."

"Up close and personal to boot," Sam agreed.

They went inside and down the stairs to the medical examiner's office located on the basement floor. Dr. Taylor sat at a desk poring over a stack of papers. He peered over his bifocals and stood when Aaron tapped on the door, flashing a smile suggesting professional courtesy rather than a 'glad to see ya' gesture.

"Hello, Aaron. Sam."

They exchanged handshakes.

Dr. Taylor was fifty-seven, with salt and pepper hair, and broad shoulders. He shoved his hands into the pockets of his green surgical scrubs. "Ready to have a look at your victim?"

"Why not? Did anyone confirm his identity?" Aaron asked while they walked to the autopsy room.

"Yes, his widow, Jennifer," Dr. Taylor said. "She came in late yesterday afternoon. A strong woman, kept it together better than most."

"How long was she here?" Aaron asked.

"Maybe ten minutes."

"That's all?" Aaron asked.

"It's not unusual," Taylor said with a shrug. "People react differently in this situation. Some can't bear to be in the same room, others we can't get to leave. Her father is Harlan Grayson, President and CEO of ChemPhen Pharmaceuticals."

"I've heard the name," Aaron said.

"Most have," Dr. Taylor agreed. "He donates a ton of money to the community, and has substantial influence in city government. His company is on the forefront of cancer research."

There were six steel tables in the autopsy room, three currently occupied with cadavers. The room was cold, and the odor of formaldehyde hung in the air like a hot air balloon. Two morticians were examining a body at the far right table.

Dr. Taylor indicated a table on the far left. "Mr. Prescott is over here."

The three moved to the table, and Dr. Taylor drew back the white sheet covering the body.

"Jared Prescott, thirty-seven years old," he said. He picked up a plastic bag and handed it to Aaron. "Here's the bullet that killed him. It hit him dead center, death was immediate."

Aaron took the bag and examined the bullet. "Looks like a three-fifty-seven, but ballistics will confirm," he said, then handed the bag to Sam.

"The angle of the wound was slightly downward. No powder burns or gunpowder residue on the clothing," Dr. Taylor added.

"No powder burns means the shooter stood at least sixteen inches away, but I would expect someone like Prescott to defend himself if the shooter was within reach."

"There were no defensive wounds, nothing under the fingernails or on the hands," Taylor said. "Here's something that might interest you. He rotated the victim's head to the left side and pointed to the gash on the side of the neck.

"We noticed that at the scene. What do you make of it, Wes?" Aaron asked.

"It's deep enough to suggest someone took their time, although with the condition of the wound and the surrounding area, they didn't use anything sharper than a butter knife. The condition and color of the bones indicate the killer inflicted the wound postmortem."

"That suggests it was personal since the bullet already did the job," Aaron mused.

Dr. Taylor moved the sheet to expose the victim's left leg. "There's a long scar on the outside of the left knee, the result of a surgical procedure. Other than the bullet wound and the neck wound, I found nothing unusual. Physically, your victim was in top physical condition, like an athlete."

"He was a star football player at Northwestern with a future in the NFL until he tore his knee in the championship game his senior year. I suspect the scar relates to that injury. What about the time of death?"

"I'd say between nine and eleven o'clock p.m.," Dr. Taylor said.

Aaron gazed at the body and blew air over his upper lip. "Okay, I guess that's it for now, Wes. If you find anything else, give us a call."

"I will, Aaron, and I'll let you know when the tox results come in."

The three left the autopsy room and stood outside Dr. Taylor's office.

"Any idea who is applying the pressure, Wes?" Aaron asked.

"My boss said this case is at the top of our list, regardless of our workload. We shifted everything else, so it's someone with significant clout. An educated guess would be Harlan Grayson, the victim's father-in-law. We deal with more than our share of unsuspected deaths and suicides, but you know how it is in this city, never a dull moment. Fortunately or not, nobody else is hounding us for autopsy results, so I didn't have a strong enough reason to resist the order, although I doubt it would have done any good."

"It's just another case where authority wields its power, despite how it might adversely affect other people. It disgusts me."

"I agree with you one hundred percent, Aaron, but unfortunately it's not my place to say. I have to answer to my superiors, same as you."

"That still doesn't make it right."

***

Aaron frowned and made a humming noise when he and Sam stood outside.

"Something wrong, Aaron?"

"The mark on the neck could be significant. We'll need to check the case files for history of signature killings. Who leaves signs on their victims?"

"Psychotics, serial killers, religious fanatics, the list goes one," Sam replied.

"That's what I'm afraid of."

Chapter Three

Aaron arrived home at four-fifty p.m. He felt fortunate his apartment complex was less than a half hour from work. Nothing frustrated him more than sitting in traffic while traveling from point A to point B. He lived on the third floor of an apartment on W 47th St. in Archer Heights, a neighborhood of residences and businesses, most notably the J.B. Hunt Transport Company.

His apartment was a drastic contrast from the thirty-five hundred square foot, four-bedroom, two and a half bath monstrosity he lived in with his ex-wife Brenda, but it suited him better, more like the twenty-two hundred square foot house he lived in with his parents.

His apartment consisted of one bedroom, a small family room with a sofa, recliner, end table, coffee table, a kitchenette, and a dining room big enough to accommodate a small table and four chairs. An apartment suited his needs since he was never much for the responsibilities, especially yard work, that accompanied owning a home. Everything was downsized, including a bare-necessity wardrobe. Six pairs of pants, two sports coats, one suit he rarely wore, and a dozen shirts of various colors. His one luxury item was a forty-six-inch Sony television.

He put the key into the lock, and then turned to the sound of a click behind him.

Harriet Fletcher, his neighbor from across the hall, stepped out into the hallway. She wore a light blue housedress spattered with pink and yellow flowers, her hair covered in light blue curlers. She held a white trash bag in her left hand.

"Hello, Mr. Randall. I didn't expect to see you home so early. Are you feeling all right? Not coming down with one of those horrible summer colds, I hope."

Since her husband Earl passed away eight years ago, Mrs. Fletcher treated Aaron like a son, insisting he eat healthy, get plenty of rest, spend more time enjoying the finer things in life, not allow the stress of the job to bring him down.

Easier said than done.

"How are you, Mrs. Fletcher? No, I'm not sick. It's just been a long day."

"Okay, I won't keep you, Mr. Police Inspector," she said, showing her palm. "I'm just taking the trash out, keeping the home in order. You know what they say, cleanliness is next to Godliness." She closed the door and walked down the hall.

"That it is," Aaron agreed.

She waved a hand over her shoulder. "Have a nice evening."

"You do the same, ma'am."

Aaron watched her turn the corner at the end of the hall to make sure she didn't return to continue the conversation. She was a nice woman and meant well, but he wasn't in the mood for small talk. A trace of guilt nagged at him for feeling unsociable, but what could he do?

He entered the apartment and closed the door, tossing his keys on the end table. He went to the refrigerator and took out a Coors light beer. A twelve-pack usually lasted him two to three weeks, depending on the stress of his job. Tonight was one of those nights.

The inside of his refrigerator screamed bachelor. Other than the usual ketchup, mustard, and pickle condiments, he stocked enough TV dinners for the week, not the healthiest of cuisine, but at least he was eating vegetables. There was a pound of ground sirloin on days he felt ambitious enough to slap a patty or two on the grill.

Tonight, it was too hot. The demands of his job weren't conducive to dining often at restaurants, but he didn't care to sit and eat alone anyway. His erratic schedule meant he couldn't always be home at a decent hour to spend time preparing a meal, even if it meant microwaving a TV dinner. The concept of a home-cooked meal was a pipe dream.

He returned to the living room and flopped into the recliner, thankful Mrs. Fletcher wasn't in a more talkative mood. He wasn't much of a conversationalist, and didn't go out much socially, likely burn out resulting from interviewing potential suspects, witnesses, family members, and friends of victims. By the end of most days, he was talked-out. He wanted to trust people, but those he dealt with on a day-to-day basis made trust an elusive commodity.

Most conversations were small talk, anyway. People talked about what they'd accomplished and how much money they made. Such people were terrible listeners who thrived on one-way conversations.

Aaron settled into the recliner and pushed the power button on the remote, sipping on beer while surfing the channels. He found *Dirty Harry* on HBO. Clint Eastwood was issuing an ultimatum to the villain in the movie's final scene. He enjoyed movies when the heroes ignored proper procedure and dealt with criminals their own way. Clint Eastwood's Dirty Harry character, flaunting the rules and restrictions of law enforcement to obtain results, was his favorite.

Action movies were straight to the point, where criminals received the justice they deserved. In Aaron's world, justice usually came after piles of red tape, determining whether the perpetrator's rights were violated, delayed trials, appeals, fancy talking defense attorneys, and sympathetic judges who believed in second and third chances.

Aaron put the beer on the end table, rested his head on the recliner, closed his eyes, and thought about the Prescott investigation. The brief discussion with Dr. Taylor resulted in more questions than answers, typical of most cases.

Just after he drifted off to sleep, the phone rang. He didn't have caller-ID, so let the machine answer. *Put the onus on the caller to leave a message if it was important.*

After the answering machine failed to pick up, he reluctantly got up and answered the phone. It was better than listening to the annoying ring. "Hello?"

"Aaron, it's Rachel. Did I catch you at a bad time?" Rachel Cameron was Aaron's closest friend he met while attending Ohio State.

"Not really," Aaron lied. "I just got home from work."

"What are you doing?"

"I'm watching HBO and drinking beer."

"Have you eaten dinner yet?"

"No. I think Swanson is cooking tonight, why?"

"I had a taste for Veal Parmigianino at Sabatino's, and wondered if you wanted to join me."

Aaron squeezed his eyes shut and massaged his forehead. Getting dressed and driving to a restaurant to eat on a cook's schedule were all valid reasons to turn down the offer.

"Sabatino's, huh? I don't know, Rachel. It's been a rough couple of days. I'm not sure I'm up for socializing tonight."

"If that's true, then you deserve to get out of the apartment and put work out of your mind," she said.

"Sounds like a sympathy dinner," he said.

"Actually, it's a celebration dinner, and I'm treating."

"I see, so now you're trying to bribe me. What are you celebrating?"

"We just closed a big deal with a client after three months of negotiation. I figure it's a good excuse to have someone else do the cooking, and Sabatino's beats the heck out of Swanson."

"Wonderful," he said, hoping he sounded more excited than he felt.

"I can tell you're ecstatic, but I know how you love their Chicken Fettuccini Alfredo with extra sauce, hot garlic bread, fresh green salad, and great atmosphere, not to mention the company of a good friend. You must admit, it doesn't get any better than that, and certainly far better than a boring TV dinner, and watching a movie I bet you've already seen."

"You sound like a commercial," he said, although Sabatino's was his favorite Italian restaurant, and Chicken Fettuccini Alfredo his favorite Italian dish. "I don't know, pasta sounds kind of heavy," he joked.

"Come on, how can you pass up a free dinner?"

"You don't give up, do you?"

"Not easily."

"All right, I cave," he said. He hadn't seen Rachel in a while, and a free dinner was mentally healthier than sitting at home thinking about his latest case. "But I don't want you to think I'm going along because you're buying. I can pay for my own dinner."

"I wouldn't hear of it. I offered, so just accept it. I know you don't like dining in a social setting, so I'll settle for your acceptance, although a little enthusiasm would be nice."

"I don't mind dining out, just not alone, and you are good company. How's that for enthusiasm?"

"I'll take it," she said. "What time do you want to eat?"

He checked his watch. "Give me time to shower and change. How about seven-thirty?"

"It's a date," she said. "I'll see you then."

He said goodbye and hung up the phone.

Chapter Four

After a short nap, Aaron showered and put on a green sport shirt and khaki pants, and left the apartment. He arrived at Sabatino's on Irving Park Road at 7:35.

When he spotted Rachel sitting on a bench inside the lobby, he was glad he accepted the dinner invitation. She looked good as usual in a silk blue blouse and modest gray skirt with black short heel shoes, emphasizing her toned legs, crossed at the knee. She had a flair for looking classy without flaunting her natural beauty. She flashed a wide and sincere smile, got up from the bench, and gave him a hug. He smelled perfume.

She glanced at her watch and then looked at him with raised eyebrows.

"Yes, I know, late as usual, right?" he said.

"Actually, I was going to say you're almost on time," she replied with a twinkle in her eye.

"I'll bet. You know, predictable isn't necessarily bad."

"I prefer reliable," she countered.

Rachel was five foot five with a trim figure, kept in shape with daily jogging and frequent trips to the gym. Her skin was smooth, and a beauty mark above her lip reminded Aaron of Cindy Crawford. The soft curls in her light brown hair cascading down her shoulders highlighted her brown eyes.

Aaron met Rachel at Ohio State in 1980, and they became close friends. In 1981, he graduated with a Bachelor of Science in Criminal Justice, returning to Chicago to follow a career in Law Enforcement. He worked six years in the Patrol Division before passing the Detective exam.

Rachel stayed at Ohio State to pursue a Master's degree in Business Finance, returning to Chicago two years later to accept a position with Deloitte & Touche, a Big Six accounting firm.

When they broke the hug, Aaron looked her up and down.

"Is something wrong?" she asked.

"You look thinner since I last saw you."

A smile lit up her face. "Our company installed a fitness center two months ago, so I decided to substitute cardio classes for lunch three times a week. I still go to the gym, but this helps me fight the temptation to eat a big lunch."

"You look good," he said.

"Thanks, that keeps me from feeling guilty splurging on pasta tonight," she said, and then added, "You look like you've slimmed down a little yourself."

"I've lost a few pounds, but it's due more to running around all the time and not having time to sit down for a big meal. I guess it's the one benefit to this job."

"Well, if you ever want to come to my club, I can get you in as a guest."

"I'll be sure to let you know," he said, knowing his schedule made the chance between slim and none.

"Not too many cars in the parking lot. Maybe we can actually hear ourselves talk," she said.

"Did you get us a table?" he asked, angling his head toward the dining area.

A playful grin crossed her face. "I sure did. I just flashed my baby blues and winked at the maitre'd."

"Very funny, except your eyes are brown, and one look around the restaurant tells me we have our choice of at least ten tables."

"Listen, don't spoil my moment of glory or you'll pay for your own dinner."

He made a zipping motion across his lips. "Subject is closed. Why don't we grab a booth?"

"I see you're wearing your khaki pants tonight," she said. "You know, Dillard's has a sale on Dockers, twenty-five percent off. You can upgrade your wardrobe and join the style of the twenty-first century."

If it was anyone else, he would suggest they mind their own business, but Rachel had a knack to offer advice without sounding condescending.

"You know me, Rachel, if it's on the rack, it's in style. Twenty-five percent off or not, pants are pants. You know, I can still change my mind and eat the TV dinner."

She laughed. "You know I'm just teasing you, Aaron."

"I know, but I have to defend myself. I don't want to be known as the guy without a comeback."

"Not much chance of that."

A cute blonde girl appearing no older than a high school freshman escorted them to a booth.

"They're getting younger all the time aren't they?" Rachel commented after they sat down.

"What do you mean?"

"Kids get out into the workplace younger than we did, don't you think?"

"It's technology. They need to pay for cell phones and iPods, although I suppose it's better than relying on mom and dad's checkbook. I applaud those parents who can instill discipline in their kids to work for what they want."

"I agree," she said.

He opened the menu. "My parents delivered newspapers, shoveled snow in the winter, raked leaves in the fall, mowed lawns in the summer, and I even did some of that as a kid. Today, kids have televisions in their bedrooms, personal CD players, hand-held computers, and stereo systems costing more than cars my parents drove. I guess that's what they call progress."

"You sound like my father," she said.

He glanced up from the menu. "How so?"

"You know, back in the good old days, we didn't have this, we didn't have that."

"I'm not sure the comparison is good or bad," he said with a frown, recalling his father preached in a similar manner.

"Neither, really, although I do have one question."

"What's that?"

"Why are you looking at the menu? You know what you're eating."

He rested his chin between thumb and forefinger. "I don't know. I might try something different tonight."

"Bull crap," she whispered.

He shot her a mock look of disapproval. "Watch it, young lady, or I'll arrest you for obscene language in a public place. I'm a cop you know."

She put down her menu and showed her palms. "But officer, ain't nuthin' wrong with the word *crap*."

Before he could reply, the waiter arrived at their table with pen and pad in hand. "Excuse me, folks, can I get you something to drink?"

"I'd like a glass of red wine please," Rachel said.

"Just ice water for me," Aaron said.

"Just ice water for me," Rachel mocked in a bass voice after the waiter left.

"Is there something wrong with the way I ordered?"

"You could be more cheerful."

"Why? You have enough cheer for ten people."

She smiled. "Aaron, you know I'm just trying to push your buttons and help take your mind off work."

"I know, and I appreciate it. It *has been* a rough couple of days."

"So, have you heard from Brenda?" she asked. Rachel and Brenda knew each other through Aaron, who met his ex-wife a year before he met Rachel. Like Aaron, Rachel was divorced, married less than a year to a man she met at work. They split when she discovered he cheated on her with a co-worker.

"Not since she moved out to California with her husband. I'm sure she's too busy rubbing elbows with royalty, and wondering where to spend all her money to care about what I'm doing."

"I saw the news last night. The man killed at that motel was pretty important, I guess."

"Jared Prescott, Vice President for ChemPhen Pharmaceuticals. He played football at Northwestern and would be playing in the NFL if he didn't bust up his knee. I remember Northwestern beat Ohio State all four years he played there."

"I thought his name sounded familiar. Those were bad years for the Buckeyes," she agreed.

"He lived in Lake Forest."

"Wow, that's big money," she said. "Our CEO lives there. I was at his house once for a company party. Those houses are spectacular. How's the case going? I mean, if you can discuss it."

"Most of what I can tell you has or will be made public, so sure, if you want to hear about it, okay. It might be a drug deal. We found traces in the motel room. A woman we have yet to identify rented the room, so it might have been a tryst." His face grew long. "I'm interviewing Prescott's widow tomorrow."

"I don't envy you that job. Losing a loved one is never easy, but losing one to violence must be unbearable."

The waiter returned with their drinks and took their meal order.

Rachel ordered Veal Parmigianino and a small salad with bleu cheese dressing. Aaron settled on the Chicken Fettuccine Alfredo.

"I knew it," she said with an 'I told you so' expression.

"Just bring on the garlic bread," he said with a smile.

"Followed by the after dinner breath mint," she teased. "You look tired, Aaron. How is the job otherwise?"

"It's a living," he said with a shrug. "Dealing with death after the fact takes its toll. I'm sure getting old is lowering my resistance."

"I doubt that," she said.

"I'm not sure I feel the passion for the job I once had."

"Don't beat yourself up too much. It happens to almost everyone at some point during their career. That's why people discuss retirement before they can afford to stop working. Have you given any more thought to another career?"

"*More* thought? What makes you think I'm looking for another career?"

She cocked her head, and a tiny grin formed at the corners of her mouth. "You have that look in your eyes tonight, and last time we were together, you mentioned it."

"You're nothing if not perceptive," he said with a chuckle. "There I go, being predictable again."

"Reliable," she corrected.

"Right," he said. "Even if I had thoughts along those lines, I'm forty-five and have worked in law enforcement my entire adult life. A new career probably means going back to school."

"That might not be so bad. I remember you had a tremendous work ethic in college," she said.

"Sure, I was in my twenties and expected to accomplish something with my life. A good work ethic was easy because I had passion and ambition. Don't get me wrong, education is a wonderful thing, but a whole course curriculum to pursue another career makes me tired just thinking about it."

"I can't believe for one second you've lost your ambition."

"Lost–no, but I'm too old and tired to start over. I have little enough personal time as it is now, let alone time to write papers and study for exams."

"I can't say I blame you there. Everybody needs down time. What about another position in the department where you don't deal so up close and personal with death?"

"You're talking about administration. I'd be one of the brass," he said then shook his head. "I don't even like saying the word. Sorry, as bad as it gets on the streets, I don't see myself in that position."

"It might not be so bad. How do you know if you've never done it before?"

"I've seen enough of what goes on above me to know. Granted, that means my career has limits, but life is full of tradeoffs."

"I know the personnel director at Deloitte & Touche," she said. "I'd be glad to check to see if anything is available."

"Thanks for the offer, but I'm a firm believer in the merit system. I have enough trouble dealing with people that inherit or fall into money, so accepting your offer would make me the biggest hypocrite on the planet. Besides, I don't see how my background and resume would fit at an accounting firm."

"I'm just trying to help," she said.

"I know, and I appreciate it."

"What about an attorney? Lots of law enforcement people go into law," she said with a twinkle in her eye, which to him meant a mix of sarcasm and humor.

"Spend another six years in law school? I don't have enough patience for it, besides, that's a no-win situation. The prosecutors have to deal with families of the victims who wonder why they can't put someone in prison and keep them there. Defense attorneys are loved by the accused, despised by the victims and their families. Too much reading and researching with not enough payback. I'm embarrassed to admit I don't think I've read two books since college."

"Well," she said, her shoulders sagging with a sigh, "I guess you'll have to continue being a detective. Look at the bright side, it *is* job security."

"Not exactly raving reviews for the profession, but not even my job is guaranteed. The city's constantly talking layoffs–fire, police, even city administration. They say budgets are shrinking. That translates to more unemployment which leads to a higher crime rate because crime has no budget restrictions."

The waiter returned with their entrees, and they were silent while they ate.

Finally, Rachel broke the silence. "You know, Aaron, you're not alone in your thinking. Most people get exhausted with the same routine day after day, year after year, and a lot believe the grass is greener on the other side. They make a career change, but find the other side is covered with weeds and crabgrass."

"Maybe you should have been a philosopher," he said with a laugh, while twisting strands of fettuccine with his fork.

She stopped a forkful of pasta halfway to her mouth. "Now, there's a thought. Maybe I should consider that my next career. You know, I've been Senior Accounting Manager for four years. Promotions are rare at this level unless you're willing to relocate, even on a temporary basis."

"You know, it seems we discuss this every time we see each other," he said.

"I agree, but sometimes it's good to get it off your chest and realize things are better than you thought."

"I see. So, for now, keep doing what I'm doing."

"Right," she said with a bob of her head, "then next week you can bring it up again."

"I guess the problem is when I chose law enforcement, I had this grandiose ambition to save the world from the criminal element, keep innocent people from becoming victims. Now, when I get involved, it's already too late. Granted, not all victims are innocent, but defense attorneys and shrinks convince the courts the guilty parties are too sick to understand their actions. Their idea of justice is to throw them in a psychiatric ward for six months and call them rehabilitated. It's frustrating to see a killer released for good behavior, only to go out and kill again. I've been in that situation. What do you say to the families of the victims? How do you explain why a killer was released in the first place? I don't have all the answers. Certainly, there are those that can and do rehabilitate. In a perfect world, we lock up the real killers and throw away the key, save the ones worth saving. Unfortunately, our world isn't perfect, and we have people in position making that call."

"So, you think you've failed, is that it, Aaron?"

"I don't know. It sometimes feels that way."

"Well, I'm no psychology expert, but I think you're being way too hard on yourself. You're one man and can't fix society by yourself. Who knows how many lives you've saved by taking these killers off the streets? Sure, some get out and break the law again, but you can't control the courts."

"Our judicial system is another issue altogether. The ones doing life or get the death penalty are usually the ones who can't afford their own attorney. I've seen it time and time again. The worst criminals are too rich and connected to get what they deserve. It would be nice to hook a big fish just once."

After they finished their entrees, Rachel ordered the flamed Baked Alaska and a cup of coffee. Aaron settled for coffee and they talked while customers drifted in and out of the restaurant.

"So, what are you going to do when you get home?" she asked.

"I think it's Jean Claude Van Damme night on HBO," he said with a wink and a smile.

She shook her head. "How you can waste two hours on a movie you've already seen, probably more than once, is beyond me. You already know what happens."

"I had the same conversation with Sam. Like I told him, I deduce facts from clues all day long. I watch TV to enjoy the characters and the action scenes. Surprises are overrated. It's like working at a fast food restaurant. After ten hours flipping burgers, the last thing you want is a burger. Besides, I like when the good guy wins, especially when they bypass politics and red tape. It's a happy ending I can rely on."

"I like happy endings too, but you can have a happy ending in a love story, you know."

"To each his own, I guess," he said. "The best I can hope for in my job is to find the perpetrator and give closure to the victim's loved ones, even though the worst has already happened."

"What about when the killer is acquitted due to a technicality, then the good guy blows him away in the end of the movie?"

"Bottom line, justice is served," he said. "Like I said, that's why I got into law enforcement in the first place–to enforce law. I guess I hoped it would be more clear-cut, although I wasn't naïve enough to believe I would turn the justice world on its ear."

"The good will inherit the earth," she said.

"Something like that."

"I don't believe you think violence is the answer, Aaron. That doesn't sound like you."

"I think a character in Clint Eastwood's *Magnum Force* said it best. 'It's not a question of whether to use violence. There simply is no other way.'"

She laughed. "Maybe I should call you Dirty Aaron."

"That's a new one," he said with a raised eyebrow.

She ate dessert, and they sipped on coffee. When they finished, she paid the bill with a credit card, including a twenty-five percent tip.

"You're sure in a giving mood tonight," he observed.

"Tis better to give than receive," she said with a wink.

On their way out, she scooped a handful of mints from a tray at the cash register and handed them to Aaron. "There's your dessert," she said. "It will get rid of the garlic aftertaste."

He cocked his head and popped the mints into his mouth when they stepped outside the restaurant. "Hell, it feels hotter now than when I got here. This weather is getting old."

"Don't worry, it won't last forever," she said, hooking her hand in the crook of his arm. "In a few minutes, you'll be in your air-conditioned car on your way to your air-conditioned apartment."

"I suppose," he said, patting her hand.

He escorted her to her car, thanked her for dinner, they hugged and said goodnight.

***

Inside, two men seated in the smoking section watched Aaron and Rachel leave the restaurant.

"You think that's his old lady?" one man asked. "She's got a nice rack."

The second man shook his head and puffed on a cigar.

"I doubt it. They came in separate cars and look too happy."

"You're probably right," the first man said, then crushed his cigarette in the ashtray. "Come on, let's get out of here."

Chapter Five

The next morning, Aaron sat in his car in a Burger King parking lot, sipping coffee and eating an egg, sausage, and cheese croissant, pondering the impending interview with Jared Prescott's widow.

It was the ugliest part of the job, but necessary. He never recalled a time when he didn't feel guilty, as though intruding on their grief. The last thing people wanted during arguably the worst time in their life was a series of questions from a nosy inspector.

Two days had passed since Jennifer Prescott identified her husband at the morgue, which was little enough time for even the strongest of heart to come to terms with the tragedy. Some *never* did.

People had reacted to his questions in various ways. Some slammed the door in his face; other times he'd dodged punches and objects thrown in his direction. Others asked how he could allow it to happen, as if blaming him personally for their loss.

The Prescott home sat on a corner lot at Stony Woods and Emerald Oak, adjacent to the Skokie Highway 41 in Lake Forest, an affluent suburb of Chicago where the mayor, a Congressman, and several Chicago Bear football players lived.

The front of the house had double Palladian windows downstairs, with two balconies on the upper level, large enough to accommodate a patio table and chairs. Four Corinthian columns supported the roof. The home's exterior was a blond brick.

Aaron got out of his car and approached the home, admiring the mahogany double front doors with beveled glass and a transom. He knocked on the door.

A man wearing black pants, white shirt, and black bow tie answered the knock, standing in the doorway with feet shoulder width apart. He folded his hands in front, as though trained on what posture to assume, depending on the circumstance. This must be the 'stranger approaching in less than $100,000 vehicle stance.' His eyes indicated a rehearsed stare, all part of the greeting etiquette, Aaron supposed.

This must be the butler, manservant, or hired help.

"Good day, sir. May I help you?" the man said in a manufactured voice. He would do well auditioning for a role in a British movie.

Aaron presented his badge. "Inspector Randall, Chicago Homicide. I'm here to see Mrs. Prescott."

The man leaned in and squinted at the badge as though studying an eye chart, then moved aside as a guard at Buckingham Palace might at shift change. He extended his arm. "Please, come in, Inspector. I'll notify Mrs. Prescott of your arrival."

The name is Bond… James Bond.

Aaron stepped into a large foyer. The man closed the door and walked down a long hallway before disappearing around a corner, leaving Aaron to marvel at the inside of the home. His first thought was why two people needed so much space, especially with no children. Homes in the area typically ran eight to ten thousand square feet. He guessed the Prescott home was at the upper end of that range.

A crystal chandelier, which would have appeared more appropriate in the middle of a lavish hotel ballroom, hung in the middle of a twenty-foot high ceiling. Large bay windows and an extensive skylight allowed an abundance of natural light to illuminate the interior. To the left, a winding staircase branched into two directions at the top. Three large landscape paintings adorned the wall leading to the upper level.

Aaron entered the room to the left of the staircase, curious to see how the other half lived. A four foot high by two foot wide portrait of Jared Prescott in his Northwestern University football uniform hung over a gray stone fireplace. A baby blue sectional sofa flanked by two brown leather armchairs occupied a sizable portion of the room. A grand piano with a candelabrum on top stood in the corner next to the window. He had yet to meet Mrs. Prescott, but found it hard to believe the piano got much use. Perhaps the butler entertained on cold and rainy evenings.

He glanced at the portrait of Jared Prescott, and shook his head before walking across the foyer to the room on the other side.

An entertainment center on the wall faced the front of the house. Built into the wall was a big screen TV with a DVD and CD player with enough lights and buttons to rival a NASA shuttle control room. To the left of the entertainment center, a fifteen foot long wet bar with a large mirror behind the shelves was stocked with liquor. Mahogany wainscot paneling covered the walls.

A large white sofa sat in the middle of the room, with two black marble end tables on either side, each with a green lamp on top. Two oversized maroon leather recliners faced the television, with a black marble coffee table between the sofa and a white armchair. Floor-to-ceiling windows with a door leading to a patio and a backyard spanned the west wall.

Aaron walked to the windows and gazed outside. The backyard was the size of a football field, with a built-in propane barbeque large enough to serve the day shift at the Fifth Precinct. A short hallway to his left led to the kitchen.

The sound of a woman's voice interrupted his unguided tour.

"Good morning, Inspector. I'm Jennifer Prescott."

Aaron turned.

Mrs. Prescott was slender, five foot six, with a full-lipped mouth, glossed with pink lipstick. Large and striking green eyes highlighted her long blonde hair, arranged in loose curls. She wore a white button-down blouse and green skirt. Her bare legs were dark tan with enough muscle to indicate she spent time in a gym. She smiled and as she walked toward Aaron, he noticed bloodshot eyes.

She wasn't alone. The butler stood behind her left shoulder. A blond-haired, blue-eyed man flanked her right shoulder. He was six foot three, mid-twenties, with a bull neck and thick arms folded across his chest. He wore a blue short-sleeve t-shirt, and black Lycra cycling shorts with 'Nike' printed on the left leg.

Aaron stepped forward and shook Mrs. Prescott's hand. It was firm and warm. "I'm Inspector Aaron Randall. I'm sorry to be here under the circumstances, Mrs. Prescott, but I need to ask you some questions concerning your husband." He turned to meet the tall man's stare.

"I understand," she said, "and please, call me Jennifer." She followed Aaron's eyes and placed a hand on the man's left shoulder. "Forgive me, Inspector, this is Mitchell Walker."

Walker stepped forward and threw out his hand without speaking. His biceps flexed when he squeezed Aaron's hand with more pressure than Aaron believed necessary.

"Charmed," Aaron lied.

"Mitch works security at my father's company," Jennifer said. "Dad insisted. He's a little overprotective."

Aaron wondered why Harlan Grayson believed his daughter needed protection, not to mention Walker looked more like a personal trainer than a security guard. Valid questions, but they could wait.

"Do you mind if we sit down?" she asked.

Aaron sat down on the white armchair and took out a notepad and pencil.

Jennifer sat on the sofa. Walker stood behind her, hands resting on his hips, posing as though auditioning for a lead role in the next *Terminator* film.

She glanced behind her. "Gordon, would you fix me a Scotch and soda with ice, please?" She turned to Aaron. "Would you care for one, Inspector?"

So, it's Gordon, not Benson.

"No, thank you," Aaron said. A hard drink this early in the morning wasn't a good sign, but he abstained from judging. After all, she did just lose her husband to a violent crime.

She leaned forward and massaged her forehead, then exhaled and sat back, draping her arm across the top of the sofa. She crossed her legs, and the motion raised her skirt a few inches above her knees.

Aaron swore she was posing. "You have a nice home," he said.

"Thank you. I realize it's a little big for two people, but Jared's father made a killing in the stock market, and we figured if you have it, why not spend it?"

Money marries into money–how appropriate.

"I don't work for a living," she said. "Some call it being a homemaker, but I spend a lot of time at clubs, shopping, and the hairdresser, so others might say I'm a spoiled bitch." She eyed Aaron as if expecting a comment, but he said nothing.

She exhaled deeply. "I hope you're here to tell me you've arrested the person that killed Jared. Or are you here to ask me who would want to kill him, and where was I that night?"

Aaron frowned. He didn't expect someone who just lost a spouse to be so direct. Her attitude was anything but typical bereaved widow.

Gordon returned and handed her a glass.

"I may seem pretty composed under the circumstances, Inspector, maybe even apathetic, but please don't misunderstand. I loved my husband," she said, then paused and squeezed her eyes shut for a moment. "I apologize for being so direct, but I don't believe in wasting time. The truth is, Jared and I spent more nights apart than we did together. I must say, with all the running around he did, I can't say I'm surprised this happened. He had more than his share of women friends. A secretary, a client, or some bimbo he met at the club."

"Are you suggesting a jealous lover was responsible for his death?"

"I'd be surprised if it was anyone else," she said with a shrug.

"Do you have anyone particular in mind?"

"Talk to the husbands and boyfriends of the women who work at his company, I expect you'll find enough suspects to fill six of your little notebooks."

"That sounds like a long list," Aaron said.

"Of course, it might just be one of his golf partners who got tired of losing. You see, Inspector, Jared was a winner at most everything he tried. Golf, tennis, poker, you name it. Winning came naturally for him."

"You said he was a winner at most things," Aaron said.

"He was a *lousy* husband."

"So, he played around and you spent little time together. Anything else?"

"I see where you're going, Inspector, but I can assure you, Jared was a very good lover."

"That's not what I meant."

"Sorry," she said with a weak shrug, then shook the glass above her head.

"Gordon, will you please pour me another drink," she said, and then looked back at Aaron. "Last one, I promise. Are you sure you won't join me?"

"It's a little too early for me. Did you ever confront your husband regarding his extracurricular activities?"

She smiled. "Extracurricular activities. I like how you put that, but yes, I did. Of course, he denied it, but I realized before long, our marriage was probably doomed from the start. Jared was a playboy, even in college. He needed to be the center of attention."

"Why did you marry him?"

"I fell in love and married an icon. What can I say, love is blind," she said with a shrug.

"Did you ever consider leaving him or asking for a divorce?"

"Sure, I thought about it," she said, "but father insisted I try to work it out. He said Jared would outgrow his adolescent behavior. He even offered to talk to him about it, but I didn't want him to interfere with something I should handle myself."

"Your father knew of your husband's infidelity?"

"Yes, he did."

"So, you decided to live with it and do nothing, let's say, a little more impulsive?"

She stared at Aaron through narrowed eyes. "Do you mean was I angry enough to kill my own husband?"

"Those are your words, not mine," he said.

"Do I really look like a killer, Inspector?"

"I've worked homicide a long time, Mrs. Prescott. Killers come in all shapes and sizes."

"Touché. Regardless, the answer is no, I wasn't angry enough to kill my husband, but I would guess most killers deny it, so I imagine my saying so doesn't mean much."

"Actually, very little."

Gordon returned and handed Jennifer another glass.

"That's your second drink since I got here," Aaron said. "I hope you don't say anything to incriminate yourself."

"Loose lips sink ships, is that it?" she asked.

"Sorry, I don't do much sailing, ma'am."

"So, now it's ma'am?" she asked. Ice cubes rattled against the side of the glass as she sipped her drink. She uncrossed then crossed her legs in what Aaron believed was exaggerated slow motion, exposing more of her thighs.

Was she flirting or attempting to distract him because she was hiding something? Then again, this might be normal behavior.

He gestured at Walker, still rooted behind the sofa.

"Why does your father think you need a bodyguard? Does he double as a personal trainer?"

She downed half of her drink with one gulp, then her eyes squinted with mischief. "I know what's on your mind, Inspector, but I don't see how that's relevant."

Aaron shrugged, knowing the comment was borderline accusatory, but he wasn't sure she would notice the difference. Her behavior wasn't typical, given the situation. Frankly, he never saw anyone so composed, almost uncaring.

"You'd be surprised what's relevant."

"You're very direct, aren't you?" she asked.

"It's in my job description, ma'am. I've learned anything less than direct wastes valuable time, and you said yourself you don't believe in wasting time."

Jennifer raised her eyebrows, but didn't respond.

Aaron nodded at Walker. "Is he helping you cope with your loss?"

Walker folded his arms and glared at Aaron as though he considered himself a knight in shining armor tasked with defending a damsel's honor. *Arnold would be proud.*

"That's not very polite," he said in a phony-sounding baritone voice.

Jennifer raised her palm. "That's okay, Mitch. I deserved that. Give us some space, please."

Walker's nostrils flared for a few moments before he surrendered and left the room.

"Can he sit and roll over, too?" Aaron asked.

"You're quick with your comebacks, Inspector," she said.

"They do a fine job in detective school," he quipped, then sat back and rested his left ankle on his right knee. It was time to direct the conversation to the relevant topic. "Did you speak to your husband on the day he was killed?"

"No, but that's not unusual."

"So, to your knowledge, he didn't come home that night?"

"I went out with friends, so I can't say for sure one way or the other. I just know he wasn't home when I returned, although the flashing light on the phone indicated he called, but didn't leave a message. Gordon was off that night."

"Do you know what time he called?"

She shook her head. "No. He didn't leave a message, so I deleted it."

"Most caller ID logs store the last fifty calls," Aaron said. "Would you mind checking your phone?"

"Gordon, hand me the phone, please," she said.

"Yes, ma'am," Gordon said and complied.

Jennifer punched the button a number of times. "Here it is. Nine-o-seven, Tuesday night," she said, then handed the phone back to Gordon.

"Weren't you concerned when he wasn't home the next morning?" Aaron asked.

"Honestly, I didn't give it a second thought. It wasn't the first time he stayed out all night. He's not a big drinker, but when he does, he's smart enough to get a ride home or stay at a motel. He probably spent the night with one of his conquests. I slept late the next day, and was only up for about an hour before the priest and officer…" The words stuck in her throat.

At least she still showed a sign of grief.

"Did you husband mention any problems at work?" Aaron asked.

She massaged the cushion on the sofa. "Nothing Jared did surprised me. He was quite the practical joker, though. He had a talent for putting people down and exploiting their weaknesses. I suppose that earned him more than his share of enemies."

By this time, Walker had reappeared, and was leaning against the wall next to the kitchen.

Most dogs would obey their masters and stay out of the room.

"Is there anybody in particular at work you think had a strong enough motive to kill him?" Aaron asked.

"I do recall one incident with a co-worker I met at a company office party. Jared was always dragging me along to those things. I think his first name was George, but don't remember his last name."

"Dragged you along?" he said, then pointed at the glass. "I expect you'd fit right in."

She inhaled and held her breath for a moment. "Are you in the habit of insulting all of your suspects?"

"Not all of them, and what gave you the impression you're a suspect?"

She raised the glass to drink but paused. "I thought all spouses were automatically suspects. I mean, on all the cop shows on TV… well, you know."

"Don't believe everything you watch on TV."

Jennifer arched her eyebrows in reply.

"Tell me about this George fellow."

"I recall Jared played a sick practical joke on him, something to do with a football game and a fake head. Sorry, but I don't remember the details."

"Is there reason to believe this guy might want to get back at your husband?"

She hunched her shoulders. "I wouldn't be surprised. I understand Jared embarrassed him pretty bad."

"I don't know if you're familiar with the area we found your husband, but it's not a place I would expect to find someone of his… let's say, economic standing. Do you have any idea why he was in that part of town?"

"Probably meeting a woman," she said with a weak shrug.

"So, you're not familiar with the Tremont Inn on Lazy Willow in Harwood Heights?"

"Never heard of it."

"Do you own a pair of sunglasses, and a red, white, and blue scarf?" he asked, throwing a curve to gauge her reaction.

She furrowed her brow. "What?"

"Never mind," he said.

"Listen, Inspector, if you want to know why Jared was at that motel, check his briefcase. My husband was obsessed with organization. He wrote down every appointment and meeting in his planner."

"We found no briefcase at the scene."

Her mouth fell open. "No briefcase? That's hard to believe. Jared never goes anywhere without it."

"You said he didn't come home that evening. Perhaps he left it in the office."

"It's possible, but I doubt it. That briefcase was Jared's bible. He hung onto it like it was his most prized possession." She laughed.

"Is something funny?"

"It's weird using the word bible and Jared in the same sentence. I bought him that briefcase for our first wedding anniversary. It cost over four hundred dollars."

"When I talk to your husband's co-workers, I'll ask about the briefcase," Aaron said, wondering what a four-hundred dollar briefcase did differently than one costing sixty dollars.

"Say hi to father for me if you see him," Jennifer said with a smile lacking sincerity.

"I'll do that. I have to ask, was your husband ever involved with drugs?"

Her hand flew to her chest. "Drugs? Jared? Not a chance. He was obsessed with physical fitness and more health-conscious than anyone I've ever known. He exercised every day, rarely ate fried foods, and drank a ton of water. I've never even seen a cigarette in his hand. Why would you ask such a question?"

"We found traces of drugs in the motel room."

"How do you know they weren't there before?"

"Unlikely. The rooms are cleaned every day, and that room hasn't been rented for over a month. The drugs were in plain sight."

"Well, you can forget that theory, Inspector," she said with a dismissing wave. "Jared would never be involved with drugs in any way, shape, or form."

Aaron nodded then tapped the notepad with the eraser end of the pencil. "You said before you were out that night. Where did you go?"

"Then I *am* a suspect."

"It's a standard question," he said, growing annoyed with her answering a question with a question. *Just give me the facts and we can move on.*

"I had dinner with friends then we went to The Mid, a dance club on North Halstead. I got home a little after midnight. I'll be more than happy to give you their names if you'd like."

"I'd like to have those names."

"I'll get a pen and paper," she said.

When she uncrossed her legs and got up from the sofa, Aaron caught a glimpse of white panties when she spread her knees several inches apart. It wasn't Sharon Stone in *Basic Instinct,* but it would do. He wondered whether she did it on purpose or the liquor made her oblivious to her actions.

Just before she reached the doorway to the kitchen, a crash deafened the room when the patio window shattered and glass showered the floor. She threw her hands to her chest and screamed, frozen in place. Walker, who was leaning on the wall, fell to the floor and grabbed his leg. Blood oozed between his fingers.

Aaron leaped from his chair and drew his gun in one move, then vaulted over the coffee table. He wrapped his arms around Mrs. Prescott and they dropped to the floor. "Everybody, get down. Walker, are you okay?"

Walker glared at Aaron, pain etched on his face. "I'm fine, just a couple pieces of glass. No big deal."

Gordon lay on the floor in front of the pantry door, his face ashen, eyes blinking rapidly.

"Are you hurt?" Aaron asked.

"I don't think so, sir," Gordon said. "What happened?"

All of a sudden, it was 'sir.' How quickly attitudes change when danger arises.

Aaron relaxed his hold on Jennifer, but she held tight and squeezed his arm. He patted her arm and released her after making sure she wasn't injured.

"You'll be all right. Just stay down," he said. Their eyes met. Fear and shock had replaced her glassy stare.

He removed a handkerchief from his pocket and crawled to Walker.

"I'm all right, cop," Walker growled.

Aaron placed his gun on the floor and grabbed his leg. When Walker resisted, he said, "Let go of your leg."

Walker pressed his lips together, but reluctantly released the hold on his leg, allowing Aaron to wrap it with the handkerchief. Walker threw his head back and bared his teeth, wincing when Aaron applied pressure.

"Hold this in place," Aaron said. "You might need stitches."

Walker glared at Aaron, but remained silent. He had lost his *Terminator* look. Arnold would be disappointed.

"Mrs. Prescott, are you all right?" Gordon asked.

"She's fine," Aaron said, "but everybody stay where you are, and keep your heads down."

"What was that?" Jennifer asked, her voice shaking.

"I don't know, but there's nothing left of the patio window and there's glass all over the floor in here," Gordon said.

Aaron picked up his gun and crawled around the island in the middle of the kitchen. Raising his gun to eye level, he looked out at the patio. The backyard appeared deserted.

He scrambled to his feet, aiming his gun straight ahead.

"What is it?" Jennifer asked.

Aaron showed his palm and moved toward the patio. Shards of glass crunched under his feet. He searched the bushes for movement, and then stepped through the frame onto the patio, taking cover behind a pillar. There was no one in sight.

He backed into the house, closed the drapes, and looked at the kitchen floor. Wood splinters were scattered among the shards of glass. He holstered his gun, put on plastic gloves, squatted, and carefully sifted through the debris. He removed a plastic bag and a pair of tweezers from his pocket.

"Did you find anything?" Jennifer asked.

Aaron raised an object to eye level and turned it in his hand. "It's a rubber bullet casing," he said, then dropped the casing into the bag and stuffed the bag in his pocket.

She grabbed her elbows and hugged herself, as though the temperature in the room had dropped thirty degrees. Her eyes glistened, and she looked like she never had a drink in her life.

Nothing better than a perceived brush with death to scare someone out of a liquor-induced coma.

"What's going on, Inspector?"

Aaron stood, took out his cell phone, and called the Lake Forest Police. "Yes, I need two units and an ambulance," he said and provided the address. He put his cell phone back in his pocket. "Help is on the way," he said, and looked at Jennifer. "Until we determine exactly what happened here, I'll work with the local police to arrange a twenty-four-hour watch on your house."

Jennifer crinkled her eyebrows. "Do you think that's necessary?"

"Under the circumstances, yes."

She chewed on her lip and wrung her hands. "I suppose you're right."

Four minutes later, two police units and an ambulance screeched to a stop outside the home. Aaron greeted two uniformed officers at the door. Two paramedics holding a gurney stood behind them. Two officers from the second unit were already preparing to control the people who emerged from their homes for a closer look.

Aaron motioned to the paramedics. "In the kitchen, we have a man with an injured leg."

He addressed the two officers at the door. "I want you to check out the immediate area. Talk to the people out here. Make sure there isn't anyone that shouldn't be here," he said, although he figured whoever did the shooting was long gone.

One officer returned to the street, the other walked around the house to the backyard.

When Aaron returned to the kitchen, Jennifer Prescott was sitting in a chair, arms wrapped around her shoulders, staring at the floor.

She raised her head when Aaron entered the room. "What should I do about this?" she asked, waving a hand to gesture at the floor.

"Sweep up the glass and replace the window as soon as possible," he replied, stating the obvious.

"I'll clean it up right away, Mrs. Prescott," Gordon said.

Jennifer forced a smile. "Thank you, Gordon," she said, and then turned to Aaron. "How could someone get into our neighborhood and do this? We're supposed to be safe. Why would anyone want to hurt me?"

"Let's not jump to conclusions. It might have been an accident, someone target practicing in the backyard, a bored teenager looking for kicks. In the meantime, like I said, I'll arrange for a twenty-four-hour watch," he said, then moved toward the door.

"Are you leaving?" she asked, disappointment evident in her voice.

"I need to get back to the precinct. The officers will search the area."

She nodded. "I should call my father and let him know what happened."

"That's probably a good idea," he agreed.

He watched the paramedics cart a reluctant Mitchell Walker out of the house before looking back at Jennifer then left the house. His scheduled visit to interview Jared Prescott's boss and co-workers just got a little more interesting.

Chapter Six

Aaron arrived at ChemPhen Pharmaceuticals Corporation in Cloverleaf Industrial Park, five miles from Chicago O'Hare International Airport, at 10:45 a.m. He passed through security at the main gate, and found a space in the 'Visitors Only' lot.

The main building stretched eight stories high, and appeared as wide as it did tall. A two-story white brick structure identified as a 'Research Laboratory' sat to the right of the main building. A blue and white sign in an empty parking space in front of the main building read 'Jared Prescott, Vice President.' A late model black Lincoln Continental occupied a space closest to the entrance, marked with a sign indicating 'Harlan Grayson – President and CEO.'

ChemPhen was dedicated to the research and development of better drugs for the treatment of serious illnesses and diseases. The company had the largest number of employees in Chicago, and their net earnings the highest in the city, allowing them government grants for continued research in the treatment and preventions of all types of cancer.

Aaron walked up a short flight of steps and entered the main building through a revolving door, to a lobby large enough to function as a small convention center. Palm trees in wooden planters sat in every corner, with a bonsai tree resting in the middle of a large fountain, surrounded by boxed geraniums.

He approached a uniformed man sitting behind a reception area labeled 'Security Desk,' and presented his credentials. "Good morning. I'm here to see Harlan Grayson."

The guard studied the badge without expression, then handed Aaron a red and green laminated clip-on visitor's badge.

"Please wear this at all times while in the building," he said with a robotic expression, then pointed to his right. "The elevator bank is over there. The executive offices are located on the eighth floor. Please check in with the receptionist when you get off the elevator."

Aaron wondered how many levels of security were required before he reached Harlan Grayson. Not that he was complaining. Most would applaud a high level of safety conscious behavior. Others might call it paranoia. Such are the times we live in. He clipped the badge to the lapel of his jacket, and headed for the elevators.

On the eighth floor, he entered a large reception area with a coffee table stacked with magazines, a black end table with a gray lamp, and six bright yellow leather armchairs. It looked more like a doctor's waiting room.

A redheaded middle-aged woman sat behind a large desk, typing furiously on a computer keyboard, so focused she didn't as much as raise an eyebrow to acknowledge Aaron's presence. Good thing he wasn't a disgruntled former employee with an Uzi submachine gun. She would never know what hit her.

He approached the desk and placed his hands on the counter. "Excuse me, can you tell me where Harlan Grayson's office is?"

The woman raised her head and studied him over a pair of bifocals. "Do you have an appointment?"

Her gaze softened when he flashed his badge.

"Oh, I see, you must be here about Mr. Prescott," she said, then shook her head. "It's so terrible what happened." She pointed to the left. "Go down this hallway to the first corridor on your left. Mr. Grayson's office is the last one at the end of the hall."

He thanked the woman, and then proceeded down the hallway, stopping in front of a door with Jared Prescott's name stenciled on the glass.

"Excuse me, can I help you?"

Aaron turned.

A man wearing a white shirt, blue tie, and navy pants approached, his index finger raised as though he was hailing a cab. He was mid-forties, six feet tall, with an average build and neatly groomed brown hair.

Aaron identified himself, and told the man the reason for his visit. The man stopped and showed his palms as though Aaron had pulled out a gun and demanded his wallet.

"I'm sorry, I wasn't told you'd be coming into the office."

At ease, private.

The man shoved his hands into his pockets and gazed into Jared Prescott's office. "We were all so shocked to hear the news about Jared," he said, then looked at Aaron. "What's happening in this city, Inspector?" he asked, as though unaware of the concept of a newspaper or the evening news.

Where has this guy been?

"And you are?"

The man extended his hand. "I'm Warren Kirby, Senior Financial Manager."

Aaron shook his hand.

A woman appeared in the hall behind Kirby. "Mr. Kirby, your meeting starts in two minutes."

He turned. "Thank you, Diane, I'll be right there," he said, then turned back to Aaron. "I'm sorry, Inspector, duty calls. Can I have my secretary get you a cup of coffee?"

"No, thank you, but I'd like to talk to you after I meet with Harlan Grayson, if you can spare a few minutes. I'd also like to look around Mr. Prescott's office."

"I don't think that will be a problem at all. The door is unlocked. My office is just around the corner." Kirby glanced at his watch. "My meeting should be over by eleven thirty."

"That will be fine," Aaron said. He watched Kirby walk down the hall, then entered Jared Prescott's office.

An oversized mahogany desk with brass handles on the drawers and a high-back brown leather swivel chair sat in the middle of the office facing the door. A green lamp and a five by seven photograph of Jared Prescott sat on top of the desk. In the photo, Prescott was dressed in a burgundy smoking jacket with his right arm resting on a mantel above a fireplace.

A glass-enclosed credenza sat against the wall to the right, its top shelf lined with books on accounting, business management, and Dale Carnegie's *How to Win Friends and Influence People*. On the bottom shelf were books on football, golf, hunting, and fishing. Aaron wondered how many of the books Prescott actually read.

Photographs of Prescott holding trophies in various sports occupied almost every corner of the office. In each photograph, his chin pointed forward, as if to say, 'I'm the man.' Perhaps these were reminders of how much he accomplished in other sports to lessen the disappointment of missing the opportunity to play professional football.

On top of the credenza was an eight by ten photograph of the 1989 Northwestern championship football team. Northwestern and Stanford, both undefeated, were ranked number one and two, respectively. On January 1st, 1990, the two teams played for the National Championship in the Rose Bowl in Pasadena.

Jared Prescott had the game of his career, rushing for 152 yards and two touchdowns in the first half to give Northwestern a 24–7 lead.

After three quarters, Northwestern led 38-10. Prescott had rushed for 190 yards and scored four touchdowns. With three and a half minutes left in the game, and Prescott approaching an NCAA bowl game rushing record, he suffered an Anterior Cruciate Ligament tear, commonly referred to as an ACL. The injury required surgery, followed by physical therapy and a long recovery period. The best game of Prescott's career was the last time he played competitive football. The injury was the catalyst to an emotional tailspin. After recuperating from knee surgery, he started drinking and wrecked his car, and spent three months in jail on a DUI charge.

A voice interrupted Aaron's reminiscing. "Hello there."

He turned. An attractive blonde woman wearing a green dress stood in the doorway. "Hello," he said, and identified himself.

"I'm Irene Kennedy, Mr. Prescott's secretary." She looked around the room and shook her head. "I can't believe he's really gone."

"How long did you work for him?" he asked.

"A little over three and a half years."

"Do you remember whether he was in the office this past Monday?"

"Yes, he was."

"Did you notice anything unusual about his behavior that day?"

She gazed at the ceiling for a moment in thought. "Actually, not that day in particular, but the last couple of weeks he did seem more preoccupied than usual, but I expect that's typical for a VP. I had to leave early that day for a doctor appointment. After lunch, he was behind closed doors, but that's not unusual."

"From what I heard, he was a ladies' man. I'm sorry if this embarrasses you, but did he ever come on to you, make advances, or harass you in any way?"

"I see word travels fast," she said with a slight smile. "Yes, Jared was a skirt chaser. He didn't flirt with me any more or less than with the other young women in the office, but he never put his hands on me, nor did I ever feel threatened. The truth is, some of the girls liked the attention and flirted back. Most call it harmless, although nowadays, it could be considered sexual harassment. There were rumors of affairs, but I guess in companies this size, those are inevitable. Some people live for stirring the pot. Frankly, I don't think anybody cared, and being married to the boss's daughter, I'm sure Mr. Prescott knew where to draw the line."

"I see," he said. "Sorry I had to ask the question."

"I understand," she said, and then turned to leave.

"Mrs. Kennedy, one more question. When I talked to Mrs. Prescott, she mentioned her husband usually carried his briefcase, and was surprised we didn't find it at the scene. I wonder whether it's in his office, perhaps locked up in one of his drawers."

"She's right. Mr. Prescott was meticulous in keeping his planner up to date on all his personal and business appointments, and always carried it in his briefcase. If you like, I can get keys to his desk and cabinets for you."

"Thank you."

She returned with the keys, and after an exhaustive search of the credenza, desk, and file cabinet, with no sign of the briefcase, she locked up and left the office.

A minute later, Aaron's back was facing the door when he heard another voice. "It's quite the shrine, isn't it?"

Aaron turned. A mid-fifties stocky man stood in the doorway, his hands buried in the pants pockets of an elegant gray three-piece suit. He had thin graying hair, and a ruddy and weather-beaten face suggested he spent time outdoors. Intensity brewed in his dark and deep-set eyes.

He stepped forward and extended his hand. "The receptionist informed me of your arrival. I'm Harlan

Grayson, President of ChemPhen Pharmaceuticals." Aaron swore he was looking down his nose and rocked back on his heels when he introduced himself, as if 'President' was a title reserved solely for him.

Aaron shook Grayson's hand. It was large.

"I see you've made yourself at home searching through Jared's office."

"Is that a problem?" Aaron asked, sensing a tone of accusation in Grayson's voice.

Grayson shrugged like he was urging a mosquito to fly off his shoulder. "I suppose not, but what do you expect to find?"

"Everything in this office has potential to provide information," Aaron said.

"Don't you think you should have presented a search warrant?" Grayson said with an air, as though he was an expert in search and seizure laws.

"I'm not searching, just browsing."

"Semantics, Inspector."

"Depends on your perspective," Aaron countered. *This guy is already off my Christmas card list.*

"Find anything interesting?"

"Like you said, it's quite the shrine. I'm here simply to inquire."

"Inquire," Grayson repeated, as though dissatisfied with the word. He made a half-turn and extended his arm. "I'm sure we'll be more comfortable talking in my office."

Aaron pointed to the photograph of the Northwestern football team. "I'll need to take that photograph when I leave."

"I don't see how it will help your investigation, but you're welcome to it. I'm here to cooperate, but we *will* need it returned."

"You'll get it back. Do you recognize anyone in the photograph?"

"Sorry, not my generation," Grayson said flatly. "Jared didn't talk much about his college football days. I suspect his failure to play professional football made the subject too painful to discuss. Let's continue this discussion in my office, shall we?"

Chapter Seven

The outside of Harlan Grayson's office was spacious, with a conference table and a variety of plants. A middle-aged woman with silver hair sat behind a desk.

"Hold my calls, Jean," Grayson said.

"Yes, Mr. Grayson."

Grayson opened the door to his office and extended his arm. "Inspector."

Grayson's office was larger than the two biggest rooms in Aaron's apartment combined. A number of photographs on the walls indicated him as an accomplished sportsman.

Talk about a shrine.

Grayson pointed to a photograph on the wall. He and another man dressed in camouflaged outfits stood over a large buck.

"That was three years ago in Canada. Fifty yards away, I caught him right between the eyes. He dropped like a sack of cement."

Poor defenseless animal.

"I noticed similar photographs in Mr. Prescott's office," Aaron said with no interest, wondering whether the two men were in competition to see who could display the most trophies. "Did you two ever hunt together?"

Grayson ignored the question. Instead, he reached into a box on the desk and took out a cigar.

"Care for one? It's a Stradivarius, made in Havana."

"No thanks," Aaron said. "What brand of cigarette do you smoke?"

"I don't smoke cigarettes, just cigars, occasionally a pipe."

"I see," Aaron said and waved his arm. "I don't think I've ever seen an office this large."

Grayson flashed a smug grin. "Running a company does have its benefits," he said, then fished a gold lighter from his jacket pocket and lit the cigar. He sat down in the chair behind the desk, took a puff, eyeing the cigar as he might a trophy. A wisp of smoke rose to the ceiling, and the air grew rich with the aroma of tobacco.

"Forgive my manners," he said. "I hope you don't mind."

Aaron wondered why Grayson didn't ask before lighting the cigar, but there was already too much idle banter. Another irrelevant comment would only provide the man an opportunity to waste more time. "I'm surprised you permit smoking in the office."

"Our filtration system is state-of-the-art. Of course, I provide my employees separate designated smoking areas," Grayson said, then switched topics as though bored. "I just got off the phone with Jennifer a few minutes ago. Needless to say, she's still shaken up over the shooting. I asked her to stay with me."

"Did she take you up on your offer?"

Grayson shook his head. "She said she didn't want to bother me, and would stay with a friend. One thing for sure, whoever killed Jared is a coward, and will get everything coming to him."

"Don't jump to any conclusions, and I hope you're not making threats," Aaron said. "We don't know yet if it even *was* a man. Let us handle it."

"Exactly what are the police doing about the shooting at my daughter's home?"

"We've requested more frequent patrols in the area, and arranged for a twenty-four hour watch on her home. Does your daughter have any enemies?"

"I can't imagine, but it's conceivable she was a target because of her relationship to me," Grayson said.

"Why you?"

"Don't be naive, Inspector. People in my position have enemies, but it's usually based on jealousy of money and power."

"So, you assigned her a bodyguard because you thought her life was in danger?"

"I err on the side of caution, and I'm not sure bodyguard is the right term. I simply wanted someone to watch over her until things settled down."

"You could have requested police protection. Some people might think Walker was more of a male companion than a watchdog."

"The police force has other priorities, and the notion of male companionship is absurd. Personally, I don't give a damn what people might think. I do what is necessary."

"That's considerate of you," Aaron quipped.

"Given the incident at the house yesterday, you'd have to admit in hindsight I did the right thing," Grayson said with a wide grin.

If you're fishing for a compliment, cast your rod in another pond.

"Let's discuss Jared Prescott," Aaron said. "Tell me about Monday. His secretary said he seemed preoccupied for the last couple of weeks. Do you know why?"

"Jared and I were scheduled to meet that evening at six o'clock. I wanted to talk to him about assuming control of the company, although I'm not planning to retire for at least another year. He wasn't aware of the reason for the meeting, but we've discussed the subject from time to time, so perhaps he assumed that was my agenda. I've run this business many years, and recently decided it was time to relax and enjoy the finer things in life." He gestured at the wall. "As you can see, I enjoy the outdoors. Hunting, fishing, I might even take golf lessons."

"That's real interesting," Aaron said with a roll of his eyes.

If Grayson noticed, he didn't react.

"Did anyone else know about the meeting?" Aaron asked.

"I kept it off the radar due to the nature of the discussion. You'd be surprised how people react to rumors of change at the top. They assume mass overhaul and downsizing, imagine the worst-case scenario. Such panic is unfounded in my opinion. In any case, Jared canceled the meeting for personal reasons."

"Did he say what those reasons were?"

Grayson looked at Aaron and lifted a single eyebrow. "I guess you didn't hear me say the word *personal*. He didn't say, and I didn't ask, although I was aware he and Jennifer were having problems. I didn't want to pry."

"I'm surprised, especially since it involved your daughter."

Grayson narrowed his eyes. "Some things are best left alone for those to work it out between themselves."

"Did your daughter know about the meeting?"

"I don't discuss company business with Jennifer. Whether Jared told her, I couldn't say. In any case, why does it matter? I don't see how…"

Aaron stopped Grayson with a show of his palm. "If you don't mind, I'll ask the questions."

Good guys 1, bad guys 0.

Grayson looked away. "Fair enough," he said, barely audible. "Frankly, I found it interesting Jared was killed around the same time we were going to discuss him taking over the company."

"As if someone didn't want him to succeed?"

"It's certainly plausible. Anyway, I called Jennifer about eight o'clock that night to make sure everything was all right between her and Jared. Nobody answered, and I didn't leave a message. The next time we talked she gave me the bad news about Jared."

"I expect the same people who didn't want to see Mr. Prescott in charge might have taken exception to his being hired. Were you aware of his drinking problem and time in jail?"

"Of course I knew about his past. I'm where I am today by knowing everything about the people working for me. I hired him despite his troubled past because I saw a bright young man with a good head for business. He would have made a great leader. I don't believe any man should suffer the rest of his life because of a little jail time for a nonviolent crime."

"I guess that goes for you allowing him to marry your daughter."

"Jared overcame adversity and straightened out his life. I respected him for his resolve. Most men don't recover from a shattered dream. I wanted to give him the chance he deserved. It turned out I was right."

Take a number and stand in line to kiss my ass.

"So, your daughter had no influence in your decision to hire him?"

Grayson's nostrils flared. "I hire people based on talent, ambition, and ability to add value to the company, not for personal reasons."

"Did you approve of their marriage?"

"Jared initially seemed to be good for Jennifer, and I wasn't going to pass judgment even if I was inclined. She's a grown woman, and I respect her decisions. Besides, she didn't approve of my second marriage. She and Patricia were never close. I can't say I blame her. Nobody can take the place of one's biological mother." He looked away for a moment before looking back. "Have you ever lost a loved one, Inspector?"

"My parents live in Phoenix, both retired."

"Are you married?"

"Divorced."

"That's too bad. Jennifer was thirteen when her mother died. Charlotte suffered with breast cancer for almost two years, and that gave me incentive to lead this company in cancer research. It also strengthened my resolve. Unfortunately, my dedication to the company prevented me from being the perfect father to Jennifer."

"Sounds like an excuse to me," Aaron said.

"I did the best I could under the circumstances," Grayson continued without reaction. "I remarried seven years ago. Patricia was a casualty of the September eleventh terrorist attacks. She was on the plane flying out of New York. Now this business with Jared."

Aaron found it peculiar Grayson glossed over his second wife's death in one of history's greatest tragedies, and his son-in-law's murder as 'business,' but he chose to guide the conversation back on track. The more time he spent with Grayson, the less he liked the man.

"Your daughter said her husband didn't get along well with some of his co-workers. Want to comment on that?"

"Nobody gets along with all of their co-workers. Jared was ambitious, maybe too ambitious for his own good."

"What do you mean by that?" Aaron asked.

Grayson shrugged as though the answer was obvious. "He often came across as someone that would step over people to get what he wanted."

"Did he?"

"Ambition builds empires," Grayson said with an air of finality, as if it was a one-sentence textbook for how to be successful in business.

"Did he?" Aaron repeated, determined to force Grayson back on topic.

"Did he what?" Grayson asked with a frown.

"Step over people."

"Let's be honest, Inspector. People envy success. Professionally, Jared was a sharp individual, but he was arrogant and carried a hefty chip on his shoulder. His attitude might have alienated him from some of the staff, but that same attitude grooms leaders."

Takes one to know one.

"Do you know anyone that would want to kill your son-in-law?" Aaron chose a direct question, hoping to entice Grayson to respond in kind.

It did just the opposite.

Grayson got up from the chair and walked to the window, put his hands behind his back, and rolled the cigar with the tip of his fingers, as though he fancied himself a king looking down on his subjects.

"Jared was a former All-American football player," he said as though it was a revelation. "He was financially and socially successful. Right or wrong, that success breeds jealousy. Jealousy often turns to hatred, and I expect is an appropriate motive given a certain psychological profile."

Now who's watching too much TV?

"The sad truth is, Inspector, I'm afraid you'll find more than your share of suspects."

"What about his infidelity?"

"What about it?'

"It's a strong motive for murder."

Grayson turned and studied Aaron through narrowed eyes. "That's a ridiculous inference that doesn't deserve a response, and I don't care for the accusation."

"It's an observation, not an accusation."

"I'll accept that," Grayson said. "In any case, if I gave you the impression I would provide you with a list of names, you've misunderstood." He sniffed and stuck the cigar into his mouth as though signaling an end to the interview.

Aaron wasn't ready to leave just yet. "Do you know what time he left work that day?"

"I went by his office at six-thirty and he was already gone."

"Your daughter said he didn't come home that night. Do you have any idea where he went from the time he left work until the time he arrived at the motel?"

"He probably went out to dinner," Grayson said with a shrug.

"There's a question about his briefcase," Aaron said. "Both your daughter and his secretary were surprised he didn't have it, and we didn't find it at the scene. It wasn't at his home or in his office. Is it possible it contained confidential documents that if found or sold might be harmful to the company?"

Grayson flashed a wide grin. "I see. CIA, NSA, spy stuff, very good, Inspector. You have a flair for the dramatic, but I assure you, there is nothing secretive about what we do here at ChemPhen."

"I don't waste time with frivolous questions. I was serious."

"Jared had no reason to sell company secrets, even if we had any to sell. He was a rich man, and as I told you, in line to take over the company. He was loyal and would not dare cross me or break the trust we had. It's ludicrous to make such a statement."

"I see. If you happen to run across his briefcase, we'll need to know."

"We'll see that you are informed," Grayson said, as though the statement was no more than an afterthought. "So, tell me, do you have any leads on Jared's killer?"

"It's early in the investigation, but we have a description of a woman who rented the room where we found him."

Grayson turned back to the window. "So, you have a suspect then," he said as more of a statement than a question.

"At this point she's nothing more than a person of interest."

Grayson shook his head and clucked his tongue. "Like I said before, semantics. Now, is there anything else? I have a company to run."

"We found drugs in the motel room, so we're looking into the possibility of a drug deal, although we don't know who bought or who sold. Is it possible…"

Grayson stopped Aaron with a hard laugh. "That's more ridiculous than your company secrets theory. Nobody working for me uses drugs and gets away with it, especially my son-in-law."

"We'll check Mr. Prescott's office, home, and cell phone records for the past month. I expect you will inform your staff to give us their full cooperation. We may want to talk to some of your people. Of course, we'll obtain the proper warrants when appropriate."

"I'd expect nothing less, and trust your superiors will make it clear I expect minimal disruptions of my operation," Grayson said, as though suggesting Aaron's sole function was to follow orders.

"I hope you're not saying you won't give us anything but your full cooperation."

Grayson pressed his lips together. "I'm more anxious than you to find out who killed my son-in-law, and see that they pay for what they did. The quicker we put this behind us, the better for everyone involved."

"Right, you have a company to run. Is that why you pulled strings to rush his autopsy?"

Grayson squinted at Aaron, but didn't answer.

"We've discussed your son-in-law's death from a company standpoint. How has it affected you personally?"

"I joined the Marine Corps at eighteen, fought in the Tet Offensive in Vietnam in sixty-eight. I lost two wives, one to the most heinous acts of terrorism in our country's history."

At least he finally acknowledged the magnitude of 9/11.

"I'm sympathetic to grief from losing a loved one, but either you pick yourself up and move forward, or allow it to destroy you. I chose to move forward."

Aaron had the option of standing and applauding, or redirecting the line of questioning. He chose the latter. "Where were you Monday night?"

"I left work at eight o'clock, went home and had a light dinner, then watched television before going to bed at ten o'clock."

"That's very precise. Most people wouldn't recall such details," Aaron said, feeling an uncontrollable urge to get under Grayson's skin.

"I'm a creature of habit," Grayson stated without reaction.

"How and when did you hear the news about your son-in-law?"

"I already told you, my daughter called me on my cell phone the next morning."

"Do you have any idea why Mr. Prescott was in that part of town? It seems a little bit, let's say, off his beaten path."

"I understand the area has high crime," Grayson said, dodging the question like a matador facing a charging bull.

"If you answer every question with a question, or give me a history lesson, we'll be here all day." This time Aaron detected a flinch.

"Knowing Jared, I suspect he was there to meet the woman who rented the room."

"Since he won't be around to assume control of the company, it's a shame you won't be able to retire and enjoy those finer things you mentioned, unless you have someone else in mind."

Grayson sighed heavily with annoyance, but recovered quickly. "I once considered my Senior Financial Manager as the next logical choice, but I'm not sure he possesses what it takes to run a company this size. Perhaps in five years. I'll stay as long as necessary. It's not what we call in business a showstopper. Golf lessons can wait. Besides, I don't see how my retirement planning relates to your investigation."

"As much as your career in the Marine corps or trips on your private jet," Aaron stated firmly, not knowing whether Grayson even had a private jet. Things were getting nasty.

"Very good, Inspector," Grayson said with a sarcastic smile.

"You never did answer my earlier question."

Grayson wrinkled his brow and appeared genuinely baffled, giving Aaron a sense of satisfaction. "Which question was that?"

"Whether you and Mr. Prescott ever hunted together."

"We may have gone out once or twice. I own a cabin and go there every winter during hunting season. Jared preferred to socialize with his own generation. So do I."

Aaron gestured toward a photograph centered on the wall above the credenza. Grayson and another man stood in front of a cabin, both holding shotguns.

"Is that the cabin?"

"Yes. Do you recognize the other man?"

"No, should I?"

"That's Illinois Senator Nathan Caldwell."

"Is that a fact?" Aaron said, although wanted to say 'so what.'

"We've known each other since before the war. Despite our busy schedules, we make time to get away to hunt and fish a couple weeks during the year."

Grayson crushed the cigar into an ashtray, sat down, and folded his hands on top of his desk.

"Nathan and I served in the same unit in Vietnam. I once considered a career in the Marine Corps, but was discharged from duty after receiving the Purple Heart for being wounded in action. Too bad, the Corps needs leaders."

A ringing phone interrupted the conversation.

Thank God for small favors.

Grayson punched the button, but kept his eyes on Aaron. "Yes, what is it, Jean?"

"I'm very sorry, sir. I know you didn't want to be disturbed, but Mr. Huber said it's urgent."

"Thank you, Jean, tell him I'll be with him in a moment."

"Problems?" Aaron asked.

"I prefer to call them opportunities," Grayson said. "Kurt Huber is our top research scientist managing one of our major projects. The man is a little eccentric and sometimes overreacts, but I suspect that's the case with most geniuses." He stood and pressed his knuckles against the top of the desk. "Now, if there's nothing more, I have work to do."

Aaron stood. "We're finished for now, but I expect we'll be talking again. In the meantime, I've arranged a meeting with Mr. Kirby."

"Warren's a good man, and he'll cooperate. Hopefully, he can help you with your issues," Grayson said, emphasizing the word 'issues' as though Aaron was a fish without fins in the middle of the Pacific Ocean. "If you run into any problems getting what you want, let me know and I'll take care of it."

Aaron took a business card from his pocket and tossed it on the desk. "I'll expect a call if you remember anything else you think is appropriate, just in case something slipped your mind."

Grayson thrust his hands into his pockets, giving the card as much attention as he would to a falling leaf in autumn. "Good day, Inspector."

Aaron walked toward the door, then turned back after he put his hand on the knob. "One more thing. I haven't ruled out anyone as a potential suspect, and that includes you, Mr. Grayson."

Grayson's mouth formed a straight line. "I'm sure you'll do the right thing, Inspector."

Aaron closed the door, sensing a stare burning a hole in the back of his jacket.

Chapter Eight

Warren Kirby was talking on the phone when Aaron entered his office.

"I have someone in my office," he said, then hung up the phone and stood. He gestured to a brown leather chair in front of his desk.

After seeing Prescott's and Grayson's offices, size and décor appeared to be directly related to position in the company. After the verbal skirmish with Grayson, that wasn't the least bit surprising.

The furnishings in Kirby's office were limited to a desk, one visitor chair, a small round table with two chairs, and a four-drawer filing cabinet. The quality of the furniture lacked in comparison to the furniture in both Grayson and Prescott's offices.

Aaron sat down in a chair and opened his notepad.

Kirby sat down and swiveled his chair to look out the window. "Sure is a hot one today. It would be nice if we got some rain."

Aaron was in no mood for small talk, even less so after fencing with Harlan Grayson. "Let's dispense with the weather report, shall we, Mr. Kirby?"

Kirby turned back to face Aaron and swallowed a lump in his throat. "Of course. Sorry. Was Mr. Grayson able to help? I know he's pretty broken up about Jared's death."

"Funny, I didn't get the sense he was overcome with grief."

Kirby smiled. "Yes, well, he is a tough old bird. Now, how can I help you, Inspector?"

"I have some routine questions."

"Sure, go ahead."

"When did you first hear the news about Mr. Prescott?"

"Mr. Grayson called a meeting of the department managers and told us. He said to keep it as low profile as possible, and asked us to announce it to our individual staff."

"How did you feel when you heard the news?"

Kirby creased his brow. "Obviously, we all were shocked, especially how it happened."

"Tell me about your professional and social relationship with Jared Prescott."

Kirby's head moved back. "You don't waste any time."

"I'm investigating a murder, Mr. Kirby. I don't have the luxury of wasting time."

"Of course," Kirby said, and then cleared his throat. "Professionally, Jared and I have a standing meeting at the end of every month to review the company's financial reports. We also meet when Mr. Grayson schedules a session with the department managers."

"What about socially? Did you and Mr. Prescott ever have a beer after work, for example?"

"No, nothing like that, not on our own. We ate lunch together occasionally, but always discussed business. We had company parties, you know at Christmas time and such. Those always include departmental staff."

"What did you think of Mr. Prescott personally?"

Kirby unfolded his arms and forced out a breath. "I won't lie to you, Inspector. Quite frankly, I've never met anyone with an ego the size of Jared's, but I have a feeling you've already heard that. He considered himself better than everyone."

"Did he ever insult you or put you down?"

"Not directly, but he was subtle in his sarcasm. Sometimes, it was what he said, but more often, it was his condescending tone of voice. Other times, it was the way he looked at people with his nose in the air, as if they shouldn't be allowed to walk on the same ground. He considered himself an answer man, constantly offering unsolicited advice. He had a saying, what was it? Oh yes, 'you got to stay ahead in the game.'"

"Were you involved in the decision to hire Mr. Prescott?"

"No, Mr. Grayson made the decision himself, but that's expected since Jared came in as Vice President, directly under Mr. Grayson."

"Were you surprised Grayson looked outside the company to fill the position?"

"Some people were surprised, but Jared came highly recommended."

"How did you feel about that?"

"If you're asking whether I resented Mr. Grayson hiring Jared from the outside, I'll tell you a number of managers, myself included, believed we were as qualified."

"Yes, but realistically, other than you, who else did Grayson consider for the position? I mean, that must have been a short list."

"Yes, but it came down to Prescott and me in the end. Naturally, I was disappointed and spoke to Mr. Grayson about his choice. He assured me I was being considered, although I was never actually interviewed for the position."

"Just disappointed?" Aaron asked.

"That's all."

"Did you think Prescott was hired because of his relationship with Grayson's daughter?"

"Harlan Grayson didn't get to where he is today by playing favorites, even if it involved his daughter," Kirby said.

"How long have you worked for ChemPhen?" Aaron asked.

"I'll have twenty-two years at the end of September. I was hired as an accounting clerk out of college and worked my way up."

"I would guess a Senior Financial Manager makes good money working for a company this size."

"I do make a very good living," Kirby said with a grin.

"How long have you been Senior Financial Manager?"

"Almost three years."

"How many positions have you held since you've worked for ChemPhen?"

"After accounting clerk, I was promoted to Supervisor, and then manager of Accounting. I made Senior Manager of Accounting before I was promoted to Senior Financial Manager."

"What's the next logical promotion?"

A knowing smile crept across Kirby's lips. "I see where this is going."

"Well?"

"Vice President," Kirby said flatly.

"Vice President," Aaron echoed. "I assume that would include a healthy pay raise."

Kirby folded his arms and his face turned a shade of red. "I'm sorry, but I don't have knowledge of the salaries of staff other than those working directly under me."

Something in Kirby's eyes told Aaron he had hit a nerve. "Can you think of anyone with strong enough motive to kill Mr. Prescott?"

"I'm not an expert in psychology, but I expect it would have to be a strong reason for someone to commit murder."

"It usually is," Aaron agreed.

"I won't accuse anyone based on speculation," Kirby said. "I can only speak for myself."

"I'm not asking you to accuse anyone. I'm just looking for someone with motive."

"I don't know anyone with a hate strong enough to kill, and nobody I know in this company fits that mold."

"Did you see Mr. Prescott on Monday?" Aaron asked.

"I'm sure I did, but we didn't meet that day, and I left at five o'clock. I can't say whether he was here or not when I left. He often stays late."

"Did you talk to him at all?"

"No, unless we're in the same meeting, Jared and I don't typically engage in idle conversation."

"Can you account for your whereabouts that evening?" Aaron asked.

"I was home all night, my wife can attest to that," Kirby said, with more than a trace of irritation.

"Mrs. Prescott mentioned an incident with her husband and a co-worker involving a fake head. She thought his name was George. Do you know what she was referring to?"

Kirby laughed and appeared to relax. "She must be referring to the football bet with the head in the bag. I said before, Jared played no favorites, but did seem to ride George more than most."

"What's George's last name?"

"Thompson. He's my chief accountant."

"Care to give me the details?" Aaron asked.

Kirby shrugged. "I heard the story second-hand and don't want to misrepresent anything. It would be better if you talked to George about it."

"I'll do that. Where is his office?"

"He's out sick, but my secretary can give you his home address."

Aaron put his notepad and pen away and handed Kirby a business card.

"Thank you for your time, Mr. Kirby. Give me a call if you think of anything else that might be relevant."

"I certainly will, Inspector."

They stood and shook hands.

After obtaining George Thompson's address from Kirby's secretary, and the photograph from Jared Prescott's office, Aaron drove to Thompson's house. He sensed today's conversations would not be the last with Kirby or Grayson.

Chapter Nine

George Thompson lived at 1229 Harvest, Oak Park, a two-story home with blue and white shutters, and a one-car detached garage in back. A lonesome pine tree stood in the front yard, and four evergreen shrubs in front looked starved for water, casualties of the recent drought.

Aaron parked in the driveway behind a dark blue, older model Honda Civic, got out of his car, and approached the house.

A note taped to the front door read 'Doorbell out of order – please knock.'

He knocked on the door, and a fortyish, five foot seven bald man wearing glasses, a wrinkled light gray t-shirt, and gray sweat pants opened the door a crack.

"I'm Inspector Randall, Chicago Homicide," Aaron said, holding up his badge in plain view. "Are you George Thompson?"

The man squinted at the badge and swallowed. "Yes, I am. What can I do for you, Inspector?"

"I need to ask you some questions about Jared Prescott. Do you mind if I come in?"

Thompson glanced behind him before he opened the door and stepped aside. "Yes, come in please."

A high-pitched voice sounded from the second floor. "George, did you say something?"

"It's for me," Thompson said, and then turned to Aaron and smiled, his face flushed. "My mother."

The living room was furnished with a dark green sofa, a brown coffee table, and two matching chairs, on dark green pile carpeting looking worse for wear. A thirty-two-inch Samsung TV sat inside an entertainment center in an alcove. On a mantle above the fireplace was a photograph of Thompson with an older man and woman Aaron assumed were his parents.

Thompson sat on the sofa and gestured to a chair. "Please, have a seat. My mother has rheumatoid arthritis and has trouble getting around," he said, and then gestured to the photograph on the mantle. "My father died seven years ago. I couldn't leave her alone, so I sold my house and moved in with her. A live-in nurse costs too much, and I don't feel right putting her into assisted care living. As it is, I have to pay a part-time nurse to care for her when I'm at work."

"That's a noble gesture," Aaron said, not sure why Thompson felt it necessary to explain why he still lived with his mother. "I hope you're feeling better."

"Huh? What do you mean?" Thompson said with a tilt of his head.

"Your boss said you called in sick."

"Oh yes, that. I think it was a stomach virus. I took vacation last week, although I stayed here and worked around the house, you know, because of my mother's condition. I must have picked up something right before I was supposed to return to work. Some timing, huh?" Thompson wrung his hands. "The news about Mr. Prescott didn't help."

"It sounds like you were friends."

Thompson looked up and snickered. "Hardly," he said, and then paused and swallowed. "I mean, we worked for the same company, but were not friends in a social sense." He rubbed his thighs and looked away. "He would never socialize with someone like me."

"What do you mean?"

Thompson looked back. "He was Vice President, and socialized only with rich people or people that could help his career."

"I see," Aaron said with a nod. "Your boss said you're the chief accountant. What does that mean?"

"I maintain the company books, prepare the balance sheet, in short, I'm responsible for the company's financial reporting. ChemPhen is doing very well. They had record earnings last year."

"That's good to hear. Listen, Mr. Thompson, I don't want to take up a lot of your time, but your boss mentioned a practical joke organized by Jared Prescott, something about a head in a bag. I'd like to hear more about that."

Thompson's laugh sounded like he was traveling over a road filled with potholes. After a few moments, he gathered himself and said, "That was probably the most embarrassing time of my life. It was the middle of October last year, about halfway through the football season. A group of guys in the office organized a pool to bet on the Bears game. They were playing Dallas on Sunday night. I don't follow football that close, but know a little. They asked me if I wanted to get in on the bet. I think they were surprised when I agreed, because I don't talk much sports around the office. I figured if I didn't win, no big deal, everyone would expect it, but if I did, it would give me a chance to show those guys up."

He paused and stared at the ceiling for a moment. "Anyway, there were ten of us in on the bet. The Bears had a slow start last year, but had won three straight and the Cowboys were undefeated. I figured most would go with the Cowboys, so I went with the Bears to win by a point. The tiebreaker was total points on the Monday night game. Whoever came in last had to buy the winner's lunch and pick up lunch for everyone."

A flush crept across Thompson's cheeks. "Wouldn't you know it, I came in last and Prescott won it all, so I had to pay for his lunch."

"Bad timing," Aaron said, mildly entertained by Thompson's recount. It was a welcome respite from his interview with Harlan Grayson.

"Anyway, I wanted to get it over with, but Prescott wanted to wait a couple of weeks. I didn't understand why at the time. Two weeks later, I placed an order with Jason's Deli to pick up the sandwiches. It's about a mile from the office. It was about forty degrees and windier than usual. It's almost as if Prescott ordered the weather just for my benefit. I offered to give him the money and have the food delivered, but he didn't go for it." Thompson shook his head. "I realized later he wanted to wait so he could plan his scheme.

"The fake head?" Aaron asked.

"Yes. Anyway, when I came out of Jason's Deli, this woman walked up and handed me a shopping bag from Balani's."

"Balani's?"

"It's an exclusive men's clothing store," Thompson said, then put a hand to his chest. "I don't shop there."

No wonder I never heard of it.

"Here's a present for you, George, she said, like she knew me. She said it in a sexy, flinty kind of voice, like, you know, she was flirting." George laughed in spite of himself. "Yeah, like some strange woman would ever be interested in *me*."

"Can you describe her?"

"She was about my height, but might have been wearing high heels, I don't know for sure. She wore big sunglasses," Thompson said as he shaped his fingers into an 'O,' and raised them to his eyes, "and she was attractive. She had nice skin and wore red lipstick, wore a white fur overcoat with a blue scarf. I stared at her for a few seconds before I realized I was holding the shopping bag in my hand. I looked down at the bag for a few seconds, and when I looked back up, she was gone."

Thompson crooked his hand to mimic holding a bag. "And there I was, standing in the middle of the sidewalk, a big bag of sandwiches in one hand, a shopping bag from Balani's in the other. I must have looked pretty silly."

"What was in the bag?" Aaron asked, growing more interested by the minute.

Thompson rolled his eyes. "It felt like it weighed ten or fifteen pounds. I didn't know what to do, so I put it down on the sidewalk, and before I could open it to look inside, someone yelled 'freeze.' The next thing I knew, two men grabbed me from behind and forced me up against the wall in front of Jason's Deli. They identified themselves as FBI agents. They had guns drawn. They frisked me like I was public enemy number one."

"Frisked you?"

"Yes. Naturally, people stopped to see what was going on. They flashed badges so fast I didn't get a chance to look at them, not that I could tell real from fake. They wore black matching overcoats and black leather gloves. They turned me around and one had his hand on my chest and leaned against me, as though I was going to resist with two guys holding guns on me. They sure looked and acted official."

"I guess it's safe to assume they weren't FBI agents," Aaron said.

Thompson's face turned a bright red and he shook his head. "Not even law enforcement, let alone FBI."

"What happened next?"

"They led me to a building around the corner and took me to a room on the third floor. There was nothing there but a gray metal table and three or four folding chairs. One put the shopping bag on the table, and told me sit down. He sat next to me, the other man stood at the other side of the table." Thompson drew a breath and ran a hand over the top of his head. "It was then I noticed something red was leaking from the bottom of the bag."

"Red?"

"Yes, red, like blood. The man sitting next to me asked me where I got the bag, so I told him about the woman. He asked me whether I'd ever seen her before and I told him no. They asked me to describe her, and I did, but they said they didn't believe me. One guy made a crack, 'George, your nose is growing like Pinnochio.' By this time, whatever was leaking from the bag had dripped onto the floor. I know they saw it, but neither one said anything. It turned out they knew what was in the bag."

Thompson rubbed a hand across his mouth and shook his head. "They asked me about my relationship with Jared Prescott. I asked them what he had to do with this. One of them just said, 'we'll ask the questions, Georgie.' When he called me 'Georgie', I knew these guys were phony, although I still didn't know what was going on. Prescott is the only one that calls me Georgie, and he does it to get under my skin."

"They sat and stared at me for a few moments, then the one standing reached into the bag and pulled out…" Thompson slapped a hand to his forehead. "What an idiot I was. I actually *believed* it."

"Mr. Thompson, what did he pull out of the bag?"

Thompson looked at Aaron. "Jared Prescott's head."

"What?"

"Obviously, it wasn't really his head, but it was so lifelike, the eyes wide open, the fake blood dripping from the neck. It scared me half to death. I was so mad after, I wished it *was* his head." Thompson's eyes flitted to Aaron and away, as though he realized the bad timing of the last comment.

"What happened next?"

"They asked me whether I held a grudge against Prescott for making me buy the sandwiches and practically accused me of cutting off his head."

"What did you tell them?"

"I was so damn nervous, I just sat there and stared at the head for a few moments until…"

"Until what?"

"Prescott walked into the room. He grabbed the head by the hair and held it up. 'Perfect likeness, isn't it, Georgie, although I must say, not as handsome as the real thing.' The three of them had a big laugh over it. They told me to go back to my office and enjoy my lunch, as if I still had an appetite. Prescott said, 'don't be late, Georgie, lots to do this afternoon, and by the way, where is my sandwich? I ordered corned beef, and don't want it to spoil. It wouldn't look too good getting food poisoning from a sandwich you bought, would it?'"

Thompson leaned forward and buried his face in his hands, then looked up and sat back against the sofa. "Then he gave that line of his, 'Georgie, if you want to succeed, you must stay ahead in the game.' He emphasized the syllable *head*. I *hated* that saying!"

"What did you do?" Aaron asked.

"What could I do?" George said, throwing up his hands. "Prescott was Vice President and Mr. Grayson's son-in-law. I tried to laugh along with them, you know, try to show them it didn't bother me, but Prescott knew better. He put the head back in the bag, took his sandwich, and the three of them left without another word. They didn't even bother to clean up the mess, but that was typical Prescott, always figuring someone else will pick up after him. I waited a few minutes before going back to work. Naturally, he made sure the whole office knew about it, and I caught flack for a good month. I guess I should be grateful they didn't videotape the whole thing."

"What happened to the head?" Aaron asked.

"Darned if I know. Prescott probably put it in his trophy case."

"Your boss mentioned Prescott seemed to target you more than anyone else. Was that true?"

Thompson looked hurt, as if he felt Kirby had ratted him out. "I suppose he did, although I don't know why. It was just my lousy luck to lose that bet. I'm sure it made his day. He went through a lot of planning to get two other people involved in something that lasted only a half hour. He might be Vice President, but sometimes acts like he's still in high school."

"What about the two phony FBI agents? Did you recognize them or hear their names?"

Thompson shook his head. "I've never seen them before or since, but if I ever did, I'd recognize them. Prescott never thought I was good at anything but numbers, but I'm *real* good at remembering faces."

"Can you describe them in more detail?"

Thompson removed his glasses and rubbed his forehead. "Both men were big, like football players. Prescott probably chose them to add realism to the scam. One guy was tall, maybe six-two or three, with black bushy hair. He had wide shoulders and a gut, weighed maybe two-twenty or two-thirty. The other guy was maybe six-one, kind of mean-looking with hair graying at the temples. He was at least twenty to thirty pounds heavier. They looked about Prescott's age."

Aaron stood. "Excuse me for a minute. I'm going to get something from the car."

"Sure," Thompson said with a shrug.

Aaron returned with the photograph of the Northwestern football team, and handed it to Thompson. "This might be a long shot, but see if you recognize anyone."

Thompson studied the photograph for a time, and then tapped on the glass. "This photograph is almost ten years old, and I can't say for sure, but I think it's these two standing next to each other."

"Okay," Aaron said. "Please understand, I must ask this question, Mr. Thompson. Did you ever consider getting back at Prescott?"

Thompson pursed his lips and looked down at his hands. "You mean seek revenge?"

"You can call it that."

"I don't know if Warren told you, but neither of us liked Prescott. Frankly, I don't know too many people in the company that did like him. Most tolerated him because he was V.P. and Mr. Grayson's son-in-law, and nobody wanted to get on his bad side. Anyway, not long after the incident with the fake head, Warren and I talked about getting photographs of Prescott with another woman. Rumors of affairs were only rumors, but if we could somehow prove he was seeing someone on the side, we could take photographs and send them anonymously to Mr. Grayson. To be honest, we were hoping to get him fired."

"Did you go through with the plan?"

Thompson shook his head. "No, for a couple of reasons. Prescott was careful, and even if he was having an affair, the odds of catching him in the act were slim. Secondly, Mr. Grayson knows everything about everyone, and it's possible he already knew if Prescott was having an affair. If he found out Warren and I sent the photos, he'd probably fire us both for invasion of privacy."

"Last thing, Mr. Thompson. Where were you on the night of Monday, August fifteenth?"

Thompson exhaled through his nose and thought for a moment. "My mother and I ate dinner and watched a movie. Needless to say, because of her condition, I rarely go out myself. I don't even remember the last time I had a date."

"I understand," Aaron said, and then got up and handed Thompson a business card. "Thanks for your time. I'll see myself out."

"Goodbye, Inspector."

***

Aaron now had a longer list of people with motive to kill Jared Prescott. Thompson's description of the woman with the shopping bag sounded similar to the woman who rented the room at the Tremont Inn. The fake head brought to mind the wound on Prescott's neck, which suggested Thompson as a suspect. Then there was the plan to take incriminating photographs of Jared Prescott, although since Thompson said they didn't follow through, the point might be moot.

Chapter Ten

Aaron sat at his desk at the Precinct. Sam sat on the other side, holding a manila folder in one hand, a McDonald's Sausage McMuffin in the other. His green and beige tie hung loose, the top button of his pressed white shirt unfastened.

"You need a third hand, Sam. Where's your coffee?"

"Too hot for coffee right now," Sam said. "The air-conditioning isn't working. The technicians are working on it as we speak."

Aaron removed his jacket and draped it over the back of the chair. "I thought it felt a little stuffy in here, but that might be a blessing. I won't feel the urge to drink the chemically treated metal they call coffee."

"You should have stopped at Starbucks."

"I'm not spending five dollars to wet my whistle," Aaron said, then breathed a sigh of relief when he felt a blast of cold air.

"Thank God for technology," Sam said, and then downed the last bite of his sandwich. "I understand you had a busy day yesterday."

"Busy, tiring, and frustrating," Aaron said then updated Sam with the details from his interviews with Jennifer Prescott, including the shooting at the house. He pointed to the plastic bag sitting on his desk.

"It's a rubber bullet. Whoever shot out the patio window wanted to scare Jennifer Prescott or send a warning message, although the injuries could have been more severe. Her bodyguard needed stitches in his leg."

"So, what is she like?" Sam asked.

"She's either a very convincing actress, or truly doesn't give a damn her husband is dead, although in her defense, she was borderline inebriated. The house could support three families, and their liquor cabinet would keep the neighborhood happy for a year. She admitted her marriage was falling apart, and her husband played around. Frankly, I would be shocked if she didn't play around herself. She seems the type."

"Sounds like she's a legitimate suspect," Sam mused. "You think she could be our Nancy Edmunds?"

"I doubt it. If her husband's murder was a conspiracy, I think she's too smart to be placed at the scene, but we'll get her photo from the DMV and show it to the clerk at the motel in any case."

"What about your trip to ChemPhen?" Sam asked.

Aaron pursed his lips and looked away for a moment. "Suffice it to say Harlan Grayson is a proud man."

Sam creased his brow. "That's it?"

"If I told you what I really thought, I'd get too worked up. It's too early and my neck feels like it's in a vice."

"I hear he's very ambitious and usually gets what he wants."

"Okay," Aaron said as he massaged his neck, "if you really want to know, he's a raging egomaniac, obsessed with control, and hopelessly infatuated with himself. He spent more time promoting his life's resume than answering my questions. I know more about his accomplishments as a sportsman and his friendship with Senator Caldwell than anything else. Frankly, I'm surprised he realized he had a son-in-law. Other than that, he's a real peach of a guy."

Sam laughed. "It sounds like you two really hit it off. Maybe you can take in a Sox game sometime. You think he's involved?"

"Other than the fact the victim was his son-in-law? It's hard to say. He was grooming Prescott to take over the company."

"Well, you did say Jennifer Prescott was probably guilty of extramarital affairs herself. Maybe Grayson figured she was giving her husband a taste of his own medicine, and that was enough for him. An eye for an eye."

"That woman is a piece of work," Aaron said with a shake of his head. "She gave me the impression she expected this to happen, and didn't act like she just lost a husband. The shooting at the house could have been staged to make her appear innocent, although the possibility of someone getting seriously hurt did exist."

"Hurt, but not killed," Sam observed.

"Possible, but unlikely. The question remains, who did the shooting and why?"

"What about the fact you were there?"

"You mean me as the target? I doubt it."

"Was Grayson the only one you interviewed at ChemPhen?"

"No, I talked briefly with Prescott's secretary and the Senior Financial Manager, Warren Kirby. I didn't get much from the secretary, but something about Kirby bothers me. I can't put my finger on it, but his demeanor at times during the interview suggests something's amiss. I just don't know what."

"It sounds like your intuition is kicking in, Aaron."

"Yeah, maybe," Aaron said then gestured to the manila folder. "What do you have for me?"

"Ballistics and phone records. What would you like to hear first?"

"I'll take it in that order," Aaron said, sitting back in the chair.

Sam opened the folder. "Okay, Jared Prescott was killed with a three-fifty-seven Magnum. The bullet in the wall came from the same gun."

"We figured as much."

"The lab found no evidence of bodily fluids on the sheets from the motel," Sam added.

"Meaning Prescott and the woman either didn't have sex, or they were extremely careful. What about the phone records?"

Sam raised a finger and smiled. "That's where it gets interesting."

"I'm up for interesting."

"There were a total of four calls made that night, two from the motel room, two from the victim's cell phone. I'll give them to you in time placed order. The first call was from the victim's cellphone to his home at nine-o-seven p.m."

"His widow confirmed there was a call from her husband's cell phone, but whoever called didn't leave a message," Aaron said. "At this point, due to the time, we can't assume it was Prescott who made the call. She went out for the evening and her butler wasn't working that night. How long did the call last?"

"Twelve seconds. Do you think the wife told you the truth about no message?"

"Since she deleted it, we'll never know. Twelve seconds doesn't allow for much of a conversation, in any case. Could be an answering machine followed by a hang up."

"The coroner estimated the time of death at between nine and eleven, so we can't rule out the possibility the killer made the call, for reasons unknown. Then again, it takes only a couple of seconds to say, 'package delivered.'"

Aaron wagged a finger. "And you say you don't watch much television."

"I don't. That's second week detective school stuff."

"I assume it's too much to hope fingerprinting lifted any prints from the scene."

"If it were that easy, we'd both be out of a job," Sam said, and then referred to the document. "The next call was placed from the motel phone to 312-776-0456 at nine-ten, and lasted eight seconds. That's the number for ChemPhen Pharmaceuticals."

"Is that the main number?" Aaron asked.

"No, it's an extension belonging to an employee named George Thompson."

"I spoke to Thompson after I left ChemPhen. Warren Kirby is his boss."

"Quite a coincidence, I'd say," Sam observed. "What's his story?"

"He's a quirky sort, lives with, and cares for his mother, somewhat of a homer milquetoast, if you want to know the truth. He said he and his mother had dinner and watched a movie the night of the murder. He was on vacation last week, and called in sick this week. He feels burdened caring for his mother, and has little to no social life, along with a lot of medical bills. To say he and Prescott didn't get along is a gross understatement. Prescott apparently gave him more grief than anyone else in the company. Their history gives him motive, so he's someone we'll need to keep an eye on."

"The third call also came from the motel phone," Sam said. "It was placed at nine-twelve to 773-777-3090. That's a pay phone at Chicago Midway Airport. It lasted three and a half minutes."

"Chicago Midway? Now that *is* interesting," Aaron said, then sat forward and rested his elbows on the desk. "What about the last call?"

"It was placed at nine-twenty to 800-822-2746. That's the reservations desk for United Airlines. The call lasted thirteen minutes."

"Two consecutive calls placed to two different airports, one to a pay phone, one to a reservation desk,"

Aaron said. "Did you get any details on the call made to United?"

"Not yet, but that's on my to-do list. In any case, thirteen minutes is enough time to schedule a flight."

Aaron tapped his lips. "Sam, this murder reeks of conspiracy. We have four phone calls, all on the surface appearing unrelated. And who makes phone calls from a motel room anymore? Hell, everyone owns a cell phone these days. If the perp made those calls, would he or she be stupid enough to call from the motel room?"

"Or cunning enough to point us in the wrong direction," Sam said.

"Exactly."

Sam closed the folder and tossed it on the desk. "Right, except we both know the mind of a killer is nothing if not unpredictable."

"Or killers," Aaron added. "If someone else were involved, the call to the airport might be a diversion. Let me know what you find on the calls to Midway and United."

"Will do."

"There's one more thing," Aaron said.

"What's that?"

"Prescott's briefcase. His widow insisted he rarely let it out of his sight, and his secretary said it's unlikely he left the office without it, yet it's still missing. I suggested to Grayson it might have contained confidential documents."

"You mean like selling information to competitors?" Sam said.

"Grayson told me I was out of my mind in so many words. If the meeting at the motel was a drug deal, a briefcase could have contained a sizable sum of money. Find out where Prescott does his banking. See if we can get in and talk to the manager as soon as possible."

***

Tom Anderson, manager at First National Bank on S. Dearborn St., was mid-forties, short and slightly overweight, with graying hair on the sides. He sat behind a large desk and wore a three-piece gray suit with a white shirt and powder blue tie.

He stood and shook hands with Aaron and Sam. "How may I help you, gentlemen?"

"We're investigating the death of Jared Prescott," Aaron said. "We understand he did his banking here."

Anderson shook his head and looked down at his hands. "What happened to Mr. Prescott was a tragedy. He was one of our most valued clients."

Aaron and Sam exchanged glances.

Anderson showed his palms. "I'm sorry, I didn't mean to sound callous."

"We'll come right to the point," Aaron said. "We need to know whether he recently withdrew a large sum of money."

"Yes, as a matter of fact, he did, and I thought about that after I heard the news. He came into the bank this past Monday and withdrew one hundred thousand dollars. I talked to him myself."

"That's a lot of money to withdraw at one time," Aaron said.

"I agree, but the bank never questions withdrawals, especially from clients like Mr. Prescott."

"Of course," Aaron agreed. "Do you remember what time he came in?"

"It was about three o'clock."

"Was he alone?"

"Yes, sir."

"Could anyone in the bank have seen him withdraw the money?"

"Absolutely not. We always handle transactions of this magnitude behind closed doors."

"Other than it being a larger than normal withdrawal, was there anything else unusual about the transaction, perhaps with Mr. Prescott's behavior?"

"That's funny you should ask," Anderson said. "I've known Mr. Prescott a long time, and he always seemed at ease, joking around. But that day I noticed he didn't seem himself."

"In what way?" Aaron asked.

"He seemed impatient, in a hurry, a little preoccupied, like his mind was a million miles away. When I asked him how things were going, he just gave me a funny look. I'd never seen him like that before." Anderson shifted in his seat. "There was something else. Cash withdrawals of this size are usually done with electronic funds transfers, but he requested the money in fifties, tens, and twenties."

"That's interesting," Aaron said. "How did Mr. Prescott get the money out of the bank?"

"He put it in a leather briefcase."

Aaron and Sam looked at each other, then thanked Anderson and left the bank.

"Prescott had the briefcase with him when he left the bank. Now all we have to do is find it," Aaron said when he and Sam were sitting in the car.

"What about the one hundred grand?" Sam asked.

"My first thought is a drug deal, especially given the traces we found at the motel."

"Could be blackmail," Sam said.

"You mean a spurned lover or mistress? Based on the relationship with his widow, I don't think he'd care enough to pay to keep someone's mouth shut, certainly not one hundred grand worth, but we won't know until we dig deeper."

Aaron put the key in the ignition and started the car. "Calling all cars. Be on the lookout for an expensive leather briefcase which may or may not contain one hundred thousand dollars."

Chapter Eleven

The next morning, Aaron drank coffee and ate scrambled eggs, sausage and toast, trying to determine what bothered him about Warren Kirby.

He paged through the Chicago Tribune. It was the same old news. Vandalism, suspicion of graft in city government, abandoned children, abused wives, and a weather report reeking of redundancy, with dry and humid conditions expected to continue over the next several days.

He got dressed after breakfast, ran a few errands, and bought groceries and household items at a local Wal-Mart before returning to his apartment. He relaxed in the recliner and turned on the television to catch the last five innings of the White Sox-Cleveland Indians game at US Cellular Field. It had been two years since Chicagoans knew it as New Comiskey Park, and Aaron still wasn't used to the new name. Probably never would be.

Both teams were seventeen games out of first place, battling to see who could stay out of the division cellar. Playoffs would need to wait yet another year. Aaron wasn't a die-hard baseball fan, but rooted for the White Sox and occasionally attended a baseball game. Watching television was a welcome diversion, and helped to put the stress of the job out of his mind, at least for a while.

At four o'clock, when it was obvious the Sox would lose their fifth straight game, Aaron flipped through the channels before settling on *Air Force One,* starring Harrison Ford. Since the movie was in its final scene, and he'd already seen it twice, he picked up a crossword puzzle book he kept by the recliner and chose a medium difficulty puzzle.

After stalling on a capital city of a country he didn't know was a country, he tossed the magazine and pencil on the floor and opted for an early dinner. Ordinarily, he didn't give up so quickly. He was obviously more tired than he realized.

He called Pizza Hut with the intent to order a sausage and double cheese pizza before he remembered his last cholesterol reading, so settled for a medium-sized single cheese pizza.

Every bit of restraint helps.

When the pizza arrived twenty minutes later, he turned on the news channel and ate at the dining room table, washing it down with a Miller Lite. Nothing went better with pizza than a cold beer.

Aaron reviewed his notes of the descriptions of the two men George Thompson identified as the phony FBI agents, then studied the photograph of the Northwestern football team he took from Jared Prescott's office.

The Northwestern head coach, Sheldon Nash, stood on the far left in the first row. On a whim, he put down a half-eaten piece of pizza, went to the end table, and pulled out a phone book.

There was only one listing for 'Sheldon Nash, two others under 'Nash, S.' He wasn't sure the man was still alive, let alone living in the Chicago area, but decided it was worth a try. He found the correct Sheldon Nash on the second number he dialed. They talked for a few minutes and agreed to meet at 12:30 the next day.

***

Nash's two-story house on Green Dale Glen in Meadowbrook was painted white with green shutters. Six mountain laurel shrubs standing three feet high stood in the yard, with two off-white patio chairs on the porch, which extended around the sides of the house. A blue jay perched on the gutter of the lower roof soared into space when Aaron shut the car door.

Nash opened the front door. "You must be Inspector Randall," he said and shook Aaron's hand. "Please, come in."

Nash was five-ten, mid-sixties, with a ruddy complexion and white hair. He wore a blue t-shirt and black pants. He was several pounds heavier, but otherwise didn't look much different than his picture in the photograph.

Aaron followed him into a small but cozy living room. A dark gray sofa rested between two end tables, each with a blue lamp. In the corner, under a small shelf filled with books, sat a tan reclining chair, with a blue armchair next to a red brick fireplace. Dark blue cotton shag carpeting covered the floor. Classical music played at low volume in the background.

On the mantle was a framed photograph of the 1989 Northwestern National Championship team identical to the one from Jared Prescott's office. Several other photos surrounded the team photo, including a five by seven photograph of Jared Prescott in full uniform, down on one knee, clutching a football in his right arm.

Nash followed Aaron's eyes. "I brought out that photo after I heard about Jared. It reminded me of better days," he said. "Can I get you anything? If you want coffee, it will have to be instant. My coffee maker is broken."

"A cup of instant black coffee will be fine, thank you," Aaron said.

"Coming right up. Make yourself at home," Nash said, and then went into the kitchen.

Aaron sat on the recliner.

Nash returned from the kitchen holding two identical brown ceramic mugs with steam rising above the rims. He handed one cup to Aaron, turned off the radio, and then sat on the sofa.

"Your house looks comfortable," Aaron noted.

"Thank you. I moved here eight years ago after my wife passed away. I wanted something smaller with less maintenance."

"I'm sorry for your loss, sir," Aaron said.

"It's not so bad," Nash said with a shrug. "I got used to living alone. I have two sons with families of their own, living in the area, so I see them during the holidays." He pointed his chin at the mantle. "I remember the championship game like it was yesterday. Jared rushed for over two hundred fifty yards."

"Your team thrashed Stanford pretty good," Aaron said.

"Are you a fan?"

"I follow college football, although not like I used to. Pro football is overrun with prima donnas and multi-million-dollar contracts. Every year the owners lobby for new stadiums because the turf turns brown or they run out of mustard at the concession stand. It's become more of a business than a sport. I did follow Prescott during his years in college, though." He laughed. "I went to Ohio State and you beat us four years straight."

"Sorry about that," Nash said with a chuckle. "We did have a good team. It was a tragedy when Jared hurt his knee. I think he would have made it big in the pros." He leaned back and stared at the ceiling. "You know, it's been fifteen years, and I still blame myself for the injury."

"What do you mean?"

"I should have taken him out in the third quarter."

"I think you're being too hard on yourself. He could have injured his knee the first time he carried the ball."

"I agree, and hindsight is one-hundred percent, but I didn't need to play him. We had the game in hand, and it's not like he needed the exposure. Several NFL teams were already negotiating for him. St. Louis had the first pick in the draft, but at least five or six other teams were involved in pre-draft trade talks. The truth is, I felt pressure from the media to play him, and they would have crucified me had I taken him out with him approaching a bowl rushing record. People were already using Jared and Heismann in the same sentence after his second year. He finished second in voting both his second and third years, and some were surprised he didn't win it his junior year. I know his reputation played a factor and might have hurt his chances. If the voting was done solely on football talent, he might have two or three Heismann's."

"What else could you do? It sounds like your job might have been on the line."

"I still felt in my heart, keeping him in wasn't the right thing to do, although like you said, nobody can predict injuries."

"Is that why you retired after that year?"

"That was one of the reasons. More than half the team was graduating, and I was facing several years of rebuilding. That's a demanding job for someone my age. Winning the National Title seemed to be a perfect time to leave the game, although sometimes I wonder whether I made the right decision."

"Did you ever consider coaching in the pro ranks?"

Nash laughed. "No, and I doubt I was ever under consideration. It's just as well, because like you said, the NFL is more of a business with huge egos and unreasonable owners. Coaching college was plenty of challenge for me. I always believed the boys learned most of what they'd need at the college level. In Jared's case, it was natural talent, so he didn't need a lot of what I had to offer. For the most part, the guys listened to what I had to say, although I sense over the past several years, things have changed. I don't know if it's a generation issue, but these young men today think they know it all. They're not as prone to accept or appreciate advice from the older generation."

"You did have a memorable year," Aaron said.

"It was the best year of my career. It was terrible what happened to Jared. Despite his issues, he was a fine young man, but hell, everybody has faults."

Aaron noticed genuine sadness in Nash's eyes.

Nash looked at Aaron and shook his head. "I must apologize for rambling, Inspector. I know you didn't come here to listen to me talk about my college coaching days. How can I help you?"

Aaron placed the cup on the table and took out his notepad and pen. "One of Jared Prescott's co-workers identified two men in the team photograph as participants in a practical joke Prescott played on the guy. He couldn't swear to their identities due to the age of the photograph, but was fairly sure he had the right ones."

"Yes, Jared was quite the practical joker," Nash said with a chuckle.

"I was hoping you might remember their names."

He pointed at the photograph. "I remember every young man's name on that team. Can you show me the two?"

They got up and moved to the mantle. Aaron pointed out the two men identified by George Thompson.

"That's Vic Bryant and Frank Regan," Nash said, then frowned. "You say these two were involved with Jared in a practical joke?"

"That's right," Aaron said. "You look surprised."

"I am, not so much in Regan's case, but certainly in Bryant's."

"Why is that?"

"The sad truth is, Jared didn't have many friends on the team, but between him and Bryant there was genuine dislike, perhaps even hatred. I tried to keep such issues to a minimum, but college football player's egos are hard to control."

"I think you're selling yourself a little short," Aaron said. "I've never coached myself, but I expect team unity is necessary to win a National title."

"Team unity was never an issue," Nash said with a smile. "We were stacked with talent. The other players tolerated Jared because they understood what he meant to the team, but there was definitely no love lost. Most of it was jealousy, but Jared's attitude did little to diffuse the situation."

"Did the animosity ever escalate to threats or fighting?"

Nash looked down and scratched his head for a moment. "Nothing that stands out. They had their tussles in the locker room, but I expect most teams do. I don't recall anything that stopped the show, so to speak. For the most part, bad blood was kept in check because the team knew the importance of working together when it counted."

They sat back down.

Nash sipped his coffee and then wagged a finger. "I do remember one time Jared and Vic did get into a fight, if you could even call it that."

"What happened?" Aaron asked.

"From what I heard, they were arguing over a girl one of them was dating. I don't know who was dating her, or who she was, but Bryant confronted Jared in the locker room after practice one day. They had words, pushed each other around, threw a few punches. Jared got a small cut above his eye, but the other guys broke it up before any real damage was done. From what I remember, that was the worst thing that happened."

"That was quite a few years ago," Aaron said. "Isn't it possible they buried the hatchet?"

"I suppose it's possible," Nash said with a shrug, "but I wouldn't bet on it. Vic Bryant had a chip on his shoulder. He wasn't easy to coach."

"Do you stay in touch with any of your former players?"

"I hear from some of them from time to time, but not Jared. He was more focused on where he was going than where he'd been. I can't say I blame any of them. They have more important things to do than reminisce with their old retired football coach. I haven't talked to Regan in years, and I wouldn't expect to hear from Bryant in any case." Nash waved his empty cup. "I'm getting a refill. How about you?"

"No, thank you, I'm still working on this one."

Nash returned after a minute with a fresh cup of coffee. "Vic Bryant played running back behind Jared, and that itself caused problems from the beginning. Vic didn't get much playing time during his career for obvious reasons. Most of the boys accepted their role on the team, but Vic considered sitting on the bench an insult. I'm afraid he let it fester inside, and sometimes he let off steam. Of course, he wanted more playing time, but given the circumstances, it wasn't realistic. The truth be known, Vic was gifted enough to start for a number of Division I schools. He might have considered changing universities, but attended Northwestern because of his father, William, who made All-Conference linebacker three straight years when he played there. I believe deep down, Vic knew it wasn't Jared's fault, but in his mind, Jared's existence was the reason he didn't get the playing time."

"How deep was his resentment for Prescott?"

Nash rubbed his arm. "If you mean was Vic capable of killing Jared, my immediate answer is no, but then again, I've never met *anyone* I considered capable of murder."

"Did Bryant's father ever talk to you about his son getting more playing time?"

"No. William was a levelheaded player who knew his role, although he started his entire college career. That might be why Vic was so adamant about not starting. I'm sure living up to his father's legacy created pressure for him."

"Did Bryant and his father get along?"

"That I couldn't say, but to say William strongly urged his son to attend the university would be an understatement. He and I talked a number of times, but he never pressured me to give Vic more playing time, because he understood the situation."

"Do you know whether Bryant still lives in the area or what he does for a living?"

"The last I heard, he was selling real estate in Denver, but that was probably four or five years ago. I should tell you though, Vic had a drinking problem in college. I talked to him several times about it, even suggested he get counseling, but my advice fell on deaf ears. Twice during his junior year, he came to games drunk, and I warned him if he did it again, he'd be off the team. That seemed to hit home because it never happened again, although we did suspend him for two games. His subordinate role on the team, combined with family pressure, was maybe too much for him to handle. His drinking gave him a reputation. The word was, if you wanted to hear the latest gossip, buy Vic Bryant a drink."

"What about Regan?" Aaron asked.

"I don't recall any problems between him and Jared, although Frank and Vic were good friends during college, so there might have been animosity by association. As far as I know, Frank still lives in the Chicago area."

"It shouldn't be too hard to find him then."

"I suspect not."

Aaron stood up and extended his hand. "Mr. Nash, here's a card with my number. I want to thank you for your time, especially on a Sunday. You've been a big help."

Nash stood up and took the card. They shook hands at the door.

Aaron was at his car door when Nash called to him.

"Inspector, I hope you catch the person who did this. Jared had his faults like we all do, but he didn't deserve this."

Aaron answered with a nod.

Chapter Twelve

The next morning, Aaron updated Sam on his discussion with Sheldon Nash.

"Assuming I can locate Regan and Bryant, they don't need to know I'm aware of the practical joke. I'd rather not give them a chance to deny their involvement with Prescott, especially Bryant. Nash was surprised he was involved because he and Prescott had a history of bad blood."

"I see," Sam said. "By the way, Dr. Taylor said the toxicology on Prescott came out negative. Also, I showed Mrs. Prescott's photo to the desk clerk at the Tremont. He said that was definitely not the woman who rented the room."

"No drugs in Prescott's system means he wasn't using, but could have been dealing," Aaron said. "And I'm not surprised Mrs. Prescott didn't rent the room."

"By the way, the chief wants to see you in his office."

Aaron exhaled a heavy sigh. "He probably wants a status report."

"That's what I figure."

"I haven't talked to him since the investigation started, so I guess now is as good a time as any."

Status reports were Aaron's least favorite responsibility of the job. They were an administrative nuisance that didn't change the facts, approach, or outcome to an investigation, but protocol demanded they couldn't be avoided.

He poured himself a cup of coffee before walking up to the second floor to Bureau Chief Vince Sherman's office. "Good morning, Vince."

Sherman gestured to a chair in front of his desk. He had a Roman nose and high cheekbones. He was six feet four and a solid two hundred twenty pounds, the benefit of a consistent and rigorous exercise regimen. He wore a short-sleeve cream-colored shirt with a light gray and navy-striped tie.

"Have a seat, Aaron. How's the coffee today?"

"No better or worse than usual."

"That bad, huh? Don't worry, it's no better on my floor. Ever try Starbucks?"

"The day I pay five dollars for a cup of coffee will come the day after a pay raise. I remember when three dollars bought you a decent meal. Today a piece of meat between two slices of bread sets you back six dollars because the company has a catchy name."

"No argument there," Sherman said.

"Anyway, I'm guessing I'm not here to discuss the state of the economy."

"No, you're right. I want to know what's going on with the Prescott murder investigation."

"I've interviewed the victim's widow, his boss, and father-in-law, Harlan Grayson, two co-workers, his secretary, bank manager and his college football coach."

"That's quite a list. Come up with anything solid?"

"One of the victim's co-workers, George Thompson, identified two of Prescott's college football teammates from a team photograph. The three of them played an elaborate practical joke on the guy. The college coach gave me their names. I'm hoping to track them down today."

"Sounds promising. What did you find out from the others?"

"Jared Prescott was never going to win any popularity contests. His marriage was falling apart, and most of his co-workers resented him. Some hated him. There were rumors he was involved in more than one affair, yet despite the allegations, Harlan Grayson was priming him to take over the company. To be honest, we have a number of potential suspects."

"Suspects? Plural?" Sherman asked. "You think there is more than one involved?"

"Very possible."

"Sounds like you have a challenge on your hands, Aaron."

"I do, but so far this seems more a waste of time than a challenge. It doesn't sound like anyone is going to miss Jared Prescott, including his widow."

Sherman got up and walked to the window, and clasped his hands behind his back. "Harlan Grayson. What's your opinion of him?"

"In a nutshell? He's a pompous ass with an ego the size of California."

Sherman turned back and smiled. "At least you're honest. I assume you are aware of his position in the community."

"He made sure I was aware of his influence and political connections, but you know how I feel about people with money and power. They're just as…"

"Just as likely to be a suspect in a murder case, I know," Sherman said.

"I know that tone of voice, Vince. It's your 'be careful where you tread, Aaron.'"

Sherman sat back down and folded his hands on the desk, drew a breath and exhaled. "Harlan Grayson is one of the most influential and powerful men in Chicago. He's managing director of IEEE, former chairman on the Council for Pharmaceuticals Corporations, and serves on the board of the Chicagoland Chamber of Commerce. He donates sizable sums of money to various charitable organizations, and is actively involved in a number of them. Personally, I don't know how the man finds time to eat and sleep."

"He probably delegates everything, but if you ask him, I'm sure he'll give you an answer in a thousand words or more," Aaron said with more than a trace of sarcasm.

"The key point where you and I are concerned is recognizing he's good friends with the commissioner, and they've already talked on the phone. The commissioner called me, so we're already feeling the pressure. Grayson complained that you grilled his daughter pretty hard, especially given the circumstances."

Aaron closed his eyes and shook his head. "I did nothing more than react to her behavior. She seemed more interested in getting drunk than in answering my questions," he said, and then leaned forward. "Vince, we've known each other a long time. You know my work ethic. I treat each homicide case with equal importance, regardless of what the victim did for a living, and especially how much their estate is worth. I am sure the commissioner realizes putting a higher priority on a case doesn't mean the perpetrators will walk into the precinct with their hands raised. I can't conduct a thorough investigation if I'm walking on egg shells, and can't afford to worry about stepping on toes or offending somebody because of who they are or how much they're worth."

"I don't question your ability or your dedication, Aaron. It's just that one of Grayson's closest friends is Senator Nathan Caldwell, and as much as we'd like to treat every victim with the same respect and attention, reality is different when people with power and influence wield their scepters."

Aaron sat back and blew out air. It was bad enough listening to Grayson crow about his relationship with the Senator, now he had to hear it from his boss. "That doesn't mean Grayson is untouchable."

Sherman answered with a shrug.

"Vince, believe me, I'm aware of the relationship between Grayson and the Senator. He made it crystal clear during our conversation. He also fed me with a wealth of other information I couldn't care less about, nor had any relevance to the investigation. He was more interested telling me about his life achievements than in discussing his own son-in-law's murder. The way he avoided my questions, he'd do well as a professional tap dancer. I'm not surprised at the pressure. It was obvious from the beginning, someone powerful was involved when they pulled strings at the coroner's office to move Prescott's autopsy to the top of the list. God forbid other families waiting for autopsy results should be given any consideration."

"I understand your position, Aaron, and I know you're doing everything you can. I simply ask you to understand mine. I have to play in the court where they throw the ball. Some will say I'm covering my ass, and I suppose that's true."

"You have your job, I have mine," Aaron said, then pointed at his boss. "That's why I'll never be sitting in that chair."

"It is often a dirty job, but somebody has to do it. One more thing, I'd like you to consider help on this one. It would show the commissioner we're being proactive and going the extra mile. I ask this only to keep him off my back. That way I can stay off yours."

Aaron's squeezed his eyes shut then opened them. "Sam is handling the research and administration legwork. Believe me, Vince, it's under control. If you want to assign someone to keep up appearances, give help to Sam. You know I work best with less clutter."

"I agree with you, Aaron, and don't like it any more than you do, but it's the way things are. However, we'll leave it status quo for now, and I'll tell the commissioner we have it under control."

"Thanks, Vince."

"Keep me posted, Aaron."

Aaron smiled. "Don't I always?" he said, then got up from the chair and returned to his desk.

Chapter Thirteen

Frank Regan lived at 10237 Timberbrook in Royal Ranch, an upper middle class subdivision, in a two-story brick home with a two-car garage. An iron gate guarded the front yard with a basketball goal on the lawn next to the driveway.

Aaron knocked on the door.

"I'll get it," a young boy's voice said from inside, and the door opened a moment later. A red-haired boy squinted up at Aaron.

"Hello there, young man. Is your father home?"

The boy gaped at Aaron without answering, and then a man with wire-rimmed glasses perched on the end of his nose appeared in the doorway. He was six foot three, two-hundred thirty-five pounds with wide shoulders, and a barrel chest. He wore a white golf shirt and dark green pants. Time and age had expanded his midsection.

He frowned at Aaron. "Can I help you?"

Aaron identified himself. "Are you Frank Regan?"

"Yes, I am. What can I do for you, Inspector?"

"I'd like to talk to you about Jared Prescott. I understand you and he played football together at Northwestern."

Regan's shoulders sagged. "Yes, Jared and I were teammates," he said, and then patted the top of the boy's head. "Michael, I need to speak with this gentleman. Go upstairs and play with Frankie."

The boy craned his head to look at his father, and then turned and broke into a run.

"Come in, Inspector," Regan motioned. "My wife is out shopping. We can talk in the study."

Aaron stepped into the foyer and Regan closed the door behind him.

There was a staircase in the middle of the lower floor with a hallway on each side. The living room was to the left of the staircase and the dining room to the right.

Aaron followed Regan through French doors into the study. The room had a large executive desk with a computer workstation. On one wall was a built-in bookcase filled with reading material. The maroon and white curtains were open on two large picture windows.

"I had a conversation with Sheldon Nash yesterday," Aaron said.

Regan's eyebrows arched. "Is that right? I haven't talked to the coach in years. How's he doing?"

"He appears to be comfortable," Aaron said with a shrug. "He gave me your name and the name of another teammate, Vic Bryant."

"Yes, Vic," Regan said with a slow nod, and then walked around the desk and sat down. He waved his hand. "Please, Inspector, have a seat. You know, you read about violence every day, yet somehow never think it will touch you or anyone you know. Jared's death is still surreal to me. I keep waiting for the news to tell us they made a mistake, that it was someone else."

Aaron sat in a brown chair and took out his pad and pen. "Believe me, it was Jared Prescott. You might be wondering why, out of all his teammates, the coach gave me your and Bryant's name."

"That thought did cross my mind."

"Jared Prescott worked with a man named George Thompson, who…"

Regan threw back his head and laughed. "Don't tell me, the fake head scam, right?"

"That's right," Aaron said.

"Jared lived for practical jokes. In college, it was a rubber snake in the locker, Ben-Gay in the jockstrap, but over time, he went in for more elaborate scams. He said if it wasn't complex and planned out, it wasn't worth doing. He called me because I have a friend who is a makeup artist for Twentieth Century Fox." Regan shook his head. "If I didn't know better myself, I would have sworn it was Jared's head in the bag. I can see why the guy freaked out. In retrospect, I suppose it was an adolescent thing to do, but was pretty funny at the time. We didn't think any harm would come of it." Regan frowned. "Say, you don't think this guy Thompson had anything to do with Jared's murder, do you?"

Aaron ignored the question. "Mr. Thompson said a woman gave him a bag with the fake head. Did you know her?"

Regan shook his head. "No, Jared told us she was part of the scam. By the time Vic and I came around the corner, she was already gone."

"Did Mr. Prescott tell you her name or anything about her?"

"Nope, just said she was a friend of his," Regan said, and then folded his arms and laughed. "It was kind of fun playing an FBI agent."

"Why did you agree to go along with the scam?"

"What the hell," Regan said with a shrug, "it sounded like fun. Besides, it was an easy two grand."

"Prescott paid you?" Aaron said with a frown.

"Yeah, but that was Jared. The one thing he liked better than a practical joke was throwing money around. He offered it because he said there was a certain amount of risk involved. After all, we did impersonate FBI agents, and it was done on a public street. I expect there might have been consequences, but it was a harmless prank. The guns were BB guns from Wal-Mart, so nobody would have gotten hurt."

"Harmless except for the emotional pain it caused the victim," Aaron said, staring into Regan's eyes.

Regan pressed his lips together and looked away. "Okay, I'll give you that."

"Mr. Nash said he was surprised Vic Bryant agreed to participate due to history of bad blood between the two."

"Jared was the one who suggested I call Vic and ask him to participate. When Vic heard about the money, he said okay. I didn't sense any animosity between them during the scam."

"What was your relationship with Jared Prescott?"

"I can't honestly say we were good friends, but we got along, for the most part. The truth is, Jared had one of the biggest egos I ever saw, but you've probably already heard that. He strutted through the locker room with an attitude. That didn't sit well with a lot of guys on the team, but we were winning, so we tolerated his behavior."

"Mr. Nash said Prescott and Bryant got into a fight over a woman. Do you recall her name?" Aaron asked.

Regan's eyes shifted, and he hesitated before answering. "That was a long time ago. I don't remember anything about it. You'll have to ask Vic."

"What was your relationship with Vic Bryant?" Aaron asked.

"Vic and I roomed together at Northwestern. We hung out, drank on the weekends, typical college roommate stuff."

"Did you and Mr. Prescott ever get into a fight?" Aaron asked.

"No, we argued a few times, got in each other's face, nothing more. It was guy stuff, nothing out of the ordinary for football jocks. The truth is, I played defense, less opportunity to, you might say, develop animosity. I let the offense wrestle with Jared's ego."

"Do you and Bryant stay in touch?"

"We did until Vic moved to Denver. He sold real estate for a while, but it didn't work out, so I heard he moved back to Chicago about a year ago. Last fall when we got together with Jared was the first time I'd seen or talked to him since he left for Denver."

"I heard Bryant drank a lot. Did his drinking ever get him in trouble?"

Regan smiled and nodded. "Vic did like to slam down the beers, that's for sure, but as far as I know, he never got violent. It mellowed him out more than anything."

"Do you know where I can find him?"

"I don't know his address, but the last I heard he was working at McCarthy Ford on South Pulaski."

"Just one more question. Where were you on the night of Monday, August fifteenth?"

Regan looked away for a moment. "Monday, let's see, oh yeah, I was at home watching the baseball game. Sox beat the Mariners in ten innings."

"You could have read that in the newspaper. Can anyone attest to that?"

"My family was here with me the entire evening. My boys watched most of the game with me before they went to bed."

Aaron closed his notepad and then they both rose and shook hands. He handed Regan a business card, and they parted without another word.

Aaron had one more stop before returning to the precinct.

"Inspector, I didn't expect to see you again so soon," George Thompson said when he opened the door. "What's this all about?"

"This shouldn't take long," Aaron said. "May I come in?"

"Of course, but can we please keep it down? My mother is sleeping."

"Sure," Aaron said, then stepped inside the house and followed Thompson to the living room. They remained standing.

"Was there something else you needed to ask me?" Thompson asked.

"When we spoke last, you said you were ill last week after taking vacation."

"That's right. I returned to work this morning," Thompson said.

"So, you were out of the office for two weeks?"

"Yes. Why do you ask?"

"Did anyone fill in for you while you were out?"

"Not really," Thompson said with a shrug. "My job doesn't have daily deadlines. Other than certain times of the month and quarter, most work can wait until I return. Any emergencies are escalated to my boss, Warren Kirby."

"What about your phone messages?"

Thompson cleared his throat. "My phone messages? I checked them last Friday from home. We can do that remotely with a password. I updated the message to indicate I would be out of the office after I called in sick."

"Do you recall how many messages you had?"

Thompson thought for a moment. "Three, I think, but none were urgent, so I deleted them. Most callers don't leave a message when they hear I'm out of the office. They'll either call Warren or wait until I return."

"Were all the calls made during normal working hours?"

"If I recall correctly, two were from co-workers during working hours, the other one was after hours, but the caller left no message, so I deleted it. Sorry, I don't remember the exact time of that call."

"Is it normal to get phone calls after hours?"

"It's not unusual. The company has suppliers and customers all over the world, but because of the situation with mother, I work overtime only when necessary. I don't understand. What's this all about?"

Aaron studied Thompson's face. If the phone call from the motel suggested he was involved, his expression didn't indicate such.

"There was a phone call made from the motel the night Jared Prescott was murdered, about the time of his death. It was placed to your office phone."

Thompson's jaw dropped. "What?" he asked, and then swallowed and raised his hands. "Inspector, I have no idea why anyone would call me from that motel."

"Could someone else have deleted a message?"

"Not without having my password."

"Could someone have obtained your password?" Aaron asked.

Thompson sat down in a chair. "The truth is, I need access to several different systems at work, and it's impossible to remember all of them. The company suggests we don't use the same password for everything, but asks that we don't write them down. I can't keep track, so I recorded them on a separate file on my computer which itself has a password I committed to memory."

"What happens if you forget a password?"

"I call the IT department."

"So, it's possible someone in the IT department retrieved the password and deleted the message?"

"Yes, I suppose it is, although I don't know why they would do that. It seems a lot of trouble to go through just to erase a message on my phone."

Aaron thanked Thompson and returned to the precinct. The murder of Jared Prescott was becoming more complex with every conversation.

Chapter Fourteen

The next day, Aaron pulled into the parking lot of McCarthy Ford on South Pulaski Road.

Heat waves rose from the pavement as he got out of the car. Despite the weather, the dealership was abuzz with activity. Sales people lured shoppers with the promise to give them the deal of a lifetime as the new model year approached. Pressure to clear existing inventory was evident with signs and flyers posted throughout.

He had just shut his car door when a man in a white shirt, gray tie, and programmed smile approached with enough bounce in his step to hurdle an NBA center. His hair was thick and wavy and neatly groomed, a poster boy for new car sales. He extended his hand from three feet away.

"Good morning, sir. My name is Noel Hudson. What can I help you with today?"

Aaron expected the next words out of the man's mouth would be, 'What can I do to put you in a new car today?'

"I'm here to see Vic Bryant," Aaron said, shaking the man's hand, but sparing the introduction. "I believe he works here."

The smile on Hudson's face vanished quicker than air escaping from a punctured hot air balloon. "Uh… you should probably speak to our Sales Manager," he stammered after a few moments of hesitation. "Please, follow me."

Inside the showroom, the temperature felt thirty degrees cooler, a welcome respite from the oven-like conditions outdoors. A number of car shoppers milled around the showroom, ogling the new model cars on display. Sales staff sat with potential customers to entice a buyer to invest their hard-earned money in a brand new vehicle loaded with more options than most people would need.

Aaron followed Hudson through a door leading to a number of small offices. The last office on the right had a plaque on the wall labeled 'Todd Conway – Sales Manager.' Hudson rapped on the doorframe and the man inside looked up.

"Yes, what is it, Noel?"

Hudson pointed a thumb over his shoulder. "This gentleman is asking to see Vic Bryant," he said, and then looked back at Aaron. "This is Mr. Conway, our Sales Manager."

Conway was mid-forties with a pencil-thin black mustache. He wore a white short-sleeved shirt with a red, white, and blue tie. He stood and extended his hand, flashing a warm and sincere smile.

"Please, call me Todd," he said, and then glanced at Hudson.

"Thank you, Noel," he said, and then walked around Aaron and closed the door before sitting back down.

Aaron sat in a gray metal chair.

The office was small, with a desk, a computer on top, and a gray five-drawer metal filing cabinet. A number of plaques adorned the walls, testimony to Conway's success as a salesman. A small table fan sitting on top of the filing cabinet struggled to circulate air in the office.

"I'm sorry, I didn't get your name," Conway said.

Aaron pulled out his badge. "Inspector Randall. I'm investigating the murder of Jared Prescott. Vic Bryant played football with him at Northwestern."

"Oh, I see," Conway said. "Yes, that killing is getting more attention than the O.J. Simpson case."

"I was told Mr. Bryant works here. Is he in today?"

Conway's expression hardened. "He did work here, but we had to let him go last month."

"Let him go?"

A sheepish grin played at the corners of Conway's mouth. "That's the politically correct way of saying we fired him."

"Why did you fire him?"

"In a nutshell, he practically assaulted one of our mechanics. Fortunately, it occurred in the service department, so none of our customers witnessed the event."

"Tell me about it," Aaron said, intrigued that an altercation between two employees seemed to concern Conway less than the image of the dealership.

You're a born salesman.

"It happened in the early afternoon. Bryant, apparently, had a few too many drinks at lunch. He went back to the service department to check on the status of a customer's car. The mechanic told him it wasn't ready, and Bryant started yelling and screaming, scared the poor guy half to death. A couple of other guys intervened and got Bryant under control before he did any physical harm to the man. He stormed out of the dealership and didn't show up for work the next two days. We fired him the following Monday."

Conway ran a finger on the edge of the desk. "That wasn't the first time we had problems with him. He was already on notice for drinking on the job, although this was the first time he lost control. I recommended terminating him, but the owner is a Northwestern alumni and follows football religiously. That was how Bryant got the job in the first place. Anyway, the owner wanted to give Bryant a chance to clean up his act, but he stepped over the line this time, and the owner finally admitted he wouldn't last here. In my opinion, the termination was long overdue."

"What did Bryant do here?" Aaron asked.

"He was a sales consultant."

"Meaning he dealt with the customer?"

"Yes. He explained the operation of the vehicle, the maintenance schedule, things of that sort. We, that is, the owner, had plans for him to go into management, but it was clear to me from the start he didn't have the personality or temperament."

"How long did he work here?" Aaron asked.

"About ten months. His application stated he worked as an independent real estate broker in Denver. In my opinion, he doesn't have enough self-discipline to run a faucet," Conway said with a chuckle.

"How did he perform on the job?"

"Mediocre at best. He lacked ambition, and probably wouldn't have lasted long in a job dealing with the public in any case. Personally I think he's more suited for construction."

"Tell me more about his drinking problem."

"I might have overstated that a bit. It's not like he was constantly drunk except for the incident with the mechanic, although when he did drink it was obvious."

"Did the customers ever complain?"

"None on record, which is somewhat surprising. Bryant was either good at planning, or just got lucky in that respect. If we did have complaints, we would have terminated him much sooner."

"Did he have any close friends or socialize with anyone at work?" Aaron asked.

"I don't think so," Conway said. "He usually ate lunch in his office or went out by himself."

"Did he ever talk about Jared Prescott?"

Conway looked away for a moment and stroked his chin. "No, I can't recall he did. Bryant was moody, to say the least. One day he'd talk your head off and treat you like his best friend, the next day, it took an Act of Congress for him to say hello."

"Have you seen him since you fired him?"

Conway gave an emphatic shake of his head. "No, and I hope I never do. He's not someone I'd want to meet in a dark alley, particularly since I was the one who gave him the news."

"How did he react when you fired him?"

Conway creased his brow and shook his finger. "That's the odd part. I expected him to explode, which is why we had security standing by when I told him. He took it in stride, almost as if he expected or wanted it to happen. He packed up his belongings and left without saying a word. I don't know, maybe I caught him in one of less surly moods. In any case, good riddance."

"Do you have a current address on him?" Aaron asked.

Conway raised a finger. "Just a second, I'll call Human Resources," he said, and then picked up the phone. He talked for a few minutes then scribbled on a piece of paper and handed it to Aaron.

They stood and shook hands. "Thanks for your time, Mr. Conway."

"My pleasure."

"Do me a favor, will you, Inspector?"

"What's that?" Aaron asked.

"If this conversation comes up, tell him I left the country," Conway said with a laugh.

Chapter Fifteen

Vic Bryant lived at 1465 Ramrod Drive in Norwood Park, in a two-story brick and veneer home. The outside of the house screamed for a paint job, and the front lawn begged for a power mower and a healthy application of fertilizer. A ratty green and white lawn chair on the front porch didn't look strong enough to support the weight of a six-week-old kitten.

Aaron climbed the porch and knocked on the door.

When it opened, despite the passing of the years, he recognized Vic Bryant as the man from the team photograph, although he looked thirty pounds heavier, mostly in the gut. He was six foot one, about two-hundred and fifty pounds, with salt and pepper hair in dire need of a comb. His face hadn't seen a razor in several days. Purple earrings in the shape of a wildcat, Northwestern's team mascot, rested in his ear lobe. His waistline stretched the material of a wrinkled and stained T-shirt hanging outside a pair of faded blue jeans. His muscles had softened with age. A bear of a man, his eyes held the look of someone who lost a battle with a hangover.

He squinted and looked Aaron up and down. "Yeah, whaddya want?" he said, his voice thick with sleep.

"I'm Inspector Randall, Chicago Homicide," Aaron said, refraining from showing his credentials at first, because he doubted Bryant could tell the difference between a badge and a magazine subscription. "Are you Vic Bryant?"

"Yeah, I'm Bryant," he said, running a hand over his stubble.

"I need to ask you some questions about your recently deceased friend, Jared Prescott." Aaron emphasized the word 'friend' hoping to get a rise out of Bryant, but it didn't work.

"Come on in," Bryant said, and then turned and walked back into the house.

Aaron stepped inside and closed the door, then followed Bryant into the living room. "Late night?"

Bryant turned and glared at Aaron. "I just got up."

That didn't answer my question, but hopefully, the interview will improve with time.

Aaron sat in a faded tan chair. Bryant flopped on an olive green upholstered sofa. He propped his feet on the coffee table and splayed his arms on top of the sofa.

The inside of the house resembled what Normandy might have looked like after D-Day. A Playboy magazine opened to the centerfold lay on the coffee table, and a crumpled Burger King bag lay on the floor next to the sofa. Sections of the Chicago Tribune were scattered on the floor. A number of DVD movies sat on top of a twenty-seven-inch television set sitting on a narrow stand next to a floor lamp. A cracked coffee cup and an ashtray filled with cigarette butts rested on top of a fake wood end table. The walls of the living room were bare, and the air ran thick with the odor of cigarette smoke and brewed coffee.

"Anyone hurt in this wreck?" Aaron asked.

"So, I ain't the neatest person in the world," Bryant said with a shrug. "It ain't against the law, is it?"

Aaron gestured with his chin to the ashtray. "What brand do you smoke?"

"Winston, why?"

"Just curious."

"You come here to discuss my lifestyle, or ask me about Prescott?"

Too bad you don't smoke Marlboro. I could take you in on suspicion. A few hours in a cell would definitely improve your living conditions and maybe your attitude.

"Those are interesting earrings," Aaron observed. "How long have you been wearing them?"

Bryant tapped on his left ear lobe and smiled. "What's wrong? You don't like my taste in jewelry?"

"Earrings are okay if you're a female or a teenage male making a statement, but I don't see too many men your age wearing them, unless you're a biker." Aaron had spent less than five minutes with Bryant and he had already fallen well below expectations. "Nice to see you still carry team spirit with you in your old age."

"I wear what I want, when I want. I don't care what people think. If they did care, nobody's had the guts to say anything."

Aaron decided it was time to focus on the reason for his visit. "I assume you heard what happened to Jared Prescott."

"Of course. It's been plastered all over the newspapers and TV stations. Like the guy was some kind of a god."

"You were teammates with him at Northwestern."

"That's right. Prescott and I shared time at running back," he said with a smirk, as though he considered himself an integral part of the championship team.

"How did you and Prescott get along during your playing days in college?"

"Why do you ask?"

"I talked to Sheldon Nash and Frank Regan."

Bryant's nostrils flared, and he leaned forward on the sofa and rested his forearms on his thighs. "In that case, you probably already know the answer, but I'll tell you anyway. I couldn't stand the guy. He strutted around with his nose in the air like his shit didn't stink. He expected everyone to move out of his way when he walked down the hall. He hogged all the playing time and screwed up my chance to play pro ball. He was an asshole. Does that answer your question?"

"I'm confused," Aaron said with a frown. "A minute ago, you said you and he shared time at running back. Now you said he hogged all the playing time. Which one is it?"

Bryant bit his lip and relaxed. "Yeah, well maybe I exaggerated a little. Shared don't necessarily mean fifty-fifty."

"According to your coach, it was more like ninety-ten. How many times did you carry the ball that year?"

Bryant narrowed his eyes, then looked away without answering.

"You make it sound as if Prescott destroyed your life. I mean a career in the pros? I'm no expert, but a second string running back with minimum playing time in college doesn't sound like a high draft prospect to me."

Bryant narrowed his eyes. "What are you, a smart ass?"

"Just making an observation," Aaron said with a shrug, satisfied he got under Bryant's skin.

"I still could have had a decent college career. I was second string only because of Prescott."

"Yes, your coach admitted you had talent and could have played for another school. Why didn't you try another university?"

"I figured I'd get the playing time if I waited it out. By the time I realized I wasn't going to get any, I was in my third year. Too late to go to another school. Nuthin' I could do but accept it."

"I heard you and Prescott got into a fight in the locker room over a woman. Why don't you tell me about that?"

"Why don't you ask her?"

"What do you mean?"

"He married the bitch."

Aaron suddenly understood why Frank Regan hesitated and seemed nervous when asked if he recalled her name.

"So you had a relationship with Jennifer Prescott?"

"Hardly what you would call a relationship. We went out a couple of times. She did it to make him jealous. The fight was nothing. We pushed each other around, and I gave him a little gash over his eye, that's all."

"I guess she couldn't see your charms, could she?" Aaron asked.

"Whatever."

"I understand you saw Jared Prescott last fall. You ran an elaborate scam on one of his co-workers, something about a fake head. Want to tell me about that?"

Bryant threw his head back and laughed hard enough to jiggle his belly.

Aaron noticed tobacco-stained teeth.

"Yeah, that was a riot, man. We scared the crap out of the dude. He actually believed it was Prescott's head was in the bag."

"You and Regan posed as FBI agents."

"Yeah, it was a blast." Bryant said. He grinned as though daring Aaron to arrest him after the fact for impersonating a government agent.

"Where did you get the guns?"

"Prescott set up the whole deal, supplied us with the guns and badges. Hell, man, they were just BB guns you can buy at any Wal-Mart."

At least Bryant's answer about the guns matched Regan's version.

"What about the woman that gave the bag to Mr. Thompson? Did you ever see her before?"

"She was just someone Prescott knew. She was gone by the time Frank and I got there."

"So you couldn't identify her?"

Bryant rolled his eyes and sighed. "I just told you, cop, by the time we got there, she was gone."

"Given how you felt about Prescott, I find it curious you agreed to participate in this scam."

"College was a long time ago. Things change. Besides, he paid us two grand. It was easy money."

"So forgive and forget, is that it?"

"What's that supposed to mean?"

"Why do you suppose Prescott asked you to participate? Certainly he had his choice among other former players."

"Who knows? Maybe Regan told him I was back in town. Maybe he couldn't find anyone else. Like I said, two grand is two grand. I didn't ask… didn't care. I got my money, that's all that matters."

"Have you seen Prescott since then?"

"Nope."

"Frank Regan told me you two were roommates in college. Do you still keep in touch?"

"I ain't seen or talked to Frank since that day last fall. We ain't got much in common. He's got a family. I don't."

"I talked to Todd Conway, your former boss," Aaron said. "Why don't you tell me what happened at the Ford dealership?"

Bryant sneered. "You don't miss nuthin, do you?"

"You'd be amazed at how thoroughness increases the odds of finding a killer," Aaron said with a smile.

Bryant narrowed his eyes for a moment, and then shrugged. "It was a misunderstanding, that's all. The weasel was supposed to have a car ready for a customer, but it wasn't. The customer got on my case, so I got on his. I just came down a little hard on the guy."

"Your boss said you'd been drinking that day."

Bryant clenched his fists. "I had a couple at lunch, so what? The mechanic didn't do his job. Why are you getting on my case, and what's my work history got to do with Prescott?"

Aaron leaned forward in the chair. "I'm investigating a homicide, Mr. Bryant. It's my job to ask questions. I look for motive. I ask about past relationships with victims. I ask people where they were, and what they were doing at the time of the murder. I watch people's reactions and facial expressions. Do yourself a favor, relax and cooperate, or we'll continue this conversation at the precinct."

Bryant ran the back of his hand across his mouth and settled back on the cushion. "All right, man, you win. Sure, I drink from time to time, sometimes maybe a little too much, but so do a lot of other people. It's not like I slugged the guy."

"Why did you leave Denver?"

"I was homesick," Bryant replied with a sarcastic smile.

So much for cooperation.

Aaron remained silent until Bryant continued.

"Okay, real estate wasn't my bag. I didn't do as well as I'd hoped, and Denver was far from home. That homesick thing isn't bullshit."

"Do you have family here?" Aaron asked.

"Just my father."

"What have you been doing since you got fired?"

"Just hanging loose, looking in the classifieds."

"Real estate didn't work out, and it's obvious you're not cut out for customer service. What exactly are you looking for?"

"Just something to pay the bills," Bryant said with a shrug.

"How are you getting by financially in the meantime?"

"I had some money saved from Denver."

"What were you doing on the night of Monday, August fifteenth?"

"So we finally get to the real meat of the conversation, huh?"

"Answer the question."

Bryant looked up at the ceiling and rubbed his chin. "As far as I can remember, I never left the house that day. Ate a frozen pizza for dinner, drank a few beers, watched television. I been doing a lot of that since I lost my job."

"Did you see or talk to anyone that can attest to that?"

"Like I said, I never left the house."

"You follow baseball?" Aaron asked.

"Sometimes, why?"

"I understand there was an extra-inning game between the Sox and Mariners that night."

"Sounds like a good one, sorry I missed it."

"I'm curious. How can you afford a house payment after losing your job?"

"I'm collecting unemployment insurance, and I told you before I had some money saved."

Aaron looked around the room. "It would be a shame to move into an apartment. With a bit of work, this house could become livable. I'm guessing it's what... twenty-two hundred square feet?"

"Twenty-three, and who said I was moving out?" Bryant asked.

"This area of town is pretty upscale. I suspect your mortgage is substantial."

Bryant stared at Aaron, but didn't answer.

"Right, you had money saved from Denver."

"Don't worry about me, Inspector, I'll manage, and my house payment is none of your business."

"That's where you're wrong, Mr. Bryant. Everything is my business. When did you first hear of Jared Prescott's murder?"

"I saw it on the news and read about it in the paper the next day."

"How did that make you feel? I mean, here was someone you knew, went to college, and played football with, not to mention you bonded with each other last fall. It must have been quite a shock."

Bryan removed a cigarette from a pack on the coffee table, lit it, took a puff, and exhaled. A trail of smoke rose to the ceiling.

"Bonded?" he said with a laugh. "That's rich. Hey, what can I say? It's Chicago, people get killed. It's an unfortunate fact of life."

"What did you study at Northwestern?"

A wrinkle creased Bryant's forehead. "Marketing, why? What's that got to do with anything?"

"Not a thing," Aaron said with a shrug. "I just wanted to make sure you didn't major in education in hopes of teaching grammar to elementary school students. I've had more stimulating conversations with high school dropouts."

Aaron got up from his seat and tossed a business card on the coffee table before Bryant could reply. "That's it for now, but I'll be in touch. If anything else comes to mind regarding your past relationship with the late Mr. Prescott, be sure to give me a call."

Bryant got up and thrust his left hand into his pocket. "Whatever you say, Inspector."

Aaron walked to the door and squeezed the doorknob, then looked back at Bryant and flicked his ear lobe. "Best of luck with your job search, Vicky."

Bryant stuck the cigarette into his mouth. He waited a few moments before following Aaron out the door, and stood on the porch.

Aaron got into his car and watched Bryant flick his cigarette butt at a black and white cat sitting on the grass, as though that was the defining characteristic of a hardened and tough man.

The cat hissed and bolted.

Aaron wanted to slap the cuffs on him for attempted arson and cruelty to animals, but was confident they would cross paths again.

Bryant's account of the fake head incident matched Regan's account, maybe too closely, as though rehearsed, which would support a conspiracy theory. Either that, or neither one had anything to hide, because they truly weren't involved in Jared Prescott's murder.

Chapter Sixteen

Aaron needed a night out. He donned a pair of khakis, maroon sport shirt, slipped on a pair of brown loafers, and then drove to Quigley's Irish Pub and Craft Beer Bar in Oak Lawn, his favorite hangout.

Quigley's offered a diversified menu, including appetizers, soups and salads, chicken, seafood, and wraps. Aaron favored the half-pound Angus burger, piled high with mushrooms.

Over the years, he became good friends with Terence O'Shea, owner and operator of the restaurant, and a former middleweight boxer.

Aaron chose a barstool at the far end, allowing him visual access to the entire room. He didn't like having his back to people, a quirk he developed from working in law enforcement. Some people called it paranoia. He preferred 'vigilant.'

It was a slow night. Two men sat at the bar drinking beer and eating wings. One older man occasionally glanced up from a newspaper to check the baseball game between the White Sox and Twins. The Sox were batting in the eighth inning, behind by six runs, likely facing another loss. Some things never change.

Aaron jumped when he felt a heavy hand slap his back.

"Hey, Aaron, you haven't been by in a while. I was beginning to think you were getting too good for us."

Aaron turned. Terry O'Shea was wearing a welcoming smile.

O'Shea stood five feet eight, had square shoulders and strong hands, bright red hair, and a ruddy complexion. His nose was crooked from one too many boxing matches.

"Terry, don't you know it's dangerous to sneak up on an officer of the law? If you keep that up, I'll need to find myself another hangout. As for my absence, business has been good."

O'Shea shook his head. "That's good for job security, not so good otherwise."

"Such is life in Chicago," Aaron agreed.

O'Shea walked around to the other side of the bar. "What can I get you to drink, laddie?"

"Give me a Heineken Light."

"Comin' right up," O'Shea said, and then filled a mug and placed it on the counter in front of Aaron. "Care for the house special tonight?"

"Let me guess, half-pound Angus burger?"

"Aye, how'd ya know?"

Aaron tapped the side of his head. "I'm a detective, remember?"

"That's a pretty lethal sandwich. Too many of those will put you into an early grave."

"Where's your salesmanship, Terry? You're supposed to convince me to eat your food, not give me a reason why I shouldn't. You do have a point though. Make mine without the cholesterol and fat."

"You just ordered a tomato and lettuce sandwich," O'Shea said with a smile. "You sure you want that?"

Aaron stared into space for a moment and tapped his chin. "You know what? I've reconsidered. Give me the works."

O'Shea clamped a beefy hand on Aaron's forearm. "I'm just looking out for your well-being, laddie, something I do for only my closest friends and most loyal customers."

"That's probably why I keep coming back here."

"I'll tell the cook to pile on the mushrooms," O'Shea said, then turned and headed to the kitchen.

Aaron sipped his beer while waiting for his order, and glanced at the TV above the bar.

Channel 9 was broadcasting a tape from earlier in the day. Senator Nathan Caldwell was speaking in front of City Hall.

Caldwell was campaigning for President, and Aaron followed politics only enough to know Caldwell and President William Kelsing agreed on very few issues. Seeing his face on television was an unpleasant reminder of his emotionally exhausting conversation with Harlan Grayson.

Caldwell's credentials were a mile long. After leaving the Marine Corps, where he received the Distinguished Service Cross, he studied law at the University of Chicago. In 1975, after passing the bar exam, he went to work for the State of Illinois. A year later, he made prosecutor for the State of Illinois. Over the next seven years, he served on the Chicago City Council and Homeland Security, before he was elected Illinois State Senator in 1990. He lost his first bid at running for President in 2004.

O'Shea reappeared in front of Aaron. "I heard about that Prescott lad getting killed. He was a helluva college footballer, wasn't he?"

Aaron nodded. "Yeah, he'd be playing pro if he didn't tear up his knee. I'm working that case."

O'Shea slapped a hand to his chest. "He was killed over a week ago. You mean to tell me you haven't solved it yet?"

"I guess either the criminals are getting smarter or I'm getting dumber. Maybe a combination of both."

"Well, either way, it's too bad. All that athletic talent going to waste. I guess he didn't do too badly for himself, though. I heard he was worth millions."

Aaron shrugged. "Once it's a million, you're a millionaire until it's a billion. Then you're a billionaire."

"I can't imagine what people do with that much money," O'Shea said, "but it sure would be nice to have some of it. I guarantee I'd find a way to spend it."

"I know you, Terry. You'd still come into work and charm the pants off your customers."

O'Shea grinned and spread his arms wide. "Hey, I love hard, honest work, and love people. Besides, you know what they say about idle hands."

Aaron raised his glass. "To hard, honest work."

"Here, here."

Aaron put down his glass and glanced up when the front door opened, admiring the woman's legs before looking at her face. He blinked twice. It was Jennifer Prescott. She wore a yellow blouse with a blue skirt that stopped an inch above the knees. The two top buttons on her blouse were unfastened, no hint of cleavage, but enough to make any red-blooded American male wish another button or two would pop. She stopped in the middle of the room, posing as a model might while waiting for the cue to strut down the runway.

O'Shea followed Aaron's stare, and a low whistle escaped from his lips. He wagged a finger in her direction. "Now *that's* a fine looking lass."

"That fine looking lass is Jared Prescott's widow," Aaron said.

O'Shea spun his head around. "You don't say?"

"I do say," Aaron replied. He watched as she soaked up the stares from the men in the room.

After a few moments, she spotted Aaron, and beamed like a sunflower. She slowly walked in his direction, not the least bit self-conscious at being the center of attention. She placed her handbag on the counter, slipped onto the stool next to him, and crossed her legs. The movement raised her skirt to the middle of her thighs.

Aaron gazed at her in surprise for a few moments before speaking. "Hello, it's good to see you again," he finally said, then glanced over her shoulder.

Jennifer followed his eyes, then frowned and turned to look behind her. "Is something wrong?"

"Where's Mr. Wonderful?"

She managed a slight smile. "You mean Mitch?"

"I thought his name was Arnold."

Jennifer frowned. "Excuse me?"

"Never mind," Aaron said. "So where is he?"

"You don't like him much, do you?"

"I don't know him well enough to say one way or another."

"I gave him the night off," she said, then looked at O'Shea, who failed miserably in an attempt to avoid staring. "I'll have a Scotch and soda with ice, please, and give him another of what he's having."

O'Shea paused for a moment before gathering himself. "Coming right up, pretty lady."

Jennifer turned back to Aaron. "You're probably wondering what I'm doing here."

"The thought did cross my mind."

"I wanted to buy you a drink. I figured it was the least I could do after what you did the other day," she said.

"Okay, if you say so, but what did I do? And shouldn't you be at home under guard?"

She removed a silver case and lighter from her handbag, took out a cigarette and held it up. "Do you mind?"

He took the lighter from her hand. "Allow me."

She held his hand while he lit the cigarette, then took a drag and turned her head to blow smoke in the opposite direction.

"I didn't know you smoked."

"I never smoke in the house. Jared wouldn't allow it."

O'Shea returned with Aaron's order. Mushrooms had spilled onto the plate, and steam rose from the sandwich. The aroma of fresh meat and onions wafted into the air.

"There you go, laddie," he said. "Quigley's house special."

"Thanks, Terry," Aaron said, and then turned to Jennifer. "I can take the smoke if you can take the smell."

"Looks good, but I bet it has more calories than I can afford in a week. Do you always eat so healthy?"

He pointed to the cigarette. "I guess it all depends on how you want to go out," he said, and bit into the sandwich. Mushrooms and a piece of grilled onion laced with grease fell to the plate.

"Touché," she replied. "Anyway, I wanted to thank you for protecting me after my patio window exploded. To answer your other question, I needed a night out. I refuse to become a prisoner in my own home."

"I was just doing my job."

"I must say you do it very well."

"Thanks," he said noncommittally, "but I've had plenty of practice. Besides, the bullet was non-lethal."

"What do you mean, non-lethal?"

"It was rubber. The likelihood of serious injury was remote at best. Shattering the patio window was probably the worst that would happen."

"But Mitch was cut."

"True, but if the shooting was intentional, whoever pulled the trigger was probably watching the house, and wanted nothing more than to scare you. As to why, I don't know yet."

She hunched her shoulders. "That's scary to think someone was watching the house. Did you find anything?"

Aaron washed down a bite of sandwich with a sip of beer. "Unfortunately no, but with the twenty-four hour guard, I don't expect any more trouble."

"How long will someone need to watch the house?"

"Until we catch your husband's killer, or your local police force decides they can't spare the manpower. Hopefully they'd follow up with more frequent patrols in the area."

She sipped her drink. "Do you mind if we change the subject?"

"Fine by me," he said with a shrug, "but you didn't need to come all the way down here just to thank me. You could have called, or sent me a thank you card with a box of fine chocolates. Which raises the question, how *did* you find me?"

"I called your department and spoke with a Sergeant Richards. He told me you left for the day, and you might be here."

"Good old Sam, burning the midnight oil," he said, recalling he mentioned his dinner plans to Sam.

"I told him I had more information about the investigation," she said, then turned up her palms. "See? No mystery."

"That's good to hear, but you could have called me on my cell phone. It was on the card I gave you. What is it you wanted to tell me?"

She smiled and waved her hand. "That was just something I told your friend on the phone," she said, and then paused and looked into his eyes. "I just wanted to see you."

"Right, I got that, to thank me for my daring rescue."

"Actually, I wanted to apologize for my behavior. I'm not really a cold-hearted bitch. The truth is, I did care for Jared. I guess putting on a tough front was my way of dealing with it. We weren't getting along, and were unofficially separated, that part was true, but I did love him… once."

"It sounds like you're trying to convince me you shouldn't be considered a suspect."

Her head spun around, and she stiffened in the chair. "*Am* I a suspect?"

"Suffice it to say, at this point, you're a person of interest."

She gazed into his eyes for a few moments as if trying to read his thoughts. "I guess that's fair," she said, then shifted her focus to the TV above the bar. "Senator Caldwell."

"I'm sure we can find something better to watch," he said. "Anything else would be an improvement. Hey, Terry, can you switch this TV to the game?"

She placed a hand on his arm. "If you don't mind, I'd like to hear what he's saying. He's a close friend of my father's. He came by the house a lot when I was growing up. He and Dad knew each other before they served together in the Marines. He saved my father's life in Vietnam, you know."

"Your father didn't mention that," he said, not surprised, given Grayson's tendency to fixate on his own achievements. "What did they talk about when he came over to the house?"

This topic of conversation wasn't his preferred choice, but if she were willing to talk, he would listen. He might pick up potentially valuable information without putting her on the defensive with questions seeming like interrogation.

"Nothing that interested me," she said. "Usually, they went outside on the patio or talked in my father's study. He wasn't a Senator at the time. Sometimes they talked about hunting or fishing or golf." She laughed. "Dad isn't very good at golf. The Senator usually took his money."

"Is that a fact?" Aaron asked, not surprised Grayson didn't mention losing at golf. He wouldn't want something he might consider a failure to become public knowledge.

"Dad has a cabin near Grant Woods Forest Preserve about an hour and half from the city. They go up there one or two times a year to get away. They try and convince themselves they're regular pioneers in the wilderness, but the truth is, the cabin has more amenities than some people's homes."

Why am I not surprised?

"I saw a picture of the cabin in your father's office."

She sipped her drink, and he finished his sandwich while watching the broadcast.

"What kind of man is the Senator?" Aaron asked, after a commercial break interrupted the Senator's speech.

"I've never actually had a long conversation with him. I know he helps with my father's company research and dad supports his campaign. I guess you could say they scratch each other's backs."

"From what I know, public opinion of the Senator isn't very high. Some people think he would do or say anything to be president."

She looked at Aaron and tilted her head. "You don't think wanting to be president is a noble ambition?"

"Ambition for a noble cause is a good thing, depending on how far one goes to achieve the goal."

"Senator Caldwell is passionate about the nation's issues, particularly those dealing with terrorism. I know I don't have to tell you it's big on everybody's mind since nine-eleven."

"I didn't realize you were so up on current affairs," he said, sarcastically.

"Why, because I don't work, I'm a blonde, or both?" she asked with a chuckle.

"That's not what I meant. It's just that when we talked…"

"Yes, I can see why you might think that, but the Senator is my father's closest friend, so dad talked about him a lot."

"What exactly is the Senator's stand on terrorism?"

"He thinks our country should focus more on our own issues, at least in the short term, instead of getting involved with other countries problems. We have our own wars to fight here. Gangs, poverty, crime, and drugs are all on the rise. That's not to say he's against helping other countries, but he believes if we resolve our own country's problems first, we'd be better equipped to deal with global issues. It's a matter of shifting priorities. I respect his views because he doesn't promise a quick fix. He admits solutions will take time. Most presidential candidates make promises and never deliver. Senator Caldwell believes our current government tries to apply a band aid to the problem, when what they should be doing is attacking the source."

"You make a good point," he said.

Aaron saw a different side of Jennifer Prescott, and was impressed with her ability to articulate on current affairs. He actually felt a little guilty, because after their first meeting, he considered her somewhat of a scatterbrain. Her conversation tonight was stimulating, even about a topic he had little interest in discussing.

"You know, when you get right down to it, not many politicians get respect," she said. "It's not fair, but I guess it goes with the territory. I mean, it doesn't matter how good of a job they do, most people assume they do nothing more than attend lavish parties and cater to those who contribute the most money to their campaign. It seems the same with lawyers."

"What about cops?" he asked.

She arched her eyebrows. "What about them?"

"Does the same stereotype apply to those in law enforcement? I expect we're in the same category of a love-hate relationship. We're heroes when we save lives, villains when we stop people for speeding."

She tapped her cigarette and ashes fluttered into the ashtray. "You could probably answer that question better than I could."

"We try to do our job, same as everybody else," he said.

"Ah, I see, then I *am* stereotyping aren't I?"

"Who doesn't?" he said with a shrug.

"I suppose most people do to a certain extent. Sorry."

"Don't be too hard on yourself. It's human nature."

"You probably run into some very interesting cases. Real mysteries, I'll bet."

"Sometimes," he replied, sensing she wanted to change the subject. "Not every case gets solved."

"My father is, or at least used to be an avid mystery reader. He tried to solve the mystery before the author revealed it. He was accurate most of the time, at least that's what he told me. I think he took more time analyzing the book than reading it. I think that takes away from the enjoyment. Reading should be for entertainment. My father made it more like a project. He has a fascination with numbers and plays Sudoku in what little spare time he has. I'm surprised he didn't mention it when you talked to him."

"So am I," he said. "He told me just about everything else."

She laughed. "Father can dominate a conversation when he finds a subject he's passionate about."

"That was obvious to me," he said. "Maybe now he has other interests."

"He's out of town a lot and too busy with his career to read much anymore."

"Where does he go?"

"All over the country. When he's home, he's either in meetings or indulging in his outdoor activities, so his work schedule doesn't allow for much leisure or entertainment. It's a lot of responsibility to run a company. A lot of long days, but it has its rewards, I suppose."

"Better him than me," he said.

"You wouldn't want to run your own company? It can prove to be financially rewarding."

"Not worth it, in my opinion. Life is short enough as it is."

Jennifer traced a finger over the rim of her glass. "So, what's it like being a homicide inspector in Chicago?"

"It's a dirty job, but someone has to do it."

"Meaning you'd rather be doing something else?"

"Is it that obvious?" Aaron asked, recalling the recent conversation with Rachel on the same subject.

"You must admit, your testimonial isn't exactly a raving review."

"I believe most people would rather be doing something else."

"Come now, Inspector, there have to be some people who love their job."

"Perhaps, but I never heard anyone say thank God it's Monday."

"You have a point, but I would think pleasure comes from a feeling of accomplishment."

Aaron thought it ironic someone who admitted she spent most of her time at beauty salons and country clubs would make such a statement. Her house was a mansion with a butler and a bodyguard. What did she consider an accomplishment?

On the TV, coverage of the Senator's speech ended. The camera followed him as he left the platform to field questions from the media before the station cut to a commercial. When it came back live, a reporter from Channel 9 recapped the Senator's speech.

"So, Inspector, when you were at the house the other day, I noticed you looking at my legs."

Aaron looked at her with a start. Her comment came from left field, and his opinion of her as someone well versed and articulate in current affairs took a beating. Still, he couldn't keep his eyes from looking at her legs on impulse.

She rotated on the chair to face him. The movement inched the skirt an inch higher on her thighs. "So what do you think?" she asked with a gleam in her eyes.

"Think about what?" he asked, forcing his gaze to her eyes.

"My legs. You're a detective, need to be observant, how would you rate them?" She grinned and cocked her head to one side.

"I've seen worse," he said with a barely noticeable shrug.

She curled her lower lip into a pout. "Is that supposed to be a compliment?"

"Sorry, it's been a long day. I'm afraid that's the best I can do."

"You're a real charmer."

"That's a new one," he said with a laugh.

"You mean your wife never told you that?"

"Shouldn't you have asked me if I was married before you started flirting?"

"Who said I was flirting?"

"I suppose you were making small talk."

She stuck her tongue out and he looked away.

"I was married once," he said.

"Really?" she asked.

"You sound surprised."

"No, I can see someone being attracted to you. After all, you did save my life."

"I didn't save your life. The bullet was non-lethal."

She was silent for a while and he wondered what really motivated her to come to the restaurant. She craved attention. Perhaps the meeting was nothing more than a tease, or maybe she wanted to eliminate herself as a suspect in her husband's murder. The reason didn't matter. Getting involved with a potential suspect was morally and ethically wrong, not to mention potentially dangerous.

"Listen, since you're here, I need to ask you a few more questions," he said.

Her eyes flashed disappointment. "I thought this was a social meeting."

"What gave you that idea? Remember, you came looking for me."

"Yes, I know, but I was enjoying our conversation. It would be a shame to spoil it with a bunch of questions."

"Not a bunch, just a few."

She shrugged and jiggled the glass. Ice cubes rattled against the side. "In that case, do you mind if I have another drink?"

"Be my guest," he said, and then signaled to O'Shea, who filled her glass.

"Thank you," she said and took a sip. "What is it you wanted to ask me?"

"Your father said he scheduled a meeting with your husband the day he was killed. They were going to discuss him taking over the company. Were you aware of that meeting?"

"No, but that's not unusual," she replied. "Neither my father nor Jared ever discussed work, and considering the state of our marriage, well…"

"Does it surprise you your father planned to put your husband in charge?"

"I never really gave it much thought, but I guess it makes sense, since Jared was Vice President. My father can't work forever."

"I talked to the man your husband played the practical joke on. It seems he picked on him more than anyone else."

"That was Jared. Once he latched onto something, he wouldn't let go. Was this man any help?"

"Yes, actually he was. He pointed out two men from a photograph who participated in the practical joke. They were former teammates of your husband's. Do you know Frank Regan?"

"The name sounds familiar, but I don't think I ever met him."

He hesitated a moment, sipped his beer, and then looked at her. "What about Vic Bryant?"

Her eyes widened for a split second before she bit her lip and looked away.

"Let me save you the trouble, Mrs. Prescott. I talked to Vic Bryant, and he said you and he dated in college. Is that true?"

Jennifer sighed heavily. "Jared got more than his share of attention from other girls and wasn't paying as much attention to me. I dated Bryant to make Jared jealous, nothing more. He was a disgusting pig, but I knew he and Jared didn't get along. It was the biggest mistake of my life. I guess all it did was cause a fight between them. I was embarrassed and felt stupid."

"Did Bryant try anything when you went out with him?"

"If you're asking did I sleep with him, the answer is no. It was one date. I made sure we went to a public place because… well… I heard he had a reputation for being a little rough."

"Bryant told me you went out a *couple* of times," he said.

"He lied. It was once… once too many," she said and then looked at her watch. "Listen, it's late. I need to be getting home. Was there anything else you wanted to ask me?"

"Yes. You said you went out with friends that night. Right before the shooting, you were on your way to the kitchen to give me their names. In the confusion, I forgot to get those names. I'd like them now."

"Yes, I did promise you that. I'm sorry, but with the shooting and all…"

"It's not your fault. We were all a little distracted."

She nodded, then took out a pen and paper from her purse, scribbled down the information, and handed it to him. "There you are, Inspector," she said, and slipped off the chair. "If that's all, I really need to be going. Thanks for the conversation. If you have any more questions, feel free to come to the house."

"Can you make it home safe? I can call you a cab."

"No thank you, I'll be fine," she said.

He watched Jennifer leave Quigley's, then finished his beer and walked outside. He wanted to say something to her, but didn't have the words. It didn't matter, because she had already driven away. He stood by his car for a few minutes, staring into the darkness, again wondering what really prompted her visit.

Chapter Seventeen

Aaron returned to his apartment, took a beer from the refrigerator, and stared at the phone on the wall, considering calling Jennifer Prescott to ensure she arrived home safely. After a few moments, he decided it wasn't wise to fuel a potential fire.

Her behavior at Quigley's suggested she was interested in him, but he doubted that was her intent.

Although he wasn't significantly older, they didn't travel in the same social circles, the main reason he was no longer married to Brenda. Maybe she believed a 'one-night stand with an officer of the law' was a temporary remedy for her loneliness. He could see the headline now. 'Cop gets romantically involved with a major suspect in a murder case.' Intriguing headlines; disastrous consequences.

He forced his thoughts from Jennifer Prescott and went into the den, sat down in the recliner, and turned on the TV. He pulled the lever on the chair and stared upward for a time. Maybe the name of Jared Prescott's killer would magically appear on the ceiling.

He'd worked hundreds of homicide cases, but couldn't remember one with so many legitimate suspects. Jennifer Prescott's appearance at Quigley's only clouded the issue. He sipped the beer and considered the other people involved.

With the exception of Sheldon Nash and perhaps Frank Regan, everyone he interviewed had motive to murder Jared Prescott. Given the history between Vic Bryant and the victim, he was at the top of the list. Bryant made no attempt to hide his hatred for Prescott, although an open and honest reaction to one's feelings for a victim often ruled them out as a suspect.

George Thompson seemed dedicated in caring for his ailing mother, but the types of sacrifices he was making often drove people to act out of character. He endured more than his share of ridicule from Prescott, and seemed harmless on the surface. Still, those types were often the ones arriving at work on a Monday morning, armed with more firepower than an S.W.A.T. unit, shooting everybody in sight before taking their own life or forcing suicide by cop. The phone call to Thompson's office the night of Prescott murder suggested guilt, but could be the killer trying to frame him.

Jennifer Prescott had everything she wanted, spoiled with a lifestyle of leisure, yet all but ignored by a philandering husband.

Harlan Grayson appeared in control, but watching his daughter cast aside by an indifferent husband was certainly a motive for murder.

Then there was Warren Kirby. He admitted his disappointment when Grayson hired Prescott as Vice President, depriving him of an increase in salary and position.

Money, jealousy, revenge, infidelity–all common motives for murder, and every suspect had at least one of these motives.

Aaron recalled his boss's suggestion to use additional manpower. He wasn't above asking for help, but there were two kinds–the official kind and the unofficial kind.

***

The next morning, Aaron walked into The Union 60's Grille on S. Union Street, a twenty-four-hour diner serving breakfast at all hours. The wallpaper depicted a nineteen sixties theme, with an abundance of purple, yellow, and red colors, with images of Elvis Presley, the Beatles, and the Rolling Stones. A jukebox sitting in the corner farthest from the door was playing the final verse of "Monday Monday," a song from 1966 by the Mamas and the Papas. The music of yesteryear wasn't as jazzy or graphic as the songs of today, but at least Aaron understood the lyrics.

Twelve rectangular red tables with four matching chairs sat in the middle of the room, with six yellow booths positioned against the wall. Twelve blue stools lined the counter. The air in the room hung rich with the aroma of coffee and bacon.

Five individual customers sat in various spots.

A waitress wiping down tables glanced up and smiled. "I'll be right with you, sir."

"I'm looking for Larry," he said, referring to Larry Petersen, who operated the diner.

"He's in the kitchen, I'll tell him you're here," she said, then walked behind the counter and disappeared through a door.

Aaron sat on a stool and flipped through the menu. A few moments later, Petersen emerged from the kitchen, wiping his hands on a soiled apron. He was mid-fifties, and wore a perpetual smile. His stomach hung over his belt, and wisps of salt and pepper hair peeked from the sides of a chef's hat, which leaned precariously to the left.

"Aaron, I haven't seen you in… what's it been… six months?" Petersen boomed in a baritone voice, rocking the room like a bass drum on the first Friday night of high school football. He stopped and showed his palms. "Say, I'm not wanted by the law, am I?"

"Relax, Larry," Aaron said with a wave. "I'm not aware of any violations, and even if there were, you'd probably bribe the judge with a cheeseburger basket and homemade fudge brownies."

"Isn't that the truth?" Petersen said with a smile. "What brings you here this morning?"

"Is Eddie around?"

"Sure, he's in the back. I'll get him for you."

Aaron got up from the barstool. "That's okay. If you don't mind, I'll go back there myself."

"Be my guest. How about I whip you up one of my world famous omelets? The eggs and sausage are guaranteed to jump start your day."

Aaron patted his stomach. "Ordinarily, I would take you up on the offer, but my stomach is cursing me after one of Quigley's house specials last night."

"Ah, yes, Terry's Angus burger. I know it well."

"Maybe next time, Larry," Aaron said, and then went into the kitchen.

Eddie Rivers, his most reliable informant, stood with his back to Aaron, cleaning out one of the ovens.

Prior to working for Petersen as a short-order cook, Eddie worked various odd jobs, including a janitor at the Salvation Army, answering phones during telethons to raise money for various causes, and distributing newspapers on street corners.

In the late nineties, he made a decent living selling insurance until his wife Diane died six months after being diagnosed with liver cancer. Although she suffered for over two years, and the outcome was inevitable, Eddie started drinking heavily to deal with depression and became an alcoholic. He lost his job and fell in with the wrong crowd, developed a cocaine addiction, and served time for possession.

Aaron was a Sergeant when he met Eddie in June of 1999, when he and his partner were dispatched to an abandoned building on the South Side of Chicago.

Eddie stood on the ledge at the top of the building, threatening to jump.

Aaron asked his partner to distract Eddie with conversation while he raced up the stairs to the top floor, and entered the roof through an access door. He listened to

Eddie recount how his life wasn't worth living after the death of his wife.

Aaron used every bit of his psychology training to convince Eddie there were alternatives to deal with his loss, and forty-five minutes later, he escorted Eddie down the stairs to the street.

Aaron took ownership of Eddie's recovery, making himself available during the fourteen months it took Eddie to dry out and kick his drug habit.

Eddie repaid Aaron for saving his life the only way he knew, through his network of, let's call them 'characters of ill repute,' to gather information impossible to get using more conventional methods.

Aaron paid Eddie more than most other detectives paid their informants, not only for the information, but also because through the years they developed a mutual respect and friendship surpassing a typical detective-informant relationship. He respected Eddie's renewed work ethic, courage, and determination to put a traumatic past behind and move forward.

"Hey Eddie, how's my number one source of gossip?"

Eddie jerked his head back in surprise, then wiped his hands on his apron, and shook Aaron's hand. He was five foot seven, slight of build, with deep-set dark eyes and a high forehead.

"Well, if it isn't Chicago's number one Inspector."

"That's *Illinois's* number one Inspector, Eddie."

"Sorry, geography was never my best subject," Eddie quipped.

"It's good to see you still have a sense of humor," Aaron said. "We haven't seen each other in a while. What have you been doing with yourself?"

"I signed up for a couple of courses at the local community college. This job isn't bad and I like working for Mr. Petersen, but I don't want to be balancing pancakes on a spatula forever."

"Good for you, Eddie."

"So, are you here for business or pleasure?"

"Eddie, when we retire we can sit in our rocking chairs and reminisce, but today it's business as usual," Aaron said, and then motioned to the back door. "Can we talk outside?"

"Sure, if you can stand the odor in the alley."

"I'm a Homicide Inspector in Chicago. What do you think?"

"You have a point, but don't say I didn't warn you."

They walked out the door into the alley. Five gray Rubbermaid garbage cans stood against the wall, and the foul odor of garbage hung heavy in the air.

Aaron pinched his nose. "You weren't kidding."

"I told you. It's especially bad with the humidity. How about we get down to business and go back inside? You can bury your nose in one of Larry's omelets."

Aaron gestured to the left. "Why don't we take a walk before the smell renders me unconscious."

"I assume you heard about the Jared Prescott murder," Aaron said, when they reached a spot more tolerable.

"I'd have to be living in a cave not to know about it," Eddie said. "When I heard you were working the case, I figured you might be coming around to request my services. How's the investigation going?"

"It's coming along. I want you check out a guy named Warren Kirby. He's the Senior Financial Manager for ChemPhen Pharmaceuticals, the same company the victim worked for."

"A high roller, huh?" Eddie said with a nod.

"You might say that. Be extra discreet with this one, Eddie. We have heavy hitters in this case, and can't afford to ruffle any feathers."

Eddie slapped a palm to his chest and lifted an eyebrow. "Discreet is my middle name, old friend."

Aaron laughed. "I thought it was Gertrude."

"You're a funny guy for a cop."

"So I've heard."

"So what's up with this Kirby guy?"

"Just a feeling I have. It might be a dead end, but if anyone can pick up dirt, it's you." He took out his wallet and handed Eddie two twenty-dollar bills. "The community appreciates your service, Eddie."

"Andrew Jackson, my favorite president," Eddie said, running the bills under his nose. "Nice and crisp, too."

"My car's out front," Aaron said. "Say goodbye to Larry for me."

"Will do. Give me a few days, and hopefully I'll have something for you," Eddie said, then stuffed the bills into his pocket.

"You do that, Eddie. Make me and Andrew proud."

Chapter Eighteen

The following day, Sam sat in Aaron's office, folder in hand.

"Find anything interesting?" Aaron asked, knowing Sam rarely disappointed him.

"I have information on our illustrious cast of characters," Sam said. "Vic Bryant, Warren Kirby, Harlan Grayson, the Prescotts, Frank Regan, and George Thompson. Did I miss anyone?"

"So far, that's everyone," Aaron said.

"Except for Jared Prescott's jail time, which we already knew about, the only one with a record is Vic Bryant."

"I can't say I'm surprised. What did you find?"

"About two years ago, he was picked up in a Denver night club, charged with drunk and disorderly. The police report said he got into a fight and put a guy in the hospital with two broken ribs. There were conflicting reports on how the fight started, so they released him with no more than a fine. He joined the Army right after college, but was dishonorably discharged after six months for striking an officer."

"He and Prescott got into a fight in college over Prescott's wife, and McCarthy Ford fired him for a similar incident," Aaron said. "Violence seems to be a habit with this guy."

"I guess it's safe to assume he hasn't mellowed in his old age," Sam said.

"No, he hasn't. What did Bryant do in the Army?"

"He trained as a sniper, but he never saw action," Sam said.

"That's a scary thought. Given his history, he's our number one suspect at this point. Who's next?"

"Harlan Grayson is squeaky clean," Sam said. "I couldn't find as much as a parking ticket."

"Disappointing, but not surprising," Aaron said with more than a tinge of sarcasm.

"It could be he's just a careful driver and a law-abiding citizen."

"You're right, Sam. It's probably not politically correct to make assumptions. I guess I was hoping you would tell me he's not as perfect as he thinks. You know he's a legend in his own mind."

"So I've heard," Sam agreed. "I also tracked down the charges made on Jared Prescott's credit card the night he was killed. I found out more about that phone call to United Airlines."

"I'm listening."

"There was a charge of four hundred-fifty dollars made to United Airlines to reserve a flight to San Diego. It was scheduled to leave Chicago at ten in the morning on Wednesday, August sixteenth, returning on Friday the eighteenth, at two p.m. United confirmed Jared Prescott was a passenger on the flight."

"Anything about a rental car or where he planned to stay?"

"Nothing on a rental car, but that wouldn't necessarily be paid until the car was rented. The other charge to his card was to the Sheraton Mission Valley Hotel in San Diego. I called the hotel, and they confirmed Jared Prescott had a room reservation for two nights, checking in on the sixteenth, leaving the eighteenth."

"Assuming Jared Prescott made that call, and we can't assume it was him, what was so pressing that he needed to get out of town at the last minute? Why San Diego? Why only two days?"

"Indeed," Sam agreed. "Those are the fifty-thousand-dollar questions. Now, regarding our mystery woman who rented the motel room, I found only two Nancy Edmunds living in the area. One is thirteen years old, the other has been in the hospital the past three months. Also, I couldn't find an address of two-twenty-one Pleasant Creek Drive."

"We figured Nancy Edmunds was an alias anyway. At least the woman was creative enough not to use Jane Doe. What about Kirby, Thompson, and Regan?"

"Nothing on them," Sam said and closed the folder.

"Prescott's widow gave me the names of two women she went clubbing with the night of her husband's murder. I don't expect more than a confirmation of her alibi, but it's worth a shot."

"Good luck," Sam said.

***

Kathy Gardner, an office manager for Chicago Title on LaSalle St., confirmed she was with Jennifer Prescott and another friend at The Mid, a nightclub on North Halstead on the night in question, but otherwise didn't provide any meaningful information. She said she hadn't met Mrs. Prescott until that night, and left the club early.

The second woman had a more interesting story to tell.

Jackie Irwin managed the Women's Wear Department at Macy's on 111 North State Street.

Irwin was five feet six, attractive, with brunette hair and a model's figure. She smiled and extended her hand when Aaron entered the office on the fifth floor, showing a row of perfectly aligned and sparkling white teeth.

"Hello, Inspector Randall," she said. "Please, have a seat. On the phone you said you wanted to ask me about Jennifer Prescott." Her lips formed a tight line. "I'm still in shock over what happened to Jared. I feel so bad for Jennifer."

Aaron noticed genuine sorrow in Irwin's eyes, perhaps even more than Jennifer Prescott. "Are you and Mrs. Prescott close friends?"

"Jennifer and I met at Park Valley Country Club a few years ago. My ex was good friends with Jared, and the four of us used to go out to dinner, sometimes the theatre."

"Used to?"

"We stopped when Jared and Jennifer started having problems," she said, then bit her lip, and looked away. "I probably shouldn't have said that."

"Don't worry, Ms. Irwin, that's not news to me. Mrs. Prescott herself told me their marriage was falling apart. Tell me about the night at The Mid club. Your friend Kathy Gardner said she left the club about eight o'clock."

"Yes, eight is probably right, but she would know better than I would. I wasn't really paying much attention to the time. Jennifer and I talked, had a few drinks, and danced a few times. I left about ten."

"Do you know what time Mrs. Prescott left the club?"

Irwin squirmed in her chair, but didn't answer.

"It's a simple question."

She folded her arms and looked away for a moment as if formulating an appropriate answer before looking back at Aaron. "Jennifer came that night to meet someone."

"Who?"

"You have to understand, Inspector, Jared played around for years, and didn't go out of his way to keep it a secret. He had an enormous ego."

"I know all about his ego. Who did she meet?"

"Someone she'd been seeing."

"By seeing, I assume you mean they were having an affair."

Irwin nodded.

"How long?"

"I don't know exactly, a few months, I guess."

"Did he show up that night?"

"Yes. After Kathy left, Jennifer and I talked for maybe another fifteen minutes before he came over to the table. The two of them danced a few times, we had a few more drinks, and then they got up. I don't know whether they left the club or not, but I didn't see either one of them after that. It's a big place and was crowded that night."

"Do you remember what time you last saw them?"

"It must have been about eight-thirty, maybe eight-forty-five," she said, and then closed her eyes and shook her head as though attempting to erase the memory. "Jennifer won't like me telling you this."

"She doesn't need to know the source of the information. What's the man's name?"

"Tim Lombardi. He's… *was* a friend of Jared's. They played golf together."

"Do you know how he and Mrs. Prescott became involved?"

"Tim's ego is almost as big as Jared's. He openly flirted with Jennifer, but Jared didn't seem to mind. It was nothing serious at first, just macho guy stuff. Jennifer got a lot of that and frankly, I think Jared got off on it. Tim found out Jared was cheating, and told Jennifer about it, but honestly, I think all it did was confirm what she already suspected. They started seeing each other behind Jared's back. She did it at first to get back at Jared, but it got serious. She told me about it because, despite Jared's cheating, I think she felt guilty, and maybe was hoping I would tell her it was all right. Personally, I don't blame her for having the affair."

"Are they in love with each other?" Aaron asked.

"You'll have to ask Jennifer that question."

"Is it possible Mr. Prescott knew about the affair?" he asked. "And if so, what do you think he would have done?"

"Honestly, whether he knew or not I couldn't say, but doubted he would have cared."

"Can you tell me where I can find this Tim Lombardi?"

"He works for GHA Technologies in Tinley Park, but I know he's on the road a lot entertaining clients, so if he's not in his office, you might ask his secretary."

Aaron stood and handed Irwin a business card. "Thanks for your time, Ms. Irwin, and trust me, you did the right thing."

Irwin smiled, but it was devoid of emotion. "I hope so."

Chapter Nineteen

Aaron called GHA Technologies, and Lombardi's secretary said he was entertaining clients at the Country Club.

Park Valley Country Club was located in the exclusive Pine Forest subdivision where the smallest home was forty-two hundred square feet. Every yard of the brick two and three-story homes was immaculately landscaped with dense shrubbery and brightly colored flowers. The streets teemed with large evergreen trees.

A fifteen-foot wrought iron gate guarded the entrance to Park Valley, located on Golf Drive. Aaron drove a mile down a two-lane winding road before he reached the parking lot.

The main building looked more like a palace than a clubhouse, and with the number of Mercedes, Lexus's, BMW's, and Audis, the parking lot could double as a luxury car dealership.

Aaron got out of his car and walked through the aisles of cars, turning when he heard the click of a golf club striking a golf ball. To the right, down a path with a signpost indicating 10th tee with an arrow pointing straight ahead, a man posed while watching his golf ball in flight.

Two golf carts with four senior-looking men dressed in plaid shorts eating hot dogs passed him on their way to the tenth tee. They drove by as if Aaron was invisible.

Aaron entered the main building, and walked into a lobby half the size of a football field, with unusually high ceilings and maroon cut pile plush carpeting. To the left, the words 'Pro Shop' were stenciled above double glass doors. Aaron had seen fancy hotels that didn't have lobbies as elegant.

"Excuse me, sir, may I help you?"

Aaron turned.

A man wearing tan pants with 'Park Valley Country Club' stenciled on the left side of his white polo shirt stood a few feet away. He looked Aaron over. "Are you a prospective member?"

What made the man think he wasn't already a member? Maybe it was his less than one-hundred dollar shirt. "Hardly," he said. "I'm looking for Tim Lombardi."

The man narrowed his eyes and continued studying Aaron. "May I ask what your business is with Mr. Lombardi?"

Aaron presented his credentials.

The man stepped forward, eyed the badge, and then quickly stepped back. "Oh, I see. I believe Mr. Lombardi is playing poker in the locker room. Take a left at the end of the hall. You'll see a sign above a stairwell marked locker rooms."

Aaron followed the man's directions, and walked down a long hallway, passing a conference room where workers were busy arranging tables and chairs. A gold engraved plaque on the wall outside read 'The Lakeside Room.' An easel outside the door announced a seven o'clock dinner party with open bar scheduled at six-thirty.

Aaron walked down the stairs and entered the locker room. A few men were in various stages of dressing, others carried tennis rackets, their one-hundred dollar Adidas sport shirts dark with sweat.

He strolled through the locker room, dodging an onslaught of condescending stares, although no one cared enough to challenge his presence. He stepped in front of a man carrying a duffel bag, walking as though he was late for an appointment.

"Excuse me."

"Yeah," the man said, glaring at Aaron as if he'd just interrupted his speech to the Senate sub-committee.

"Where can I find Tim Lombardi?"

The man hesitated as though considering whether he was too busy to answer the question, before jerking a thumb over his left shoulder. "There's a room in the back. Just follow the smell of cigar smoke."

"Thank you," Aaron said then stepped through double doors into a larger room containing several round card tables with matching folding chairs. A fifty-four inch television mounted ten feet high on the wall was tuned to the ESPN classic station airing a college football game with two teams he didn't recognize.

To his left, four men were playing cards. Red, white, and blue poker chips sat in a pile in the center of the table. Smoke from each man's cigar rose and coalesced to form a cloud above the table.

As he approached, all four glanced up and instinctively covered their cards.

"Which one of you is Lombardi?"

One man placed his cards down in front of him, and removed the cigar from his mouth, studying Aaron as if sizing him for a new suit of clothes. The condescending look must be part of the membership bylaws, and frankly, Aaron was getting tired of it.

"I'm Lombardi. Who are you?"

"We need to talk."

"I'm in the middle of a game here, pal, but don't bother, I had my golf shoes polished yesterday. You must be new here. Where's your uniform?"

Lombardi's comment drew laughter from his three playing partners.

At times like these, Aaron wished he didn't have to play by the rules of law enforcement. He would grab Lombardi by the scruff of the neck, throw him up against the wall, and ask politely for his attention. He opted for tact.

"I don't work here."

"Then who let you in?"

"If that's the way you want to play it," Aaron said with a shrug. He took out his ID and walked around the table, putting it close enough to Lombardi's face so Lombardi had to move his head back to read it.

The badge did nothing to dissuade Lombardi's smug attitude.

"Homicide Inspector, huh? I think he's putting out on eighteen, can it wait?"

"Let's you and I talk about Prescott. This needs to be a private conversation. Why don't we go somewhere where your mind is not on the poker game?"

"You can talk to me right here, Inspector," Lombardi said, and then waved a hand. "These gentlemen knew Jared as well as I did."

Aaron crooked his finger and gestured to Lombardi. "Let's just you and I talk."

Lombardi stared at Aaron for a few moments before tossing the cards face down on the table.

"I'm out of this hand, boys, but I'll be back for the next one," he said, then got up from the chair.

Lombardi was six feet two, with a deep tan, blonde hair, and blue eyes, with a physique suggesting he worked out regularly, just the type of man to attract Jennifer Prescott's attention. He wore a brown Izod golf shirt with black shorts.

He angled his head to the right. "In there."

They entered a smaller room with a long table covered with a white linen cloth. Several other tables rested against the corner with matching chairs stacked eight to ten high.

"This is available to members and their families only," Lombardi said, as though suggesting Aaron should feel honored to be allowed access.

Aaron ignored the remark.

Lombardi puffed on his cigar and blew smoke into the air. "Jared's death was tragic," he said, with no more emotion than if reading the list of appetizers from a restaurant menu.

"I never said anything about *Jared* Prescott," Aaron said.

Lombardi furrowed his brow and grinned. "No, you didn't, did you?" he said, and then walked over to the table and crushed his cigar into an ashtray. He turned and faced Aaron, folded his arms, and leaned against the table. His body language suggested he was preparing to chat with a neighbor over the back yard fence. "So you want to know about my affair with Jennifer Prescott."

"I'm glad for the sake of conversation you're not denying it."

"Jennifer called me and said you might be nosing around. I have no secrets, Inspector, nor am I a fan of wasting time. How do you cops say it… cut to the chase?"

"I'm not familiar with the phrase. You watch too much TV, Lombardi."

"Anyway, yes, Jennifer and I were involved. It's been going on for a few months. Jared cheated on her, and she started looking for nothing more than companionship. I never meant to steal her from Jared. It just happened, but it's over. I haven't seen her since Jared's death."

"Why did you stop seeing her?"

Lombardi raised his eyebrows. "You're the detective–shouldn't it be obvious? I mean, how would that look? Besides, Jennifer needs time." He studied his fingernails. "I didn't expect the relationship to last anyway."

"That's too bad," Aaron said, but couldn't have cared less. "You met Jennifer Prescott at The Mid club the night of August fifteenth. According to a reliable source, you left about eight-thirty. Is that correct?"

Lombardi looked at the floor and laughed.

"Something funny about this, Mr. Lombardi?" Between Harlan Grayson and Lombardi, Aaron's patience was worn to the thickness of a toothpick.

"I follow the news and watch TV, Inspector. I know Jared was killed around nine o'clock, and yes, we left the club about eight-thirty. Jennifer followed me back to my place and no, there weren't any witnesses. We got there just before nine. She left my place around eleven-thirty."

Aaron studied Lombardi's face. It was evident he had prepared for Aaron's questions, leaving him to wonder whether he and Jennifer Prescott had rehearsed a story. She told Aaron she arrived home just after midnight, which would coincide leaving Lombardi's place at 11:30.

"How far is your house from the Tremont Inn motel?" Aaron asked.

"Sorry, I never go to that part of town," Lombardi said with a shrug, "but I would guess maybe half an hour, forty-five minutes, depending on traffic and time of day."

Aaron stared into Lombardi's eyes then put his notepad and pen away to signal an end to the interview. "Thanks for your time, Mr. Lombardi. I'll be in touch."

Lombardi flashed a smile and waved his hand. "If I can be of any more help, Inspector, do let me know."

They walked together toward the door.

Lombardi opened the door and extended his arm.

Aaron took two steps and stopped. "By the way, what kind of car do you drive?"

"A BMW 545i."

"What color?"

"Dark green… like money," Lombardi said, showing as many thirty-two polished teeth as possible without risking injury to his jaw. "Listen, I can put in a good word for you here if you want a membership."

"I'm sure you can."

Lombardi returned to his poker game, and Aaron left the locker room, returned to his car, and left the country club.

***

Aaron knocked on the door to the Prescott home.

Gordon opened the door and his eyes widened. "Inspector, what are you doing here?" he asked in a tone as if he assumed Aaron's first visit was his last.

Aaron pushed past Gordon and stepped into the foyer. "Where is Mrs. Prescott?"

Gordon looked past Aaron and swallowed, but said nothing.

"She's upstairs resting and can't be disturbed right now," boomed a voice from the hallway.

Aaron turned.

Mitchell Walker stood in the hallway, hands on his hips.

"Disturb her."

"Why should I?"

"It doesn't concern you, Walker. I'll wait in the other room," Aaron said, then went into the den, and stood next to the sofa before Walker could protest any further.

Three minutes later, Jennifer Prescott entered the room wearing a long silk purple robe. Walker was close enough to be attached to her hip.

"This needs to be a private conversation," Aaron said.

Jennifer put a hand on Walker's shoulder and whispered into his ear.

Walker nodded, then glared at Aaron for a few moments before leaving the room.

Jennifer sat on the sofa and looked more subdued than the last time he saw her. "I didn't expect to see you again so soon," she said. "Is something the matter?"

"You could say that," Aaron said. "Why didn't you tell me about your affair with Tim Lombardi?"

Jennifer lowered her head and studied her hands as though they contained an explanation. "How did you find out?"

"That doesn't matter. I just had a conversation with Lombardi, but I suspect you already know that, because you called him. What you do with your social life is your business, but the time you left the night club that night gave you plenty of time to stop at the Tremont Inn on your way over to Lombardi's house, if that's really where you went."

Jennifer looked up at Aaron, her eyes showing fatigue. "First of all, Inspector, what you're suggesting is not only ridiculous, but out of line. Second of all, I didn't mention my relationship with Tim because he has nothing to do with this. I know it looks bad, and I realize I was wrong to keep it from you, but I was trying to protect him."

"Protect him from what?"

"From getting questioned by the police for no reason. Inspector, I did not kill my husband, nor did I hire anyone to kill him. Tim and I were together that night, but I had no part in what happened to Jared. You have to believe me."

"Right now, I don't know who or what to believe, but mark my words, I *will* find out who killed your husband. Good day."

Aaron backed out of the driveway and drove away, thinking he'd like to lock the cast of characters in a cramped cell and see who flinched first.

Chapter Twenty

Vince Sherman sat behind the desk in his office, hands folded, an unfocused look in his eyes. "I got a call from the commissioner yesterday."

Aaron tried to keep from rolling his eyes, but they didn't cooperate. "How are things at Buckingham Palace?"

"Harlan Grayson and he had another discussion."

"What's the old man's problem now?" Aaron asked. Of all the things he wanted to hear, Grayson's complaints were at the bottom of the list.

"He took exception to the way you treated his daughter, and threatened to file a harassment complaint. He claims you practically accused her of murdering her husband. She was pretty upset, and I can't say I blame her. Is that how it went down?"

Aaron leaned forward in the chair. "You know, Vince, Grayson made a point of telling me how his daughter is all grown up and able to make her own decisions, but every time someone looks at her cross-eyed, she whines to Daddy. And no, that's not how it went down."

"You know, Aaron, I'm obligated to warn you, *again*, how you handle this investigation. The pressure on the department is greater than ever, especially now since Harlan Grayson has threatened action. If I didn't know any better, I believe you went out of your way to piss him off."

Aaron gave a wry smile and sat back in the chair. "I guess it's a good thing for me you *do* know better."

"We need indisputable evidence before we formally accuse anyone of anything. You know that."

"You mean like every other normal murder investigation? Grayson is overreacting. I did nothing more than rattle his daughter's cage, and had just cause. She withheld information of an affair, which in my mind makes both her and her boyfriend suspects. She must know that meeting her lover on the same night her husband is murdered will do more than just raise an eyebrow."

Sherman relaxed a little. "I wasn't aware of that."

"Of course you weren't."

"Well, like it or not, this isn't a normal investigation. The commissioner asked me to talk to you, and we've talked. Off the record, I support your actions, but understand my hands are tied. I can only do so much if Grayson decides to escalate the issue."

"I know you'll do your best, Vince."

"Tell me about the affair."

"Jennifer Prescott was involved with a man her husband knew from the country club. She met him at a club the night of her husband's murder. Based on the conversations I had with her friends, the time they left the club coincides with the time Prescott was murdered. That's too much of a coincidence."

"Did you talk to this man?"

"Yes. His name is Tim Lombardi. He's a real piece of work, but that seems to be a common trait with everyone involved in the investigation."

"Did either one of them deny the affair?"

"No. their stories matched, too closely in my opinion."

"You think they rehearsed the story?"

"It's possible. Mrs. Prescott said she kept the affair a secret to protect Lombardi."

"Do you honestly believe she's guilty?" Sherman asked.

Aaron shrugged. "I don't know what to think. Her behavior is inconsistent. I never know which personality will show up."

"Okay, like I said, we've talked, so keep me posted," Sherman said.

After the discussion with Sherman, Aaron went home, tossed his jacket on the sofa, took out a Miller Lite beer, and punched the play button on his answering machine. There was one message from Rachel.

She wanted to treat him to dinner that evening, but didn't provide details. He wasn't in the best of moods after yet another obstacle to the investigation, and wanted to tell her he arrived home too late, but something in her voice on the message urged him to return the call.

She answered on the first ring.

"What's this about treating me to dinner?" he asked. "Twice in less than a month? What will people think?"

"Since when do you care what people think?" she said. "Are you up for it or not?"

Aaron raised the beer bottle to eye level and gazed at the liquid as if the answer to his decision swam inside like a worm in a bottle of tequila. "I don't know. I thought it might be a good night to stay home and get drunk."

"Give me a break, Aaron, you haven't been drunk since college. I really wanted to get together tonight. There's something important I'd like to discuss with you."

Aaron heard anxiety in the tone of her voice. Suddenly, his frustration with the Prescott investigation wasn't as high a priority. "You sound worried, Rachel. Is anything wrong?"

"No, nothing is wrong," she said after an uncomfortable pause. "I just need to talk to you."

Rachel didn't sound like her normal vibrant self, and he decided to accept her invitation, although the promise of a meal was secondary to learning what was on her mind.

"Okay, you win," he said, and checked his watch. "It's six-thirty now. What time do you want to meet?"

"How does seven-thirty sound?"

"Seven-thirty is good. Where are we going?"

"I was thinking of Longhorn Steakhouse in Norridge."

"Sound great," he said.

"Good. I'll see you then."

"Listen, Rachel, I know my hourly rate is barely above minimum wage, but I can afford to pay for my own dinner."

"We'll see," she said, and hung up before he could protest further.

***

Rachel was standing in the lobby when Aaron arrived at the Longhorn Steakhouse at seven-twenty. "Wow, ten minutes early," she said, glancing at her watch. "What did you do, run every red light?"

He smiled. "The truth be known, I like steak better than pasta."

"I'm still impressed," she said.

They hugged, and the hostess led them to a booth in the back of the restaurant.

The table was covered with a white linen cloth, and an amber candle burned in the middle of the table. Framed pictures of the ocean, fishermen in boats, and lighthouses hung on the walls, providing an outdoorsy and borderline romantic ambiance.

Rachel wore a dark green blouse and white slacks. Her hair looked as if she spent extra time primping, and her nails were painted a light pink, complementing the color of her glossy lipstick. She smelled of expensive perfume, and didn't appear like someone who had worked all day.

"I'm glad you changed you mind," she said.

"A juicy steak sounded too good to pass up, particularly after the last couple of days," he said.

She unfolded the napkin and put it in her lap. "More drama in the Prescott case?"

"Harlan Grayson has his jockstrap in a knot. He's reacting to what he believes is unfair treatment of his precious daughter."

"Oh?"

"He called the commissioner and threatened to file harassment charges. The commissioner came down on my boss, my boss came down on me, etcetera, etcetera."

"Wow. Do you really think he'll file a complaint?"

Aaron opened the menu. "I've been through this before. He can file all the harassment complaints he wants. I'm still going to do my job. He gets off on intimidating people and believes he's got the department running scared. I think he's more concerned about his own image than his dead son-in-law."

A waiter appeared at their table to take their order.

Rachel ordered a six-ounce rib-eye steak, cooked medium, with a baked potato. Aaron opted for a ten-ounce sirloin with a side of French fries. They ordered salads and iced tea to drink.

When the waiter left, Aaron studied Rachel's eyes. They lacked their normal look of vitality, and concern knitted her brow.

"Enough about my day," he said. "One look at you tells me there is something serious on your mind. You look troubled."

She gave a quick and half-hearted smile. "What makes you think that?"

"Rachel, we've known each other a long time. I heard it in your voice when we talked on the phone, and I see the look on your face."

Rachel snapped her fingers and nodded. "That's right, sometimes I forget you're a detective."

"Detective? Hell, Mr. Magoo could read your face. Now what's going on?"

She placed her elbows on the table. "Okay, I had a long talk with my boss on Tuesday. The Tax Department

Manager in the Seattle office is retiring at the end of next month, and the company wants to fill the position from within."

"I see. Let me guess. They're considering you for the position."

"Actually, it's more than a consideration. They already offered me the job, so I have a big decision to make."

Aaron paused before answering. "I'm impressed. The company obviously thinks highly of you."

"I guess I'm doing okay," she said with a shrug.

"Seattle, huh? I guess you'll need to decide whether you prefer overcast skies, rain, and fog to the four seasons."

"You sound like you've been there before."

"I've read articles and seen pictures," he said with a chuckle.

"It's not as dreary as you think. Those weeklong rains you hear about usually happen only in winter and spring. The average temperature ranges from forty to the upper sixties, and they get less than forty inches of snow a year. That's a far cry from Chicago."

"You sound like a meteorologist, but isn't Mt. St. Helen's near Seattle?"

"Less than one-hundred miles north," she said, then cocked an eyebrow, "but Mt. St. Helen's erupted over twenty-five years ago, and every city has its share of inclement weather. Ice and snow in the North, hurricanes in the South and the coast, tornadoes in the Midwest."

"What about San Diego?"

"I know someone that lives there, and it's not always seventy-five and sunny. Besides, we don't have an office in San Diego."

"You've obviously done your homework. It sounds like you've already decided."

Before she could answer, the waiter returned with their drinks and salad, and informed them their entrees would be ready shortly.

"I haven't made any decisions yet," she said. "That's why I asked you out tonight. I wanted to hear your opinion."

"I don't know whether it means more money, and frankly it's none of my business, but have you tried putting two columns on a piece of paper and list the pros and cons?"

"That's a good approach if you're trying to decide which grocery store to shop at, but I think it depersonalizes it, reduces it to black and white, makes it too objective."

"Isn't that the point?" he asked. "It keeps your emotions from distorting the analysis. What about the cost of living?"

"It will be a factor, but money isn't the primary motivator. I'll have more responsibility, and be in a higher profile position with greater opportunity for advancement."

"Is that what you want?" he asked.

She gazed off in the distance for a few moments. "Honestly, I don't know. I'll be under more pressure. What if I don't make the grade?"

Aaron curled his lip. "Come on, Rachel, I know you have more confidence in yourself than that. I wouldn't even entertain the thought. It sounds to me like you're looking for reasons to turn down the offer."

"Maybe I am."

"I'm sorry, I didn't mean to imply…"

She showed her palm. "I know, and I didn't take it that way. I've always been a Midwestern girl, so this would be a big change for me." She paused and raised her glass, staring at the liquid inside. "Then again, maybe a change is what I need."

"Well, you do have one thing going for you," he said with a smile. "The Seahawks are expected to contend for the Super Bowl in a year or two. The Bears are still rebuilding."

She pointed an accusing finger. "You know me better than that, Aaron Randall. I'll always be a Bears fan no matter where I live."

He laughed. "Sorry, just testing your loyalty. Speaking of growing up in the Midwest, have you talked to your folks about it?"

"Not yet. I need time to think before I decide. If I turn it down, there's no use bringing it up. They're both over seventy, and Dad's had some health problems recently, although given his age, I guess you'd consider them somewhat minor. On the one hand, I know it's important to take advantage of opportunities in life, but family is important too. I don't want guilt to influence my decision."

"What do you think they'd say if you decided to move?"

"I know *exactly* what Dad would say. He's too proud to ask his little girl to sacrifice. Mom would put up an argument, but eventually give in. They both care too much to try to convince me to stay, if that's not what I wanted. They raised me to live life, to pursue my dreams, and have a satisfying and rewarding career. They would naturally prefer I stay, but would understand and respect my decision if I chose to move."

"How long did the company give you to decide?"

"Obviously the sooner the better, but I negotiated for three weeks."

The waiter returned with their entrees. Steak sizzled, and the aroma of meat rose from the plates. They dug in and enjoyed their meal, silent while they ate.

When they were almost finished eating, Aaron broke the silence. "You know, maybe you'll meet a man out there."

Rachel stopped chewing, and looked up from her plate. She didn't answer for a few moments then resumed eating. "One never knows," she said with a noncommittal shrug.

They finished eating, and the waiter took their plates.

"Moving away from a city I've lived all my life is a potential life-changing decision, and I don't know how I feel about it right now," she said. "Frankly, it's a little scary. What do you think I should do?"

"I wouldn't want to advise you one way or the other," he said, then laughed. "I don't want you to blame me if it doesn't work out."

Rachel cocked her head. "Don't be ridiculous, Aaron. I know the final decision is mine. I just value your opinion."

"I think you should consider what you want for a long-term career. If your ambition is to advance in your company, relocating is probably a smart move. What happens if you don't accept the job?"

"There's a possibility I wouldn't be considered for another promotion. It doesn't seem fair, but that's how many big companies work. It can affect my growth and earning potential, although, like I said, money isn't the deciding factor."

"That's enough reason right there to accept the offer."

She gazed down at the table for a moment, then looked back up. "What about us?"

Aaron had raised the water glass to his mouth, stopped halfway, and frowned. "What do you mean?"

"You know, our friendship," she said, then cleared her throat. "It's important to me. I'd hate to lose that."

He put the glass down, reached across the table, and clasped her hand. "We'll always be close friends, Rachel, you know that. If you decide to accept the job, I'm a phone call away, and I'm sure you'll come back to visit your parents. I might even surprise you and take a vacation to the West Coast."

"When was the last time you took a vacation?" she asked.

"That's just it. I'll have a good reason to get away from the city. Naturally, I'd wait until the winter to escape the snow and cold."

She patted his hand and smiled. "Thanks for your input. It helps a lot, and I'll just have to think about it, maybe talk to my parents and get their opinion. It's definitely not something I'll rush into."

"Glad to be of service," he said and squeezed her hand.

They got up from the table, and despite his protests, she paid the bill, and they walked outside. She thanked him again for listening, and they hugged and said goodbye.

***

Back at his apartment, Aaron sat in the recliner and switched on the TV, his mind a million miles from the TV show, thinking about the discussion with Rachel. He reflected on their conversation, and imagined his life without her. Despite their friendship over the years, neither one had broached the subject of a romantic relationship, yet he sensed she wanted him to talk her out of relocating. Was it something in her eyes? In her words? Or was he reading something that wasn't there? Was it wishful thinking on his part?

He put his head back and stared at the ceiling. Rachel was his best friend. His social life was lacking, if not downright nonexistent. His time with her over the years helped him put the stressful and often depressing duties of the job behind him. She listened and lifted his spirits when they needed lifting, which seemed far too often. She'd always been supportive, and endured his gripes, and tonight she needed him to be there for her. The conversation prompted him to think that perhaps deep down he felt more for her than he wanted to openly admit.

Should he embrace his feelings and approach the subject with her? What if she didn't acknowledge similar feelings for him? Embarrassment was bad enough, but he'd never forgive himself if it compromised their friendship.

After deciding a good night's sleep might help him think more clearly, he took two Tylenol and went to bed.

Chapter Twenty-One

The next morning, a ringing phone roused Aaron from a deep sleep. He crawled out of bed, sluggish after a night of tossing and turning, and answered the phone. He looked at the clock and realized he'd slept eleven hours, something he hadn't done since college.

"Hello."

"Hey, Aaron, it's Eddie. Did I wake you?"

"Hi, Eddie. No, I've been up for a while," he lied. "What's going on?"

"Sorry to bother you so early on your day off, but I got some information on that guy you wanted me to check out. I thought of waiting until tomorrow, but I think you might want to hear this."

"No such thing as a day off in this business, Eddie. I'm glad you called."

"Have you had breakfast yet?"

Aaron massaged the back of his neck. The conversation with Rachel the night before still nagged at him. "No, but it's definitely at the top of my list. What did you have in mind?"

"What about The Bagel on North Broadway?"

The Bagel Restaurant & Deli was one of Eddie's favorite restaurants. It was open from eight a.m. to ten p.m. and served breakfast, lunch, and dinner.

"Sounds good, Eddie. I'll meet you there at nine-thirty."

"See you then."

Eddie was sitting in a booth when Aaron arrived at the restaurant. Couples occupied three booths, five customers sat on stools at the counter, and a man sat by himself in another booth reading a newspaper. The aroma of meat and coffee wafted in the air.

Aaron ordered two scrambled eggs with sausage and coffee. Eddie ordered three eggs over easy, bacon, hash browns, toast, and coffee.

The waitress wrote down the order and filled two coffee cups, and then left.

"So, you already have something on Kirby?" Aaron asked. "I'm impressed."

Eddie inhaled and expanded his chest. "Fast is how I work, although I can't take too much credit for this one. It was one of the easiest assignments you've ever given me. That being said, you might want to buy me lunch after you hear this."

Aaron laughed. "After that hearty breakfast you ordered, you'd need lunch in a to-go box. What did you find out?"

"Your hunch was right on the money, and I do mean money," Eddie said. "Mr. Kirby likes to gamble, big time. He favors the horses, but he's dropped major bucks on football, baseball, basketball, pretty much any sporting event with a bookie."

"Lots of guys gamble, Eddie. What's so special about Kirby?"

"Either he's not very good or extremely unlucky, because he's accumulated a sizable debt over the years. From what I gathered, it's over fifty grand."

Aaron whistled softly. "That's a nice chunk of change, but I get the feeling there's more."

Eddie beamed as if he'd just received Aaron's endorsement for president. "Right you are. Kirby had to take out a loan to cover his losses."

"Let me guess. He didn't get the money from Bank of America."

"Right again," Eddie said, then stopped talking when the waitress returned with two loaded plates, and refilled their coffee cups. He rubbed his palms together. "Looks good," he said, and bit into a bacon strip.

Aaron loaded his fork with eggs and took a bite. "So where did Kirby get the money?"

Eddie pursed his lips and nodded. "Johnny Marco."

Aaron raised his eyebrows. Johnny Marco was a well-known loan shark in Chicago. Like most loan sharks, Marco employed hired muscle to collect payments. He was also a suspect in the 1999 murder of a local businessman, although the police never gathered enough evidence to charge him.

"Marco, huh?"

Eddie narrowed his eyes. "Yeah, and I'll tell you, hearing his name pop up again made me feel a little uneasy, not to mention it brought up bitter memories."

The man Marco was suspected of murdering was a good friend of Eddie's.

"I'll bet you'd like nothing better than for me to find Marco was somehow involved in Jared Prescott's death," Aaron said.

"That would be nice," Eddie agreed. "It's about time the snake got what he deserved. Anyway, the word is, your man is paying off Marco a little at a time, enough to satisfy him, at least for the time being. Apparently, he still owes around forty grand, give or take."

"The fact Kirby pays something is probably why he's not in the hospital or at the bottom of the river," Aaron mused. "Anything else I should know?"

"That's all I have so far, but I'll keep digging," Eddie said, and then popped the last bacon strip into his mouth, followed by a swig of coffee. "Thanks for breakfast."

"No problem, Eddie. I appreciate the info on Kirby. I'll even pay for dessert."

Eddie placed a hand on his stomach. "I've had plenty, thanks, and Kirby was easy. I almost feel guilty taking your money."

"In that case, maybe you should pay for your own meal."

Eddie flashed a wide grin and pointed a finger. "I said *almost*."

Aaron finished his coffee, reached into his wallet, and handed Eddie two twenty-dollar bills.

Eddie stuffed the bills into his pocket. "Always a pleasure doing business with you, Inspector."

Aaron paid the bill and they left the restaurant. "I believe it's time to have a chat with Johnny Marco," he said when they were standing outside. He pointed at Eddie's pocket. "Don't spend that all in one place."

"Maybe I'll put money down on the horses," Eddie quipped. "See if I have any more luck than Mr. Kirby," he said, and then flashed a two-fingered salute, got into his car, and headed west on 35th street.

Aaron got into his car and headed east.

***

Inside the restaurant, the man sitting in a booth by himself paid his bill and walked across the street. He got into the passenger side of a silver Honda Accord, looked at the man behind the wheel and pointed west.

"Follow him."

Chapter Twenty-Two

Johnny Marco hung out at Joe Morelli's Pizza on North Lincoln. Two Harley Davidson motorcycles sat out in front, and the lunch hour crowd was starting to gather when Aaron arrived. He opened the front door, stepping aside for two young women who flashed him a smile. He followed them into the restaurant.

Morelli's had two pool tables, two dartboards, and three big screen TV's, making it a popular spot on the weekends and Monday nights during football season.

Aaron walked to the back of the restaurant.

There was a game in progress at each pool table. Two men playing on the table closest to the wall appeared to be the riders of the motorcycles. One was six foot two, two hundred thirty pounds, with a shaved head and handlebar mustache. He wore blue jeans, and chains dangled from every pocket of a denim vest. 'Serpent Kings' in green and red letters was embroidered on the back of his jacket.

The other man was shorter and stockier, but dressed in the same outfit. He flashed Aaron a look as he passed, flexing his biceps as if to indicate messing with him was a fatal mistake.

Aaron looked away and continued toward the back of the pizzeria, where the cook was spreading tomato sauce on pizza dough. "Excuse me," he said.

The man turned and studied Aaron through a squint. "Yeah? What can I get for you?"

"Where can I find Johnny Marco?"

The man glanced over Aaron's shoulder, looking left then right. "Who wants to know?"

Aaron opened his jacket wide enough to get his badge and show his gun. He didn't usually display his firearm, but given Johnny Marco's reputation, it seemed appropriate.

The man pointed to the left. "Back room."

"Much obliged," Aaron said, then gestured at the pizza. "Looks good." He walked to the door and knocked.

The door opened, and a man with a thick neck and brush haircut poked his face out. He didn't speak, but looked at Aaron as though trying to decide on which piece of sirloin steak to buy at the grocery store.

Aaron held his badge up to the door. "Inspector Randall to see Johnny Marco."

The man kept his eyes focused on Aaron. "Just a minute," he said, and closed the door. A few moments later, it swung open, and the man moved aside. "Mr. Marco has agreed to see you."

Lucky me, Aaron thought, and entered the room. The man closed the door behind him.

Johnny Marco was playing cards with two men, while a third man stood behind him like a statue, as though he fancied himself a British citizen auditioning to stand guard at Buckingham Palace. Both men wore black suits, white shirts, and black ties. Their jackets bulged on the left side.

Marco's hired muscle.

Johnny Marco puffed on a cigar, showing no urgency to acknowledge Aaron's presence. Finally, he tossed the cards face down in the middle of the table. "I'm out," he said. He removed the cigar from his mouth, crushed it into an ashtray, and looked at Aaron. "Henry, Charles, excuse us for a moment."

"Are you sure, sir?" the man on the left asked.

"Sure, the Inspector and I are old friends. Isn't that right, Inspector?"

"Not in this lifetime, Marco," Aaron said.

Marco looked at his men and bobbed his head. The two left the room, one brushing Aaron's shoulder as he passed. Thick neck and the other man remained.

Marco indicated a chair with a wave of his hand. "Have a seat, Inspector. Can I get you anything?"

"Just information today," Aaron said and sat in the chair.

"Working on a Saturday, huh?" Marco asked. "Business must be good. It's a shame you boys don't take the weekend off. What can I do for you?"

Marco was five foot nine inches tall, forty-five years old, with olive skin. A healthy dose of gel pasted thick black hair to his scalp. A half-inch scar ran along the middle of his left cheek. The top three buttons on his blue shirt were undone, exposing a chest full of thick dark hair, and three gold chains hung around his neck. In Aaron's mind, he was nothing more than a Mafia wannabe.

Aaron looked around the room. There were three chairs, a card table, and end table next to a green sofa. A faded landscape painting with a rip in the canvas hung on the wall above a vending machine.

"I see you've improved your office décor, Johnny," he quipped.

"Well, you know, Inspector, business is in a bit of a slump," Marco said with a sardonic smile. "The ebbs and flows of the economy affect everybody. It gets harder to cover expenses after the charitable contributions. You know how strongly I believe in giving back to the community."

"Save it, Marco. I'm interested in one of your clients, Warren Kirby. The word is, he owes you about forty grand."

Marco stared at Aaron in silence for a moment. "Client, I like that, and it's funny you should mention Mr. Kirby. He came to me about a year and a half ago, wanting to borrow fifty grand. He said it was for an investment, but you know me, I don't concern myself with the details."

"Just the bottom line right, Marco?"

"That's right. I thought you said you weren't here to hassle me."

"Fortunately for you, I have more important matters to deal with, but rest assured, I can always have the IRS validate those charitable contributions."

Marco smiled. "Yeah, I heard you were on the Prescott case. There's big money in that one. This Kirby guy have something to do with it?"

"Tell me about the loan."

Marco removed a cigarette from his pocket and turned it in his fingers before lighting it. He took a puff and blew smoke in the air. "Mr. Kirby paid me what he could afford every month and never missed a payment."

"So I guess you don't have to, let's say, encourage him?"

"I run a legitimate business, Inspector."

"Sure you do."

"Anyway, a couple of weeks ago, Chuck got a call from Kirby wanting to know the balance due. Two days later, I got an envelope in my mailbox addressed to me, no return address. It contained the balance of what Kirby owed."

Aaron frowned. "Are you sure it was Kirby on the phone?"

Marco shrugged. "Like I said, Chuck took the call, but who else would it be?"

Warren Kirby was becoming more interesting by the minute.

"I assume he paid in cash?"

"Forty-one thousand and change." Marco looked away as he puffed on the cigarette. "Who knows? Maybe his investment paid off, but like I said, I don't concern myself with details or why people need the money. I supply a service."

"Was there postage on the envelope?"

"Nope, just a stuffed envelope addressed to me."

"Do you know the exact day you received the money?" Aaron asked.

Marco nodded at one of his men. "Chuck?"

"It was the seventeenth of August," Chuck said.

Two days after Jared Prescott's murder.

Marco tapped his temple and smiled. "Chuck has a good memory."

Aaron glanced at Chuck then looked back at Marco. "Nice to see you screen your employees. What did you do with the money?"

"I put it in the bank. What do you think?"

"How did he pay?"

"What do you mean?"

"I mean, all hundreds, fifties, twenties, what?"

"Gotcha. Yeah, it was mostly hundreds, why?"

"How do you know it was Kirby who paid the money?"

"He signed his name at the bottom and the balance due was to the penny. As far as I'm concerned, his account is closed. I don't expect to see him again. I got the impression he doesn't agree with my business practices."

"Big surprise," Aaron said.

Marco crushed the cigarette butt in the ashtray. "So, what do you think, Inspector, Kirby offed Prescott and stole his money?"

Aaron got up from the chair. "Thanks for your time."

"Don't mention it. You know me, always willing to help out when I can."

Aaron walked to the door and put his hand on the knob, then turned. "Make sure you stay clean, Johnny. The Better Business Bureau is watching."

Aaron sat in his car outside Morelli's. The settlement of a debt of over forty thousand dollars, and the unaccounted money from Jared Prescott's account was too much of a coincidence to ignore, and warranted another conversation with Warren Kirby.

Chapter Twenty-Three

Kirby's home was a sprawling ranch at the end of a cul-de-sac at 1675 Emerald Lakes Dr. in Jefferson Park. Kirby was standing in the driveway behind his car, a set of golf clubs at his side, when Aaron arrived.

He turned when Aaron shut his car door. "Inspector Randall? What are you doing here?"

"You got a few minutes? We need to talk."

Kirby gestured to the golf bag. "I was just heading out for a round of golf. Can it wait?"

"It concerns Johnny Marco," Aaron said.

Kirby's shoulders sagged, and his face turned a shade of red as though his blood pressure had spiked. He picked up the golf bag and put it into the trunk of the car, then turned back to Aaron. "Let's talk inside."

They entered the house through the garage. Kirby led Aaron into the study at the back of the house. An 'L-shaped' executive desk with a desktop computer sat in the middle of the room. Decorative paneling covered the walls, and two large bay windows flanked each side of a built-in bookcase, with a view of a patio fronting a large back yard.

"Have a seat, Inspector," Kirby said, and sat down behind the desk.

"You want to tell me about your business arrangement with Marco?" Aaron asked.

Kirby's eyes drifted, and he blew air over his upper lip. "I used to have a gambling problem. I got in over my head, and heard about Johnny Marco from someone at the track. I knew about Marco's reputation, but needed to settle my debts. I didn't think I had a choice. Marco loaned me fifty grand, but at a high interest rate. I hoped to make a big score at the track and square it, but it never happened.

Anyway, I arranged to pay back in installments, sometimes a thousand a month, sometimes a little more. Fortunately, he agreed. I'm not naïve, Inspector. I know how loan sharks do business, but I was desperate for the money. I still owe over forty grand. I don't know how long it will take to pay it off, but if nothing else, I learned a valuable lesson and stopped gambling–quit cold turkey." Kirby turned up his hands. "What else can I tell you?"

Aaron wondered why Kirby didn't mention the payoff. Certainly he must know Marco would have divulged that information. He decided to play along. "When and where are you supposed to make the next payment?"

"At the end of every month I meet one of Marco's business associates at Cirillo's Bar and Grille. It's a restaurant on Eighth Street."

"I know Cirillo's," Aaron said. "Does your wife know about your debt?"

"No. I never called in my bets from the house or my cell phone. I used a public phone at the airport."

"Chicago Midway?"

Kirby frowned. "Yes, that's right, how did you know?"

"Did you ever accept a call from any of the phones at the airport, like say, from one of your bookmakers?"

Kirby shrugged and his Adam's apple quivered. "No, I never took a call, just called out. Anyway, why do you want to know about my gambling debt?"

"Four phone calls were made the night Jared Prescott was killed. Two came from his cell phone, the other two from the motel room where we found his body. The last of those phone calls went to a public phone at Chicago Midway."

Kirby bit his lip and shrugged. "I don't see how that concerns me."

Aaron stared at Kirby without speaking for a few moments, before he decided it was time to drop the bomb. "What I don't understand is why you would make payments on a debt already paid in full."

Kirby cocked his head and frowned. "I'm sorry, I don't follow you, Inspector. I told you, I still owe Marco over forty thousand dollars."

"Not according to him," Aaron said with a shake of his head. "He told me he received an envelope in his mailbox with the balance of your loan, along with a note and your signature. That was following a phone call to one of his men asking for the payoff balance. He said it could only have come from you."

Kirby sat forward in his chair. "Is this a joke? I don't have that kind of money, and I never sent any such envelope to Marco. I told you, I never dealt directly with him. And I never made any phone call."

"Johnny Marco doesn't joke about outstanding loans."

Kirby's Adam's apple swam in his throat. "I assure you, Inspector, I would love nothing more than to have the loan off my back, but Marco is either lying or pulling something. One thing for sure, the money didn't come from me."

"Here's the interesting coincidence, Mr. Kirby. Jared Prescott had a briefcase full of money the night he was killed. We can't find the briefcase or the money."

Kirby's face paled, and he sat back in his chair. "Wait a minute. Are you accusing me of killing Jared and stealing the money to pay off Marco?"

"Seems plausible, doesn't it?" Aaron said with a shrug.

Kirby slammed a fist on the desk. "Damnit, someone is trying to frame me. I did not kill Jared, nor do I know how Marco got the money!"

"Then tell me, who else knew about the loan, and who would pay someone else's debt in full, and more importantly, why?"

Kirby stiffened and fidgeted in his chair before he relaxed and forced a breath. "No one else knows about the loan. I'd never admit it to anyone. It's not easy living with this problem." He paused and swallowed. His Adam's apple was getting a workout. "Are you going to arrest me?"

Aaron stood. "You're safe for now, but don't make any travel plans, and I suggest you keep your attorney's phone number handy."

"Of course," Kirby said. "I understand, but I'm not going anywhere. I need to clear my name. It's obvious someone is trying to frame me."

Aaron left Kirby's house, still unsure of the man's involvement. He didn't deny the gambling debt, or the fact he placed his bets from an airport pay phone. He was either telling the truth, or had put on a performance worthy of an Oscar. In either case, he now ranked at the top of the list of suspects along with Vic Bryant.

Chapter Twenty-Four

The next day, Aaron, Sam, and Dr. Taylor stood in the autopsy room at the morgue. The body of Eddie Rivers lay on a metal table, a white linen cloth drawn down to his knees.

"The EMT brought him in at three a.m.," Dr. Taylor said.

"Dispatch got an anonymous phone call about ten-thirty last night," Sam added. "They found the body in an alley off Glenbrook and Eighth."

Aaron gazed blankly at Eddie's lifeless form. "Glenbrook and Eighth," he said. "Any witnesses?"

"Not a soul," Sam said.

Anger burned like hot lead in Aaron's stomach, and his hands curled into fists. "Eddie had no reason to be in that part of town."

"Our preliminary examination indicates death caused by a knife wound," Dr. Taylor said. "Based on the depth of the wound, we believe the blade was about eight inches long. Time of death was between nine and eleven p.m."

"There was no blood around the body at the scene," Sam said. "Based on the amount of blood loss, Forensics believes he was killed somewhere else, and his body dumped in the alley." Sam handed Aaron a clear plastic bag. "They found this in Eddie's pocket."

"Two twenty-dollar bills torn in half," Aaron said then looked at Dr. Taylor. "Wes, let me know if you find anything else during the autopsy."

"I will, Aaron, and I'm sorry. I know Eddie was a friend."

"He was more than a friend," Aaron said with a half-hearted nod.

He and Sam left the room.

Standing outside, Aaron said, "Jennifer Prescott's house gets shot at, and I find out she's having an affair. Eddie digs up dirt on Warren Kirby, who paid off a loan shark with money he supposedly didn't have, now Eddie ends up dead. Someone is watching, Sam."

"It certainly looks that way."

Aaron returned to the precinct and poured himself a steaming cup of coffee before going to Vince Sherman's office.

Sherman sat behind his desk, rotating a can of Pepsi with his fingers. "I am sorry about Eddie, Aaron. You need anything?"

"I'll be all right. It's not the first time I've lost a friend," he said, then looked out the window. "This business stinks, you know?"

"Tell me about it," Sherman said.

Aaron updated Sherman on the information Eddie Rivers provided regarding Warren Kirby, including the loan from Johnny Marco, and his subsequent conversation with Kirby.

"Less than twenty-four hours later, Eddie's found in an alley. It's no coincidence, Vince. There's more than one person involved, and whoever they are, they're making it personal. Eddie was killed somewhere else and dumped into an area of town that's practically deserted, and then dispatch gets a call from an anonymous caller, probably Eddie's killer."

"So, Kirby was in over his head with Johnny Marco, huh?" Sherman mused. "Interesting choice for borrowing money."

"Yeah."

"Marco is as shady as they come," Sherman said. "You think he was behind Eddie's death?"

Aaron shook his head. "Marco's a snake, but he's not dumb enough to kill someone less than a day after I talked to him. Besides, it's not as if Eddie uncovered a skeleton. Marco isn't trying to hide anything. He knows we're all aware what he does for a living."

"Listen, Aaron, if you need time…"

Aaron stopped Sherman with a hard stare. "You know the answer to that question, Vince. Eddie's death is connected to this investigation, and I will find his killer, and when I do, I'll bet my badge I'll find Jared Prescott's killer as well."

"I'll assign a man to check on Eddie's activities from the time you talked with him until the time we found him. We'll check his apartment, his work, maybe somebody saw something." Sherman looked over Aaron's shoulder. "Yes, what is it, Nick?"

"There's a phone call for you, Inspector Randall, a woman. She won't give her name, but said it's urgent she speak with you right away."

"Thanks," Aaron said, and returned to his desk and picked up the receiver. "This is Inspector Randall. How can I help you?"

"Please meet me by the theater in Hollow Grove Park tonight at eight o'clock. I have information on the murder of Jared Prescott. And please, come alone."

"Listen, ma'am, why don't you come down to the station and we can…" he started.

"I'm sorry, I'm afraid I can't do that. Hollow Grove Park, eight o'clock. Please."

The phone clicked in Aaron's ear.

Chapter Twenty-Five

Aaron arrived at Hollow Grove Park in Harwood Heights at seven-fifty.

The woman's refusal to meet at the precinct smelled like a setup and he was prepared. He had his service revolver and a .38 caliber pistol strapped to his ankle.

Hollow Grove Park was located in a middle-class section of the city, with an outdoor basketball pavilion doubling as an ice skating rink in the winter months. An indoor theater featuring performances by local actors was open year-round.

He entered the park and walked slowly down the path. There were twenty people in his estimation. Some walked. Some jogged. One couple strolled hand in hand.

He kept his arms in a ready position, studied the eyes of each person as they passed, and turned in their direction after they passed. Reaching the theater, he stopped and positioned himself along the edge of a stand of pine trees, out of clear sight, and looked around.

Fifteen yards away, a man and woman huddled together on a bench. A woman standing by herself twenty yards away puffed on a cigarette. He stayed in the shadows and watched the woman. She glanced back and forth a number of times, clearly looking for someone.

He opened his jacket and unfastened his holster, then waited a minute before approaching. He was three feet away when the woman turned and looked at him for a few moments before turning away.

"Nice evening," he said.

"Sure, if you don't mind unbearable heat and high humidity," she replied with a shrug, without looking back. "Are you Randall?"

"Inspector Randall. You called me this afternoon?"

"Yes. I'm Laura Carter," she said, then tossed the cigarette butt on the ground before looking at him.

The light from the lampposts illuminated her face. Her eyes gleamed blue with long eyelashes, her lips glossed with rose-colored lipstick.

She indicated the path with a nod. "Do you mind if we walk?"

Aaron extended his arm, and she started down the path. He stayed one step behind and to her right.

She didn't waste any time, a refreshing change for Aaron. "I saw the news report on Eddie Rivers. He was my brother."

"Eddie never told me he had a sister," Aaron said, surprise in his voice.

"Probably because in his eyes I didn't exist, and I can hardly blame him. I wasn't very supportive after Glenda's death, and abandoned him after he got in with the wrong crowd. I realize now, too late of course, family should come first regardless of the situation. Eddie talked about you from time to time. He said you saved his life and he trusted you." She laughed. "He said you weren't a typical cop."

"Eddie was a good man. The coroner said nobody showed up to identify his body."

"I felt too guilty, too ashamed, and frankly, couldn't face it," Carter said. "I know that's not a valid excuse, but now I have to live with the guilt."

"You said on the phone you had information about Jared Prescott's murder."

The woman stopped and leaned against the rail in the middle of a bridge over a manmade stream running the length of the park. The gentle sound of running water provided a welcome distraction. The bounce of a basketball on blacktop echoed as six young men played a game of three-on-three on the lighted court. Trees swayed from a soft breeze, offering a welcome respite from the hot and sticky night.

"I was there the night Jared was killed," she said.

Aaron shot her a glance, then looked away. He'd been bounced around, given bogus information and, believing someone was watching, decided to test her. "You were at the Holiday Inn?"

"Tremont Inn," she said, "but I could have read that in the newspaper."

"Fair enough," he said. "What were you doing there?"

"A few days before that night, a man called me and said he wanted to play a practical joke on Jared because his birthday was coming up. He said it's time Jared got a taste of his own medicine. He didn't identify himself, and I didn't recognize his voice, but he said he knew Jared and I had history."

"Is that true?"

"Yes. Anyway, the man told me to rent a room at the Tremont Inn for the night, but to wear a wig and sunglasses just in case Jared arrived early. I didn't think much of it at the time, but he was very explicit with the details, saying it all had to do with adding realism to the joke. He said to trust him, that it would all make sense later. He told me to park the car a block away and walk to the motel. I was to give the clerk a fake name, say someone drove me to the motel and would pick me up the next day, so I didn't need to provide a license plate number. I was told to give the clerk an address of two-twenty-one Pleasant Creek Drive, and to ask specifically for Room twenty-five."

"Did he give you a reason for the specific address and room?"

"He said it was all part of the plan. I had to write it down so I could remember. The caller said it was critical for the scam to work on Jared."

"So, you're the infamous Nancy Edmunds," he said.

"Right," she said with a sheepish grin, "I was that night anyway. The caller even told me to use that name. Why, I don't know, but Jared was suspicious by nature and might want to check who rented the room. You don't think about those things at the time. He told me to buy a pack of Marlboro's, smoke one and stay in the room until no later than eight-forty-five, then leave and put the key under the mat outside the door, and drive away."

"I asked him, why Marlboro, and how do you know I smoke?"

"What did he say?"

"He said he didn't know I smoked, but the Marlboro was part of the scam," she said.

"Weren't you a little suspicious?"

Carter shrugged. "Frankly, I thought it was odd, but figured it would be fun to see the tables turned on Jared. He was a master practical joker himself, and besides, the man promised to pay me two thousand dollars. I asked him if I was doing anything illegal because two thousand dollars just to rent a room seemed a little much. He said all I was doing was using a fake name and I would understand. Naturally, I agreed, although to be honest, I didn't really expect to get paid. The whole thing seemed harmless at the time." She looked down and shook her head.

"Two thousand dollars for a few minutes of your time," Aaron mused. "Not a bad hourly rate. Is that how it went down?"

"All except the part of me leaving."

"Oh?"

"When I got to the motel about eight-thirty, there were only a few cars in the parking lot. I checked into room twenty-five under Nancy Edmunds, smoked the cigarette, and left right at eight-forty-five like the man instructed. I put the key under the mat, then got into my car, and drove around to the back of the motel out of sight. I got out of the car and stood by the corner of the building. I guess curiosity got the better of me, and I didn't see any harm in sticking around, as long as I stayed out of sight, and Jared didn't spot me. I wanted to see what the joke was all about."

"What happened then?"

A couple approached, and she waited for them to move out of range. "I waited behind the motel. About five minutes later, a red sports car pulled up and parked in front of the room, and a man got out. I assumed it was the guy who called me."

"Can you describe him?"

"It was dark, and I was too far away to see his features, but he was a big guy."

"By big, do you mean tall or heavyset?"

"Both. He stopped at the door to the room and squatted to get the key from under the mat. About ten minutes later, a gold Mercedes pulled up and parked next to the red sports car. I recognized it as Jared's car. He got out and opened the trunk, and either put something in or pulled something out. I couldn't tell from where I stood. He walked up to the door and looked around before knocking. A few seconds later, he went inside." She reached into her pants pocket and brought out a pack of Marlboro cigarettes and a lighter. She took one out and offered the pack to Aaron.

He declined then took the lighter from her hand and lit the cigarette. "We fingerprinted a Marlboro cigarette butt we found in the ashtray in the room and came up with nothing. Have you ever had your fingerprints taken?"

She shook her head. "Not that I recall."

"We also found a trace of heroin."

Carter shot a glance at Aaron and stiffened. "It wasn't mine. I smoked a couple of joints when I was a teenager, but never gave hard drugs a second thought." She took a long drag from the cigarette, and stared at the glowing ash. "I've tried hundreds of time to give these up without success."

"What happened after Prescott went into the room?"

"Ten or fifteen minutes later, the other guy came out and tried to open Jared's car door, but Jared must have locked it. The man went back into the room and came out a few seconds later. He opened the car door and stooped inside, then went to the trunk and took something out. It looked like a briefcase, maybe a small suitcase. He went to the driver's side of Jared's car, opened the car door for a second, then got into his own car and drove off."

"Did you get a make on the red sports car?" Aaron asked.

"I don't know, but I think it was a convertible. Anyway, he was in a hurry, and must not have been paying attention, because he backed into a light pole. It sounded pretty loud, so he might have done significant damage."

"I don't suppose you got a license plate number."

The woman shook her head. "Even if I thought about it at the time, it was too dark."

"You said the caller knew you and Jared had a history."

"I met Jared at one of his company functions. I used to work for an escort service. The guy I was with took off with another woman. Jared came up and we started talking and hit it off, actually became good friends. We slept together a few times, but never got romantically involved. It was mostly a physical relationship."

"Did anyone else know about your... meetings?"

"Meetings," she repeated with a chuckle. "That's a tactful way of putting it."

"Tact is my middle name," he said with a shrug, which appeared to put Carter more at ease, because she looked at him and smiled.

"Eddie was right about you. Anyway, by now I guess it's common knowledge Jared was a playboy. He did enjoy his privacy though. Who knows, maybe no one knew about us, maybe the whole world knew. I guess I was intrigued by the offer of the practical joke, because I helped him with a scam last year."

"Let me guess, you were the blonde woman with the fake head in the shopping bag."

She looked at him and cocked her head. "You know about that?"

"You'd be amazed what I've found out during this investigation. Did you ever get your money for that night?"

"Surprisingly, two days later, I found an envelope in my mailbox with the two grand." She tossed the cigarette butt on the ground and crushed it with her shoe. "My life is different now. I quit the escort service over a year ago. I'm engaged to be married."

"Does your fiancée know about that night?"

"He knows what I used to do for a living, but not about that night. I decided to keep my relationship with Jared a secret, especially after what happened."

"So you told him half the truth?"

Carter shrugged and her face blushed. "I suppose I thought half a truth was better than no truth, but I guess a partial lie is still a lie, isn't it?"

"I'm not judging you. Is it possible the man that called you was one of the men involved in the fake head scam last year?"

"Could be, but I never saw either one of those men up close, or heard them speak."

"Did the caller say how he got your number?" Aaron asked.

"I asked him and he said he got it from a friend who I worked with at the escort service, but he didn't remember her name. I should have pressed the issue, but by I guess I was distracted by the promise of the money and all the instructions I needed to write down. I normally screen my calls, but the number looked like it came from a cell phone, and sometimes are the numbers of friends I haven't committed to memory. I'm sorry now I didn't write the number down, even sorrier I answered it in the first place."

"We could trace it from your cell phone records, but there are ways to make a phone untraceable," Aaron said. He noticed genuine remorse flood her eyes. "Don't blame yourself, Ms. Carter. You had no way of knowing what was going down. Whoever killed Jared Prescott would have found someone else. Tell me, how long did you stay at the motel after the man left?"

"No more than a couple of minutes. I was afraid the man would circle the motel and find me, and I wanted to get paid. I'm embarrassed now the thought even went through my head."

"I don't want to make you feel worse, but I have to ask. Why did you wait this long to come forward?"

"Believe me, I've felt sick to my stomach ever since that night, Inspector, even though I convinced myself then, and still believe now, I had no part in Jared's death. I honestly didn't think I could help the police. Then when I heard about Eddie, and the newspaper saying it could be linked to Jared's death, it finally got to me. I guess deep down I knew someday it would come back and haunt me. I want to help if I can."

"I believe you," he said, "but it's possible you'll get subpoenaed as a material witness if this ever goes to trial. The defense attorney might even try to convince the jury you were an accomplice. I'm sorry, but I can't sugarcoat this, and need to warn you of the potential consequences. Of course, before that happens, I still need to find out who pulled the trigger."

"I appreciate your honesty, Inspector, but I need to put this behind me. I already feel better telling you. I wanted to meet you alone because I had hoped to keep it a private matter, but realize now that probably isn't possible."

Aaron opened his mouth to answer, but before he spoke, a dot of red appeared on Carter's forehead. She emitted a low moan, and her eyes glazed over. She froze for a moment before pitching forward into his arms.

The weight of her body pulled them both to the ground. Aaron released his hold on her and rolled onto his right side while pulling his gun from its holster. He took cover behind the stiles of the bridge and scanned the area. The six young men continued playing basketball without interruption. He took out his cell phone and dialed 911 to request an ambulance and backup unit, although he suspected Carter was already dead.

He stayed low and reached over to turn her on her back. Blood flowed from the hole in her forehead down between her gaping eyes. He pressed two fingers to her throat and, feeling no pulse, reached up, and closed her eyelids.

It didn't take a detective to know Laura Carter's murder was not random. Someone knew of her involvement and followed her to the park, perhaps even tapped her phone and overheard the conversation to set up the meeting. Maybe they followed him. In any case, her murder was more than just another statistic in Chicago's homicide annals. Aaron was getting closer, and the real criminal, or criminals, were getting bold, which meant they were getting desperate. Jared Prescott, Eddie Rivers, now Laura Carter–the body count was rising. It seemed anyone with information germane to solving Jared Prescott's murder was a target.

Chapter Twenty-Six

"Someone strolls through a crowded public park carrying a hunting rifle, yet nobody saw or heard anything," Sam said early the next morning, sitting across from Aaron. Ballistics had already confirmed the bullet killing Laura Carter came from a Remington 770 Centerfire Rifle, a weapon popular among hunters, chosen for its accuracy and reliability.

"Hollow Grove Park offers plenty of trees for cover, and we were standing in an area that wasn't well lit," Aaron said. "Nobody reacted to the shot, and I heard nothing but a bouncing basketball, so I'm guessing the shooter used a silencer. I suspect he used a night vision scope as well, because Carter was hit dead center of the forehead. That's not luck."

"Have you considered the possibility you were the target?" Sam asked.

"If I was, I don't think I'd be sitting here talking to you."

"But you said you dropped and rolled right away."

"Sure, but it took me three or four seconds before we hit the ground, and the shooter could have gotten in another shot, maybe two. No, I think he hit the intended target." He stared out the window. "Three murders with three different weapons. We're in the middle of a damn war here, Sam."

"Sure looks that way," Sam agreed. "What's the next move?"

Aaron buried his head in his hands and massaged his forehead for a few moments before looking up with a start. "Wait a minute. Didn't you say Vic Bryant trained as a sniper?"

"He sure did. You think he was the shooter?"

"It's certainly worth paying him another visit," Aaron said, then stood and put on his jacket.

"Are you going for a warrant?"

"I don't think because Bryant served in the military and trained as a sniper will be enough to convince a judge to issue one, and I don't feel like waiting around to find out. Besides, if he was the shooter, I doubt even *he's* stupid enough to stash the weapon under his bed."

***

Nobody answered the door at Bryant's house, and his car wasn't parked in the driveway. Aaron checked with the next-door neighbor, who said he hadn't seen Bryant in at least two days. In any case, it would have to wait until morning. He requested a unit to drive by and stake out the house, although for all he knew, Bryant was speeding down a highway, heading for Denver.

Aaron drove home and gazed at the sky. It was another muggy night, and a cloud covering from the previous night had disappeared, dashing any meager hopes of moisture. He stood in front of his apartment door, but before he could put his key in the lock, he turned to the sound of a soft *click* behind him.

Mrs. Fletcher stood in the doorway, wearing a flowered smock. Through the open door, the aroma of a freshly baked pie drifted into the hallway.

"Good evening, Mr. Randall. I baked a blueberry pie. If you haven't eaten dinner yet or perhaps want dessert…" her voice trailed off.

"That's nice of you, ma'am, but I plan to eat light and go to bed early," he said with a forced smile, then turned the key and opened the door.

"I think that's a wise decision," she said, "but if you change your mind, just knock."

Aaron entered the apartment, closed the door behind him, and flipped on the switch. He threw up his hands when the light didn't come on.

"The hits just keep on coming," he said aloud, and then walked over to the end table and turned on the lamp.

The room remained dark.

He removed his jacket and tossed it on the chair, took two steps toward the kitchen and stopped. His senses were acute with years of training, and something didn't feel right–something having nothing to do with the lights.

He stayed still, and listened to the faint sound of a television in an adjacent apartment, followed by a car horn outside from an impatient driver. Inside the apartment, it was quiet. He shook his head and blinked, thinking perhaps he was more tired than he realized, although he still couldn't shake the feeling something was amiss.

Once his eyes adjusted to the dark, he unbuckled his shoulder holster and tossed it on the sofa. He located the remote on the coffee table and switched on the television, if only to bring light into the room, although if a fuse was blown, the TV wasn't likely to come on.

He pushed the button on the remote, then heard a sound to his right. There was someone else in the room.

He wheeled, a second too late.

A heavy body slammed into his left side, knocking him off balance. Falling to the floor, he managed to grab a shirtsleeve and carried the attacker to the floor with him. The element of surprise gave his attacker a significant advantage. As they landed on the floor, Aaron twisted and turned on the floor to gain separation from his attacker.

The attacker sat on top, and as he drew back his right hand to throw a punch, Aaron noticed he wore a black ski mask.

Aaron blocked the punch with his left hand, and before the attacker could react, connected with his right fist to the side of his head.

The attacker groaned and relaxed his hold.

Aaron thrust his right hip forward and shoved the attacker to the floor, then rolled to the left side and scrambled to his feet, dazed but still conscious. Moving to the sofa, he grabbed for his gun, but the attacker had recovered and was on his feet. He tackled Aaron from behind before Aaron reached his gun. They fell onto the coffee table, smashing it to pieces.

The attacker was back on top, pinning Aaron's arms to the sides, leaning in close to his face. His breath reeked of meat and onions.

Aaron kicked and writhed, but the attacker outweighed him, rendering Aaron's arms and legs useless. With the only remaining weapon available, Aaron snapped his head forward and connected square on the attacker's nose. The attacker brought both hands to his face and fell back.

Aaron pushed the attacker back far enough to free his legs, then lashed out with his right leg. The bottom of his foot landed square on the attacker's chest.

The attacker fell backward to the floor with one hand holding his face, the other holding his chest as he moaned in pain.

Aaron scrambled to his feet and retrieved his gun, then kneeled over the attacker and put the barrel inches from his face. "Don't move," he said, then reached forward and grabbed the bottom of the ski mask.

The attacker resisted, groping blindly at Aaron's arm.

Aaron slapped his hand away. "I said, don't move."

The attacker relaxed and showed his palms.

Before Aaron could remove the ski mask to reveal the attacker's identity, he felt a sharp pain in the back of his head. The room went dark.

Chapter Twenty-Seven

Aaron's eyes flickered, and he slowly forced them open. Even slower, the memory of the evening's events crept back into his mind, although the details were still fuzzy. He lay motionless on the floor, and listened to a banging on his apartment door, which exacerbated the pounding in his head.

"Mr. Randall, it's Mrs. Fletcher. Is anything wrong? Please, open up."

He struggled to his knees and winced as searing pain shot through his skull. He rotated his head and massaged the back of his neck, feeling the crusty texture of dried blood. Pain coursed through every molecule in his head. It took another minute to stand before he staggered to the door.

"Mr. Randall, please open the door. I heard noises. Are you all right?"

Aaron couldn't let Mrs. Fletcher see his condition and notice the apartment, but he had to tell her something. She was nothing if not persistent. Leaning his shoulder against the door, he said, "I'm fine. I was rearranging the furniture and fell." It was a lame excuse, but all he could think of on short notice.

"Are you sure you're all right? Can I get you anything? Do you need an ice pack?"

"No, I assure you there's nothing to worry about. I'm sorry if I disturbed you."

"Disturb me? Don't be silly."

"I'm fine," he said, hoping she would buy his story and return to her apartment.

She was silent for a few moments then said, "Well, okay. Good night, Mr. Randall."

He gazed through the peephole. Mrs. Fletcher's hand was on her doorknob. She turned in his direction as though she could sense him watching.

He flipped the switch on the wall, and when the lights came on, he remembered they didn't work when he arrived. Whatever electrical problem existed was resolved. He turned to survey the damage to the apartment.

The coffee table lay in pieces. He picked up one of the broken legs and brandished it for a moment before tossing it back on the floor. He retrieved his gun from the floor and checked the chamber to find it fully loaded before checking the rest of the apartment. Everything appeared normal until he walked into the bathroom.

Written on the mirror in big black letters were the words LET PRESCOTT R.I.P!

He stared at the message while massaging the barrel of his gun and tightened his jaw. If someone wanted him to abandon the investigation into Jared Prescott's murder, they were wasting their time. Following the deaths of Eddie Rivers and Laura Carter, a personal attack made him more determined than ever.

He retrieved a flashlight from the drawer in the kitchen before returning to the dining room area to examine the sliding door to the patio. It was slightly ajar, and the lock was damaged.

Amateur.

He called the precinct to report the attack, but requested they send out a crime scene team in the morning. There was no need to disturb the residents in the apartment complex at the late hour.

Once the adrenaline settled, his head throbbed worse than ever. He went into the bathroom and popped two Advil, then washed the dried blood from his head. When he came out of the bathroom, he heard a knock on the door, and assumed Mrs. Fletcher had returned. Perhaps she wanted a more plausible excuse for the noise from his apartment. He stood in the middle of the room, deciding whether to answer the door.

"Aaron, are you in there?"

He breathed a sigh of relief. It was Rachel, although his relief quickly disappeared, knowing she wouldn't be as easy to convince everything was copasetic, and she wasn't likely to turn around and go home without specific details of what happened.

He went to the door and released the latch. "Come in."

She looked at him with her eyebrows drawn together, then brushed past him into the apartment.

"What are you doing here, Rachel?"

She turned. "I came to find out what's going on. I heard that…" she started and then looked at the floor and the remains of the coffee table. "My God, what happened here?"

"How did you know something…" Aaron paused and glanced across the hall. "Never mind," he said, closing the door. "I had a visitor tonight. Apparently, somebody isn't too happy with my investigation of the Prescott murder."

She looked at Aaron and her mouth dropped open. She stepped forward and gently touched his jaw.

Aaron winced and jerked his head back.

"Your concerned neighbor called me and said you might have hurt yourself moving furniture. She said you sounded strange. You're lucky I live close by."

He managed a wry smile. "Mrs. Fletcher told you what I wanted her to know. She tends to overreact."

"Well, it's a good thing she does. *Someone* has to look after you, Aaron," she said. "I for one am glad she called me. You shouldn't knock it. Someday she just might save your life."

He gestured to the sofa. "Do you mind if I sit down? I'm nursing a sore neck and a monster of a headache, not to mention a tender jaw. It's odd, but I don't remember getting whacked in the mouth. My visitor probably added that for good measure after I was out."

Rachel went into the kitchen and rummaged through the drawers. "Do you have an ice pack?"

"I must have ten, but can never find one. A rag wrapped in ice will do, thanks," he said then sat down and rested his head against the sofa.

A minute later, she returned to the living room, handed him the rag, then sat down beside him.

He placed the rag on the back of his neck, rested his head on a pillow, and stared at the ceiling.

She placed a hand on his shoulder. "I better drive you to the emergency room. You look terrible."

"I don't need an emergency room. It's just a few bumps and bruises. Believe me, I've been through worse. I'll be as right as rain in a couple of months," he said with a painful laugh.

"A couple of months," she echoed. "I'm serious. I'm worried about you. You might have a concussion. At the very least, you should see a doctor."

"Maybe. I'll see how I feel in the morning."

She shifted on the sofa and patted her thigh. "Here, lie down. I'll massage your neck. It will help ease the pain."

He looked at her, and his lips parted.

"Come on, put your head down."

"Okay, if you insist," he said with a shrug. "Be gentle."

She laughed. "Given the circumstances, I'm glad to see you haven't lost your sense of humor."

He drew his legs up on the sofa and rested his head on her thigh. He sighed when the tips of her fingers kneaded his neck. "Thanks, that helps."

"So tell me what happened here," she said.

"After you nurse me back to health, go to the bathroom and look at the mirror."

The pain and tension eased with every stroke of her fingers. "You should consider a career change to a masseuse."

She chuckled. "Maybe after I retire."

He moved his head to look into her eyes. "Speaking of careers, have you made a decision about Seattle?"

She looked at him and shrugged before looking away. "I'm still thinking. Why do you ask?"

It might have been the knock on the head, the pressure of the investigation, perhaps both, but his emotions were in turmoil. Under any other circumstances, he would think twice before squeezing her hand.

"I don't think I want you to go."

He sat up with some effort, grimaced from the pain in his head, then reached around the back of her neck, brought her face close, and kissed her.

She responded.

They had kissed before, but it was never more than a peck on the cheek, a kiss on New Year's Eve, or to wish one another a happy birthday.

This kiss was different. It breathed with a passion Aaron didn't think could exist between them, and before they could consider their actions, were lying side by side on the sofa, their bodies pressed together.

He lightly ran his knuckles in a circular motion across her back, moving lower with each rotation, while he probed her mouth with his tongue. When his hand reached her buttocks, she didn't resist.

His hands moved independently, and when he applied light pressure, a soft moan escaped from Rachel's lips, and she eased her lower body forward.

He grew hard, and moaned with a desire he hadn't felt since his marriage. A fire burned in his loins, and he slipped a hand into her slacks, feeling her bare skin, smooth to the touch.

She flinched and shifted on the sofa to allow him access, moving back and forth in rhythm to his gentle caresses.

A few moments later, as they moved in unison, the narrow space on the sofa was unable to contain them, and they tumbled to the floor. She winced when the breath was knocked out of her when he landed on top.

"I'm sorry, Rachel," he said, flinching when the impact reminded him of the pain in his head.

"No, it's not that. Get up a second. I felt something sharp pinch my back."

He forced himself from the floor with some effort and helped her to her feet.

She reached behind her. "Am I bleeding?"

He examined the back of her blouse and noticed a speck of red. "A little," he said. "Does it hurt?"

"Actually, it startled me more than anything. What did I fall on?"

"I don't know, let me take a look. Probably a wood splinter from the coffee table. I guess I should have cleaned up before we…" He paused, and they looked at each other for a moment. "I'll check it out," he said, and then squatted and slowly ran his hand over the carpet. A few seconds later, he drew his hand back. "I think I found the culprit."

She leaned in. "What is it?"

"Hang on a second. Don't touch it," he said then retrieved the flashlight from the end table, and directed the beam at the carpet. He forced air through his lips. "I'll be damned."

"What is it?" she asked.

He went into the kitchen, returning with a pair of tweezers and a plastic bag, then picked up the object and held it up. It was an earring in the shape of a Wildcat.

"My visitor was considerate enough to leave a memento," he said, and then dropped the earring into the plastic bag.

"What do you mean?"

"Vic Bryant. He was a teammate of Jared Prescott's at Northwestern. He wears earrings like this."

They looked at each other, neither one speaking for a few moments, then he gently placed a hand on her elbow. "Rachel, about what just happened, I don't know what I'm feeling right now. I don't know whether I should apologize or what. I just…"

She touched his lips with a finger and smiled. "No apology necessary. If I had a problem, I would have stopped you. Anyway, let's not discuss it right now, okay? She nodded at the plastic bag. "You have more important things to attend to."

"Okay," he said, then raised the bag. "This should be enough to bring in Bryant and get a search warrant for his house. I'll take care of that first thing in the morning."

She glanced at her watch. "Listen, I'd better be going."

He walked her to the door, and she turned, put her arms around him, and they kissed, long and hard.

"Take care of yourself, Aaron. I'll call you tomorrow."

"You get that cut taken care of."

"It's just a nick. Actually, I'm more concerned with the bloodstain," she said with a grin. "It's one of my favorite blouses." She wiggled her finger and left the apartment.

He watched her walk down the hall then closed the door, amazed at how much his life had changed for the better in a matter of minutes.

He called the precinct and requested a unit to pick up Vic Bryant and take him to the precinct for questioning, assuming the man hadn't already left town or gone into hiding. It wouldn't take long to notice a missing earring, and Bryant wasn't likely to return to claim his lost property.

Chapter Twenty-Eight

The next morning, Aaron updated Vince Sherman on the previous night's events. "I want a warrant to formally charge Vic Bryant."

"Aaron, you might have a concussion. You should see a doctor. At the very least, go back home and get some rest. We'll take care of Vic Bryant."

"We're close to breaking this case and I'm seeing it through to the end. Besides, seeing I was the one to knock the earring out of Bryant's ear, it's only proper I be the one to return it to him."

Sherman laughed. "It's good to see the blow to your head hasn't affected your sarcasm. You can return his property when we find him. He wasn't at home last night when the unit went to pick him up, which is not surprising given what you told me. We put out an A.P.B. and staked out his house. I'm anxious to put this case behind us for a number of reasons. I don't like politics any more than you do."

Aaron lowered his head.

"Something else bothering you, Aaron?"

"It doesn't add up, Vince. The shooting at the Prescott home and three killings with three different weapons. Bryant took a big risk jumping me at my apartment, when he could have killed me the night he took out Laura Carter, assuming he was the shooter. It's almost like he wanted me alive to see the warning on the mirror. Like he was taunting me."

"I agree. It makes him appear pretty stupid to announce it by writing on your mirror, but I think you're reading too much into it. Bryant might not be the brightest guy, but I would think he's smart enough not to kill a cop, although like you said, maybe your neighbor scared him away."

"Yeah," Aaron said with a chuckle, "after the team arrived this morning, it took me ten minutes to explain why I lied to her."

"The D.A. is preparing a search warrant for Bryant's house as we speak. I'm hoping we'll find enough to connect him to all the killings."

"Maybe, but don't count on it. I don't think he's acting alone, and he's not the kind of guy that would…"

A call on Sherman's phone interrupted Aaron.

Sherman raised a finger. "Excuse me for a second," he said, and picked up the phone. "Vince Sherman."

Aaron got up and walked to the window.

Sherman listened without speaking for a few moments then hung up the phone. "They just brought in Vic Bryant."

Aaron turned from the window. "It's about time. I want the first shot at interrogating him. I want to see the look on the bastard's face when I walk into the room and throw the earring in his face. Where did they take him?"

"He's not here," Sherman said.

"What do you mean?"

"He's at the morgue."

"The morgue? What the hell happened?"

"A unit found him about two hours ago at Longwood and Trent, slumped over his steering wheel. His wallet with his driver's license was on the passenger seat, but there was no money or credit cards. Preliminary indication is a robbery-homicide."

"Any witnesses?" Aaron asked.

Sherman shook his head. "None so far."

"I'll be damned."

"Aaron, I want you to go down to the morgue and see what you can find out, get as many details as you can. In the meantime, I'll expedite the warrant and meet you at

Bryant's house. We should have no problem getting it now."

Aaron frowned. "You? Why you?"

"Politics," Sherman said with a wry smile. "It will look good for the press, good for the department, and most of all, make the commissioner happy we're finally closing this case."

Aaron's mouth twisted. "Interesting choice for someone that doesn't like playing politics."

"I don't like paying taxes either, but I still pay them."

"Fair enough. I'll call when I'm done at the morgue," Aaron said, then left Sherman's office. Twenty minutes later, he stood over Vic Bryant's body at the morgue with Dr. Taylor at his side.

"The cause of death was a small caliber bullet to the temple. Time of death was between ten and eleven p.m.," Taylor said.

Aaron leaned over and examined the body. The earring from Bryant's right ear was missing, with traces of dried blood on the ear lobe. As he stared at Bryant, details of the attack at his apartment filtered into his memory.

"His father, William, identified the body," Taylor said. "He's sitting outside in the lobby area."

"Okay, thanks, Wes," Aaron said, and left the room.

He found a man sitting in a yellow plastic chair, head resting in his hands.

"Mr. Bryant?"

The man looked up. "Yes? What is it?"

"I'm Inspector Aaron Randall, Homicide. I wonder if I might have a word with you."

"You the one gonna find out who killed my son?"

"In a manner of speaking, yes."

Bryant leaned back in the chair and squinted. "What does that mean?"

"I've been working the Jared Prescott murder. Are you familiar with the case?"

"Yes, of course. Harlan and I talked about it. What's that got to do with Vic?"

Aaron frowned. "You know Harlan Grayson?"

"Harlan and I go way back. We fought together in the same regiment in 'Nam in sixty-eight." Bryant forced a laugh. "They called us the Rabble Rousers of the twenty-fifth."

"Do you two stay in touch?"

"We talk maybe once or twice a month. Both our wives died of breast cancer. Harlan came down to Denver to attend my wife's funeral and donated a sizable sum of money in her name to the Cancer Foundation. I need to call him and let him know what happened after I take care of… Vic's funeral."

"Did you know Jared Prescott?"

"I never met the man, only knew him through what Vic told me. Hot shot football player. He and Vic didn't get along well in college…" Bryant looked at Aaron and hesitated. "I shouldn't have said that. I…"

Aaron stopped him with a show of his palm. "I'm aware of the history between your son and Prescott. When was the last time you spoke to your son?"

Bryant looked at the floor. "The truth is, Vic and I weren't on speaking terms for a number of years after he graduated college. I suppose it was mostly my fault. I rode him too hard, wanted him to make a name for himself playing football, maybe get into the pros. Turns out it was nothing but a pipe dream.

"After Vic got discharged from the Army, I tried to help him, but he hadn't decided what he wanted to do with his life. He came to Denver to try real estate. I used my connections to find him a job, but he couldn't shake his drinking problem, so it didn't last long. He kept asking me for money, said he was going to open his own business, but

I knew better. He got into a couple of scrapes in Denver and got in trouble with the law. I loved my son and would do anything I could to help him, but he was freeloading and I got fed up supporting him."

Bryant stopped and massaged his forehead. "Our fragile relationship was over once the flow of money stopped. Before today, we hadn't been in contact for… hell, I don't remember how long."

"Was Harlan Grayson aware of your son's dislike for Prescott?"

"Dislike?" Bryant said with a laugh. "That's putting it mildly. They hated each other almost from the beginning, what with the competition on the football field. Vic even blamed Prescott for some of his failures, but that was a convenient excuse. Maybe if I hadn't driven him so hard…" his voice trailed into silence before he continued.

"As far as Harlan knowing, yeah, he knew because we talked about it. When his first wife died, I came to her funeral. I felt I owed him because he came to my wife's funeral. We talked about what we'd been doing since the war, and I found out Jared Prescott was his number two man. I actually called Harlan when Vic got fired from Smith Ford, wanted to know if he had any connections. It was a feeble attempt to rectify my relationship with Vic. About six months after Vic left Denver, I moved back to Chicago. I wanted to try and patch things up between us."

"Did your son and Harlan Grayson ever meet?"

"Once, at my wife's funeral."

"Were you aware your son dated Prescott's wife when they were in college? At the time she was Jennifer Grayson, Harlan Grayson's daughter."

"I knew Harlan had a daughter, but no, Vic and I never talked about his girlfriends." Bryant straightened up in the chair. "In any case, what does all this about Prescott and Grayson have to do with my son's death?"

"There's a good chance the two murders are linked."

"Are you saying the same person who killed Prescott killed my son?"

"It's possible, but right now, I can't divulge the details."

William Bryant needed to know his son was the prime suspect in Jared Prescott's murder, but now was not the time to tell him.

"I'm sorry for you loss, Mr. Bryant, but I need to get back to the Precinct. I'll make sure you're updated when we have more information."

"Yeah," Bryant said with a weak nod, then rested his head against the bench and closed his eyes.

Aaron left the morgue and drove to Vic Bryant's house.

Chapter Twenty-Nine

When Aaron arrived, Vince Sherman and four police officers were waiting in the front yard.

The D.A. had approved a warrant for an unencumbered search, permitting them to look for evidence relating to the deaths of Jared Prescott, Eddie Rivers, and Laura Carter.

Aaron approached the porch, followed by the five other men, and knocked on the door, identifying himself as a police officer. He believed Bryant lived alone, but he had to follow procedure. After a few moments without a sound from inside, he brought out Bryant's keys he retrieved from his personal affects, and unlocked the front door. The six men entered the home.

The team moved from room to room to verify the house was uninhabited before convening in the living room.

"Obviously, this guy never heard that cleanliness is next to Godliness," Sherman said.

"He didn't strike me as the religious type," Aaron added.

"Okay, men, let's tear the place apart," Sherman said.

The team started the search in the unfinished basement, looking in boxes, checking for loose boards and breaks in the walls; anywhere Bryant might have hidden potential evidence.

For almost two hours, they searched the kitchen, living room, dining room, two bathrooms, and two bedrooms, emptying medicine cabinets, closets, drawers, cupboards, and the pantry.

In the master bedroom, Aaron found a phone number scribbled on a yellow Post-It note siting on the dresser, along with a number of matchbooks from *The Strip,* an adult men's club.

The search continued without finding any evidence to link Bryant to any of the murders, until two officers searched the crawl space through an access door in the ceiling.

Two minutes later, one of the officers called out. "Chief, you and the Inspector need to see this."

Aaron climbed the ladder with Sherman close behind. In the far corner of the crawl space closest to the front of the house, against the wall, concealed under a stack of still-packaged insulation, was a Remington Model 770 rifle, a .45 semiautomatic, a .357 Magnum, and a briefcase with gold-engraved initials 'JPP' on the handle.

"JPP–Jared Philip Prescott," Aaron said.

"We got him, Aaron," Sherman said with a wide grin, then turned and addressed one of the officers. "Bag and label the evidence and take it down to the station. Let's get ballistics and identification going on these weapons."

"Yes, sir."

Sherman breathed a heavy sigh when he and Aaron stood outside Bryant's home.

"It's over, Aaron, and about damned time, too. I'm betting my pension we'll match the gun to the Prescott murder, and the rifle to the Carter murder. I don't know about you, but I'm looking forward to a good night's sleep. It will be nice to have the commissioner off my back for a change."

"Right," Aaron said, but wasn't thinking about sleep at the moment. What looked like an open and shut case felt too good to be true.

***

Two days later, Aaron sat in Sherman's office and listened to the report results of the evidence found at Vic Bryant's home.

"The three-fifty-seven Magnum was registered to Vic Bryant," Sherman said. "The forty-five automatic was registered to Jared Prescott, and ballistics matched the bullet that killed Jared Prescott to the three-fifty-seven. The bullet that killed Laura Carter came from the Remington. Mrs. Prescott confirmed the briefcase belonged to her husband. It contained forty-three thousand, two-hundred seventy dollars in cash."

Sherman closed the folder, sat back in the chair, and laced his fingers behind his head. "Good work, Aaron."

Aaron sat stoic and didn't answer.

"Something wrong, Aaron?"

"What about fingerprints?"

"We found nothing but smudges, but I don't think it matters in this case."

"That's a little odd, don't you think?"

Sherman raised his eyebrows in answer to Aaron's question.

"So what do we have here, Vince? Jared Prescott goes to the Tremont Inn with a briefcase full of money. Whether or not it was the entire one-hundred grand he withdrew the day before, we don't know. The question remains, why did he take the money with him?"

"Buying drugs, buying information, who knows?" Sherman said with a shrug. "It doesn't matter, and whether he took the briefcase with him to the motel is pure speculation, not to mention a moot point. Bryant also had Prescott's gun, which Prescott probably took with him that night, for reasons unknown."

"Except the difference between one-hundred grand and what we found in the briefcase is what Warren Kirby owed Johnny Marco, give or take a few grand."

"Come on, Aaron, that's testimony coming from a known loan shark and former murder suspect. That's weak and you know it."

"Point taken," Aaron said, "but Marco had no reason to lie. Besides, the phone number on the Post-It note I found at Bryant's house matches the number of a phone at the airport called on the night of Jared Prescott's murder. What was Bryant doing with it? Whether he called that number or why we still don't know, but it's the same airport Kirby admitted using to call his bookie."

"Are you suggesting he and Bryant were part of a conspiracy?"

"Kirby needed money to pay off Marco. Maybe he had something on Prescott and blackmailed him to get him to the motel. Maybe he didn't have the guts to pull the trigger himself, so he hired Bryant to do his dirty work. I don't have proof Bryant and Kirby even knew each other, but Kirby worked with Prescott, and Bryant was involved in the fake head scam. Maybe the scam has more to do with this whole mess. Something isn't right about this whole thing."

"Maybe Bryant paid off the loan to incriminate Kirby," Sherman suggested. "Look at the evidence. We tied Bryant to all the killings, and the earring in your apartment proves he attacked you. I'm sorry, Aaron, I respect your intuition, but I can't see there's anything left to prove. Your conspiracy theory is wishful thinking."

Aaron turned away and covered his mouth. "What about Eddie Rivers?"

"Aaron, I'm truly sorry about Eddie, but at this point, it looks like his death was an isolated incident. I admit the timing suggests it might be related, but we have nothing to prove that."

Aaron gazed down at his hands. He wasn't close to giving in. "I'm sorry, Vince, I just can't buy the timing of Eddie's death as a coincidence. I think someone has been watching from the beginning. Don't forget the shooting at the Prescott home. If Bryant did all the killing, why didn't he silence Laura Carter until that night at the park?"

Sherman shrugged. "Perhaps he figured she wasn't a threat."

"That only validates my point. How did the shooter know where she was unless he followed her? Vince, someone else is involved, I'm sure of it."

Sherman rolled his eyes. "Okay, assuming for the moment Eddie's death is related, what reason would Bryant have to kill him?"

"I don't know, maybe revenge, maybe to send me a message, like the one on my bathroom mirror. Maybe to make it look like Kirby was involved, because Eddie found out about his debt to Marco. Remember, the two twenty-dollar bills I gave Eddie weren't stolen, they were torn in half. That's a message. It's not just Eddie, there are other loose ends."

"Like what?"

"Whoever got into my apartment broke the lock on the patio door. I talked to my neighbor across the hall. She was up late that night and has the senses of a hawk, yet she didn't hear a sound. Whether it was Bryant or someone else, they got into my apartment without attracting any attention."

Sherman's eyebrows creased, and he sat back. "What do you mean–they?"

"It came back to me when I saw Vic Bryant's body at the morgue. I had the attacker dead to rights on the floor with my gun in his face and was about to take off his ski mask when I was hit on the back of my head. He couldn't have clobbered me if he was Houdini. There had to be another man in my apartment that night."

"And you think it was Kirby?"

"At this point, Vince, I won't guess who the other person was, but there's more."

"Such as?"

"Bryant was missing the earring from his *right* ear."

"I don't follow."

"I landed one solid punch during the fight. It was with my right hand when Bryant was on top facing me. The blow would have landed on his left side, his left ear. He still had the earring in his left ear."

"Give me a break, Aaron. You said yourself you wrestled with your attacker. How do you know the earring just didn't fall out from the scuffle?"

"Because his right ear showed a cut where the earring tore through the lobe. The fact we found evidence stashed in the same place is too neat, Vince, and you know it."

"Neat is how I like it. We rarely get that in this business. Bryant hid the guns and the briefcase in a place where he figured it would never be found. You said yourself he wasn't the brightest person. Besides, you know as well as I do killers aren't playing with a full deck. They all screw up somewhere along the line. A police search is never part of the plan because they always believe they won't get caught."

"So, you're telling me Vic Bryant got away with killing three people, but didn't have enough sense to stash the evidence somewhere other than his own house or get rid of the weapons all together? We got everything except a video tape of the killings and a signed confession, and he had to know we'd come looking for him after he lost the earring. I think closing the case is premature."

Sherman stared without speaking, appearing to consider Aaron's arguments. "Once the commissioner sees the report, he'll want to know why we're not closing the case. What do I tell him?"

"Tell him we still have an unsolved murder related to the investigation."

"Unsolved murder? What are you talking about?"

"Vic Bryant," Aaron said with a shrug.

Sherman cocked his head. "You must be kidding me."

"No, I'm not. Someone needs to be assigned to that homicide. I'm the logical choice. We still don't have proof Bryant was at the Tremont Inn the night of Prescott's murder, and despite the evidence we found all packaged in one tidy place in his attic crawl space, we can't prove he killed *anyone*, let alone three people. Frankly, I'm not even convinced he was one of the men at my apartment. You have to admit, Vince, it's a little too much of a coincidence he's found dead just as we're about to close in on him."

Sherman swiveled in his seat. "What do you suggest?"

"I found a number of matchbooks from a men's club called *The Strip* at Bryant's home. I'll start there, and then have another chat with our gambling friend, Warren Kirby."

Sherman tapped on his desk, clearly torn between the pressure from the commissioner and his trust in Aaron. "Okay, but I don't know how long I can keep the commissioner off my back. I can't withhold the news about Vic Bryant more than a day or two, and once that happens, I'll get pressure from the media, the commissioner, Grayson, hell, maybe Senator Caldwell. That's something I wouldn't wish on my worst enemy. That being said, I trust your judgment, Aaron, but whatever you do, avoid Harlan Grayson at all costs. The less he knows the better, and I'm risking a lot based on your intuition."

"I'll get you something, Vince, you can count on it."

It was ten minutes to five when Aaron left Sherman's office, enough time to go home and grab a bite to eat before visiting *The Strip* in hopes of finding out more about the late Vic Bryant.

Chapter Thirty

The Strip on North Clark Street was the most popular men's entertainment club in Chicago. A pink and white flashing neon sign labeled *The Strip* was visible from five blocks away. Blue, green, and purple lights hung end to end on the eaves of the roof.

Aaron maneuvered his car around a predominately male crowd while searching the parking lot for an available space, then waited in a long line to enter the club.

Ten minutes later, the attendant placed the five-dollar cover charge into a green metal box and stamped Aaron's hand with a purple imprint of the club's logo, a circle with a dancer in the middle.

Aaron entered through an inner door and moved aside to survey the crowd.

Most men were dressed casually; some wore jeans and t-shirts, while others wearing tuxedos sat close to the stages. A number of women wore revealing outfits. He wondered whether they were there for pointers, help their man live out a perverted fantasy when they returned home, or came along to make sure their man didn't cross the line.

Tobacco smoke hung heavy in the air. Music heavy on bass blasted from amps, while men catcalled and whistled to three strippers performing on separate runways. Surrounding each runway were armchairs with stools positioned behind, and a number of booths lined to the left.

Above each runway, a hexagonal-shaped Light Sphere flashed red, green, and yellow in rhythm to the music, while the strippers danced and gyrated.

The bar to Aaron's right stretched the length of the wall. Five bartenders dressed in white shirts, red bow ties, and black vests scurried like frightened mice to serve customers on barstools lined up along the length of the counter, occasionally munching from strategically placed pretzel and peanut bowls.

Aaron checked out the dancers while he shouldered his way through the crowd.

On the first runway, a Caucasian woman wearing a top hat and purple-glittered G-string, her right leg wrapped around a pole, curled her finger in a beckoning gesture, daring onlookers with more testosterone than common sense to join her on the runway.

Men resembling sumo wrestlers in training wearing matching black shirts with *The Strip* logo, stood guard in front of each runway, thick arms folded across their chests, more than willing to discourage any notions to accept the dancer's invitation.

A buxom African-American woman on the second runway stopped dancing occasionally to allow men to stuff paper money into the belt of her G-string.

On the third runway, a Hispanic woman with muscular thighs was in the early stages of her routine.

As Aaron reached the far end of the bar, a double door opened. An attractive blonde woman wearing an outfit that would make a Hooter's waitress blush emerged, carrying a platter with plates of barbeque wings and ribs.

A bartender wearing thin wire-rimmed glasses approached Aaron and bobbed his head. "What can I get you?" he yelled to be heard above the din.

Aaron took out Vic Bryant's DMV photo from his shirt pocket, and placed it on the counter. "Have you ever seen this man in the club?"

The bartender studied the photo. "Yeah, that's Vic. He's a regular here on Friday nights, but I haven't seen him tonight." He craned his neck and pointed over Aaron's shoulder. "You see those two guys at the table against the wall? He usually sits with them."

Aaron thanked the bartender and walked over to the table, past the third runway as the Hispanic dancer removed her top and tossed it into the crowd. She met Aaron's eyes and smiled as he passed, jiggled her unencumbered breasts, and threw her hips in his direction, rubbing two fingers together in a *care-to-make-a-donation* gesture.

Aaron smiled and showed his palms.

She curled her lips into a mock pout before she turned away, and gyrated in the opposite direction.

Aaron approached the table indicated by the bartender.

The first man looked mid-thirties, slight of build with thick brown hair and a dark tan, wearing a pale blue shirt and white pants. The second man was older and heavier with a barrel chest, swarthy complexion, square jaw, and a mustache to complement his five-o'clock shadow. His black hair was slicked against his scalp, and a cigarette dangled from his mouth. He wore a black shirt and black pants.

Aaron stood in front of the table, blocking their view of the entertainment.

The heavier man stood up and pressed his fists against the table. He was six foot two with a midsection suggesting a love affair with beer.

The other man wrapped his hand around the heavier man's arm. "Take it easy, Buzz."

The man called Buzz shot his friend a look, then looked back at Aaron. "You're in our way, man. Why don't you find yourself another table?" he said in a manufactured baritone voice.

The other man spoke up. "Look, mister, we don't want any trouble. Can we help you with something?"

"I'm Inspector Randall. I'd like to ask you a few questions about a friend of yours, Vic Bryant. The bartender said you three hang out here together." He gestured to an empty chair. "Do you mind?"

The man seated nodded. "Sure. I'm Eric Alberts, this is Zach Owen."

Owen flashed Aaron a token nod before sitting back down.

"Vic isn't here tonight," Alberts said. "We haven't seen him in a while. What do you want to know?"

"How well do you know him?" Aaron asked, using present tense on purpose.

"I've known Vic for about a year," Alberts replied. "I was in the market for a new car, and he overheard me talking about it to Buzz one night at the club. Vic said he worked for a car dealership. One thing led to another, and he set me up with a good deal. I offered to help him if he ever needed financial advice. I'm a CPA."

"Would you say you're good friends?"

"I would say more like business acquaintances, and drinking buddies on the weekends. The club is the only place we see each other, usually Friday nights."

"I understand Mr. Bryant likes to drink, sometimes to excess. Did he ever get drunk enough to get himself in trouble, like maybe get thrown out of the club?"

Alberts laughed and nodded. "Vic did like to slam down the beers. A few times we called a taxi, a couple of other times we drove him home, but I don't remember him ever getting thrown out."

"Did he ever come here with anyone else?"

"No, he always came alone, at least since I've known him. I got the impression he doesn't have too many friends. But we all come here for the same reason," Alberts said, angling his head toward the runway. "You know."

Aaron turned. The Hispanic dancer was teasing an older man sitting in front waving a twenty-dollar bill in the air. She shuffled closer and squatted to allow the man to tuck the bill into the band of her G-string.

Aaron turned back. "Right. You said you never saw Bryant outside the club?"

"The only time was at the dealership when I bought the car. Like I said, I promised him financial advice at a reduced rate, although he never took me up on my offer. I know he quit his job recently, and I offered to put him in touch with contacts of mine, but he declined. He said he was going to take some time off."

Apparently, Bryant didn't know the difference between 'quit' and getting fired.

Aaron looked at Owen. "What about you?"

"Never saw the man outside the club," Owen said, without taking his eyes from the runway.

"What's this all about and how did you know to come here?" Alberts asked.

Aaron removed a matchbook from his pocket and tossed it on the table. "We found a number of these when we searched his house."

Alberts looked at the matchbook, then back at Aaron and frowned. "Searched his house? I don't understand."

"Your drinking buddy was a suspect in the murder of Jared Prescott."

Alberts's eyes widened. "Are you serious?"

Owen tore his eyes from the dancers. "Damn."

"Think back to the beginning of August," Aaron said. "Do you remember anything unusual about Bryant's behavior?"

Alberts looked at Owen and shrugged. "Hell, I don't know. With Vic, it's hard to say what's unusual versus normal. He was generally a fun guy, although he did get a little loud after a few beers. Now I know why we haven't seen him in a couple of weeks. Has he been arrested?"

"Vic Bryant is dead," Aaron said, with no more emotion than if commenting on the weather.

Owen had picked up his glass, but stopped an inch from his mouth and put it down on the table without drinking. "What did you say?"

"What are you talking about?" Alberts added.

"He was found shot to death in his car less than a mile from here."

Owen's mouth fell open. "Holy shit."

"What happened, I mean who…" Alberts asked.

"We're looking into it."

Alberts frowned, and seemed lost in thought for a moment, then nudged Owen with an elbow. "Wait a minute. Buzz, what about that night he came to the club late?"

"What night?" Owens asked.

Alberts turned to Aaron. "It was about a month ago. We normally meet here around six or six-thirty, but Vic didn't arrive that night until eight-thirty. He said he had a meeting about a business transaction. Ordinarily, it was no big deal, I mean it's not like we're on a timetable, but I remember he was pretty excited. He had a couple of shots and a few beers and made a comment about better days are coming, the man is going to take care of me. I asked him what he meant, but he didn't give any details. We assumed either he found another job or it was whiskey talk."

"Whiskey talk?" Aaron asked with a frown.

"Yeah, Vic talked a lot after he drank, always bragging about striking it rich, but hell, we all probably say that at one time or another. You know, like we'll hit it big with the next lottery ticket." He paused and looked away in thought. "Come to think of it, that's the last time we saw him."

"Do you have any idea who he was referring to when he said 'the man?'" Aaron asked.

"No, I don't, but he might not have been referring to an actual person. I will say he was acting a little unusual, even for him. He was buying drinks, tipping the waitresses and strippers more than usual, almost like he came into money."

"Did you ask him about that?" Aaron asked.

"No, we figured it was none of our business."

"Did he ever mention Jared Prescott's name?"

Alberts thought for a moment. "Not that I remember."

Aaron stood and took out two business cards and tossed them on the table. "Thanks for your time, gentlemen. If you think of anything else, give me a call," he said, then gestured over his shoulder. "Enjoy the show."

***

Aaron left the club and was about to get into his car when he turned to the sound of a voice.

"Excuse me, sir. Can I talk to you for a minute?" the man said and jerked a thumb over his shoulder. "I'm Ian Francis. I tend bar here. I don't mean to pry, but one of the guys in there told me Vic Bryant was killed, and it might have something to do with the Prescott murder?"

News travels fast.

"Yes, does that mean something to you?"

"I don't know, sir, it might not mean anything, and I didn't think much of it at the time, but now that I heard he might be involved, I thought I better say something."

"I'm listening," Aaron said.

"If I remember correctly, that was a Monday night. Vic was here that night. He got here a few minutes after eight and went inside."

"How certain are you about the time?"

"Positive. It's one of my regular smoke breaks."

"Go on."

"A couple of minutes later, this red sports car pulled into the parking lot near the back, and a guy gets out and gets into the passenger side of a white conversion van. The van left the parking lot right after the guy got in."

"You said a red sports car?" Aaron asked, recalling the description Laura Carter provided.

"That's right, and the reason I remember it was because Bryant came out of the club about ten minutes after he went in. He looked like he was in a hurry. I said hello, but he just grunted. Anyway, he walked over to this red sports car, got in and took off."

"You mean he came to the club in his car and left in this other car?"

"That's right, almost like the other guy was dropping it off for him. But like I said, you see all kinds of things working here, so at the time…"

"I understand. Did Bryant come back that night?"

"Yes, and so did the conversion van. It was about nine-thirty. I was on another smoke break. The van pulled into a parking space, but nobody got out. It just sat there. Then, about ten minutes later, here comes Bryant in the red sports car. He parks next to the van, gets out of the car, walks over to his car, and leaves the parking lot."

"Did you talk to him at all?"

Francis shook his head. "No, his car was in the middle of the parking lot."

"So he didn't go into the club?"

"No, sir, but after he pulled out of the parking lot, someone got out of the passenger side of the van, opened the driver's side door of the red sports car and went to the back and opened the trunk, took something out and put it in the back of the van. I don't know, it looked like a big package, maybe a suitcase…"

"Or a briefcase?"

Francis looked away for a moment and stroked his chin. "Yeah, could have been, but I was too far away and it was dark."

"So what happened after that?"

"After the guy put whatever into the van, he got into the red sports car and left the parking lot. The van followed him out."

"Could you identify the make and model of the red sports car?" Aaron asked.

Francis shrugged. "No, didn't think of it at the time and like I said, too far away, too dark."

"What about the man who got out of the van? Can you give me a general description?"

Francis made fists and hunched his shoulders. "Big guy, football player type."

Aaron took out a ten-dollar bill from his wallet and handed it to the bartender along with a business card. "Thanks for the information, and give me a call if you see that van or sports car again."

"Yes, sir, I certainly will."

***

Aaron got into his car and started it, but sat for a while before putting it into gear. Given the testimony from the three men at the club, a conspiracy theory was a certainty, at least in his mind. Laura Carter said a red sports car was at the Tremont Inn the night of Jared Prescott's murder, although proving it was the same car Bryant drove to the club was another issue. Bryant's body was found in a green Toyota Camry, registered in his name.

There were more unanswered questions. Where did the red sports car come from? Did Bryant take the car to the Tremont Inn? Was the object the man removed from the trunk Jared Prescott's briefcase? If so, how did it end up at Bryant's home? Who were the two men in the van? Aaron had good reason to suspect Warren Kirby might be one, but who was the other? There were too many players, and if Bryant was involved, there were others to be held accountable for the murders of four people, Bryant included.

Chapter Thirty-One

When Aaron walked into Warren Kirby's office the following Monday, Kirby was talking on the phone, his feet propped on the desk, as if he didn't have a care in the world. He put his feet on the floor when Aaron walked through the door.

"I'll call you back," he said, then hung up the phone. "Inspector, I'm surprised to see you," he said, then let out a huge breath. "I heard you found Jared's killer."

Aaron closed his eyes and shook his head. He was hoping his boss would have kept the news of Vic Bryant's murder quiet. He opened his eyes and closed the door.

Kirby swallowed as though a grapefruit had lodged in his throat. "I take it this isn't a social call."

"I need you down at the precinct," Aaron said.

"Why?"

"Let's just say to help me fill in the blanks on a few unanswered questions."

"I don't understand. What questions? You found your killer so…"

Aaron showed his palm. "I'd advise you not to say anything until we get to the precinct. You may call your lawyer and have him present during questioning if you like."

Kirby ran a hand through his hair. "Why would I need a lawyer? Are you arresting me?"

"No, I'm not making any charges, not at this time."

"Please don't tell me this is still about the gambling debt."

"Like I said, we'll do this at the precinct."

Kirby forced air from his mouth, then stood and grabbed his jacket and draped it over his arm. "I have nothing to hide, Inspector. Let's go."

"We'll take my car." Aaron opened the door and stepped back.

Harlan Grayson stood in the doorway, his eyes narrowed to slits, beefy arms folded in front of his chest like a parent preparing to scold a misbehaving child. "What's going on here, Warren?" he asked, without taking his eyes off Aaron.

"I'm taking him in for questioning," Aaron said.

Grayson stepped into the office and closed the door. "You can question him here," he said, then looked at Kirby. "Have a seat, Warren. I'd like to hear what the Inspector has to say."

Aaron stared hard into Grayson's eyes. "You're interfering with an official police investigation, Grayson. If you prefer to accompany Mr. Kirby to the precinct, I have plenty of room in the back seat of my car. If not, I suggest you stay out of my way."

Grayson flashed a palm. "Save your breath, Inspector. I talked to your boss this morning, and in light of the evidence, he assured me the investigation into my son-in-law's death is closed. You found his killer—Vic Bryant. I'm a patient man, but my patience is wearing thin. I will not tolerate harassment of my staff, especially for something that is no longer an issue."

Aaron's grin reeked of sarcasm. "You don't waste any time, do you?"

The muscles in Grayson's jaw tightened. "Excuse me?"

"What's next, a call to your buddy, Senator Caldwell, to get me thrown off the force?"

Grayson's eyes turned cold, and he appeared to struggle for an answer.

Aaron relished the small victory, and didn't allow Grayson time to reply. "We still need to clear up a few issues regarding Mr. Prescott's murder. I believe Mr. Kirby can help."

"I don't see how Warren can possibly help you."

"I'm not at liberty to discuss the details, and it doesn't concern you. Let's go, Mr. Kirby," Aaron said, keeping his eyes on Grayson. "Excuse us."

Grayson reluctantly stepped aside and shoved his hands into his pockets. "Trust me, Inspector, you will be sorry you crossed paths with me."

"I'm already sorry, and that better not be a threat," Aaron said, then proceeded down the hall with Kirby close behind, turning when they reached the elevator. The doors opened and Aaron and Kirby got into the elevator, leaving Grayson standing in the hallway with a scowl on his face.

**

Aaron escorted Warren Kirby to an interrogation room, told him he could call his attorney, and then went to Vince Sherman's office.

"Come in, Aaron," Sherman said. "We need to talk. I just got off the phone with Harlan Grayson for the second time today."

"You would think the man has better things to do with his time. He already told me about the first call. Frankly, I'm surprised he didn't call the White House. What did you tell him this morning, Vince? I thought we agreed you'd give me time to follow through. He's under the impression we've closed the case."

"I told him we were wrapping up the investigation, nothing more than what the media reported," Sherman replied. "I told him about Bryant, but we needed to tie together a few loose ends based on new information. I guess he interpreted it the way he wanted."

"I'd be surprised if he didn't."

"Aaron, I warned you about him. He said you threatened to arrest him. Is that true?"

"I had sufficient cause, Vince. He was interfering with an official police investigation. Frankly, it took every ounce of self-control to keep from slapping the cuffs on him right there."

"I bet that would have made your day," Sherman said with a smile.

"You have no idea."

"Well, for what it's worth, both the commissioner and I are ragged listening to him whine every time we turn around."

"It's nice to finally hear I'm not stuck on an island without a boat."

"Between you and me, Aaron, I often can't say what I really think, but you didn't hear that from me. You have some latitude, but still need to wrap this up sooner than later. Did you bring in Kirby?"

"He's in the interrogation room. Are we done here?"

"For now," Sherman said. "Keep me informed of any progress. I don't want the next phone call from the commissioner telling me they've reassigned me to a street beat."

"Think of the exercise you'll get," Aaron said with a smile.

"That's funny, Aaron."

Sam stopped Aaron on the way to the interrogation room. "I heard you brought in Warren Kirby."

"I'm on my way to talk to him right now."

"You might want to wait on that."

"What do you mean?"

"They found the body of a twenty-three-year old woman this morning. Her name is Linda Sanchez. She lives at seventeen-seventy-two Emerald Grove."

"Why are you telling me?"

"They found an ID badge in her home. She worked for ChemPhen Pharmaceuticals."

"What?"

"It might not have anything to do with the Prescott case, but I thought you should know."

"You're right, Sam. Give me that address again. I want to go over there myself."

Sam handed Aaron a piece of paper. "What do you want me to tell Kirby?"

"I suspect he'll want his lawyer present before he says anything. If he complains, give him a magazine and tell him to smoke a cigarette."

Chapter Thirty-Two

Linda Sanchez's home was a blue and gray, two-story, brick veneer with a modest front yard and detached garage, located in Albany Park, a middle-class neighborhood.

The crime scene team had already cordoned off the yard, and two police cruisers sat in front. The coroner's wagon passed on its way to the morgue as Aaron got out of his car. An officer met him as he approached the house.

"Good morning, Inspector. We were the first unit on the scene. We found a ChemPhen employee badge."

"Yes, I heard. What do you have so far?"

"The victim's name is Linda Sanchez. Her boyfriend was here when we arrived. His name is Craig Stewart. He said he'd tried to call her but didn't get an answer, so he came over. He found her in the living room."

"How did he get into the house?" Aaron asked.

"He had his own key."

"Where is he now?"

"A black and white took him down to the precinct," the officer said, then gestured to a middle-aged woman wearing a blue and pink striped dress standing in the driveway, talking to another officer. "That's Martha Jameson, the next-door neighbor. She called 911."

"Thanks," Aaron said, then walked over and put his hand on the officer's shoulder. "I'll take it from here."

"Yes, sir."

"Excuse me, it's Mrs. Jameson, correct?" he asked.

The woman's eyes were bloodshot and rimmed with red, and it was an effort for her to nod. "Yes, that's right."

"I'm Inspector Randall. I know this is a difficult time, but are you up to answering a few questions?"

"Yes… I think so."

Aaron gestured to a bench in her front yard. "Why don't we sit down?"

"Please tell me what happened," he said after they sat down.

She looked at Aaron and folded her arms as if the temperature had dropped. "I was working in my yard when Craig, that's Linda's boyfriend, came running out of her house screaming for help. He collapsed in the front yard. I dropped my rake and went over to him. He was muttering, 'she's dead, Linda's dead, my God, she's dead.'" Mrs. Jameson's voice cracked, and she looked away.

"Take your time, ma'am."

It took several moments for her to gather her composure before she continued.

"I went back into my house and dialed 9-1-1. I told them something happened to my next-door neighbor. I really didn't know what to say, or what actually happened, but Craig was hysterical. A few minutes later the ambulance and police arrived." She put a hand to her forehead. "My God, everything happened so fast. Policemen were all over the place, putting up this yellow tape and…" She paused to wipe her eyes.

"What can you tell me about Ms. Sanchez?"

"She moved in about three years ago. She was a sweet young thing, always smiling, always seemed so happy. We say hello to each other every morning when she leaves for work. I like to work in the yard early in the morning." She paused again. "Craig feels so bad, probably worse because of the argument they had."

"Argument?" Aaron asked.

"It was Sunday, the day she was supposed to leave for a business trip to San Diego. She asked me to watch the house and pick up her newspapers and mail. Anyway, Craig came over around lunchtime. He parked in the driveway, and I knew he was mad about something, because he slammed the car door and went into the house.

The next thing I knew, he and Linda were screaming at each other."

"Do you know what they argued about?"

Jameson shook her head. "No. As a matter of fact, I had to turn up the volume on my television. I never heard language like that coming from Craig. It was very upsetting."

"How long did the argument last?"

Jameson shrugged. "I don't know, fifteen, maybe twenty minutes. I heard the car door slam and looked out, and saw Craig back out of the driveway. He was going so fast his tires squealed. I'm glad no cars were coming. He could have killed somebody."

"What happened next?"

"I waited a while then went next door to see if Linda was all right. She was crying, but said she had to get ready for her trip and didn't want to talk about it."

"When did you last see Ms. Sanchez?"

Mrs. Jameson thought for a moment. "The following Friday, a little before dinnertime, when she got back from San Diego. I was out in the yard. I asked her how the trip was, but she seemed a little out of sorts and in a hurry, so I left it alone. I guess with the stress of the trip on top of the argument with Craig, she had enough to think about. Frankly, I was surprised Craig didn't pick her up from the airport, because I assumed they made up from their fight."

"Why did you think that?"

"Because after Linda left for her trip, Craig came back a couple of hours later to pick up her car."

"Pick up her car? What time was that?"

Jameson thought for a moment. "I think it was around eight o'clock. I assumed he was going to take it for servicing because a friend of his dropped him off in a white van. It might have been one of those auto shop vans. In any case, I felt relieved, because Linda wouldn't have given him the keys to the car if they will still arguing." She looked at Aaron. "Would she?"

Aaron shrugged in reply. "Do you remember if there were any markings on the side of the van?"

Jameson rubbed her forehead in thought. "No, I don't think so, but I really didn't pay much attention. Whoever was driving the van dropped Craig off and left right away. Anyway, whatever plans Craig had for the car must have changed."

"Why do you say that?"

Jameson looked at Aaron in surprise, as though the answer was obvious. "Well, because a couple of hours later, he came back and parked the car in the garage." She wagged a finger. "I remember it was a few minutes after ten because I had just started watching a rerun of a soap opera."

"Was anyone with him?"

"Yes, the white van pulled up a couple of minutes later. Craig got in after putting Linda's car in the garage and they left."

"Are you sure it was Craig Stewart who took the car?"

"Oh, yes, I'm positive. He was wearing that funny hat."

"Funny hat?"

"I think it's called a Kangol cap. Professional golfers wore them years ago, but they're not too popular anymore. I do recall wondering why he was wearing it in front, because he always wore it backwards. Come to think of it, when I saw him today, he looked like he'd lost weight, probably due to Linda being out of town and the argument."

"Why do you say that?"

"When I saw him the night he came to pick up the car, he looked… I don't know… bigger." Jameson's eyes moistened, and she dropped her head into her hands. "She and Craig seemed so happy together. They remind me of Todd and me when we first fell in love. They loved going for drives in Linda's red sports car. I don't know what happened between them, but poor Craig will be so lost without her."

"Ma'am, I'm sorry, did you say red sports car?"

"Yes, I did, why? Does that mean something?"

"Would you excuse me for a moment?" Aaron got up and walked up the driveway to the garage. When he noticed the door handle was broken, he pulled on the bottom on the door. It opened with an annoying squeak.

A 2005 Nissan 350Z sat in the garage. On the left rear fender was a sizable dent, and the left taillight was broken. He took out his notepad and flipped through to check the notes from the aborted meeting with Laura Carter. *He backed into a light pole when he pulled out of the parking lot.*

Aaron called the precinct and requested a tow for the car to the police garage before returning to the bench. Mrs. Jameson's head was buried in her hands.

"Ma'am, I need to ask you about that car. Other than her boyfriend, did you see anyone at Ms. Sanchez's house the last few weeks?"

Jameson considered the question for a time and then shook her head. "No, and as far as I remember, Craig didn't come over until today, except for that Sunday evening." She shook her head. "It's too bad. Whatever problems they had, apparently, weren't solved. I didn't even see much of Linda after she came back from her trip."

"I see," Aaron said. "Ma'am, I appreciate your time, and I'm truly sorry about Ms. Sanchez."

"You're welcome, Inspector. I just pray Craig gets through this."

"I'm sure he'll be fine," Aaron said, more to ease her mind than make a prediction. After a cursory check of the crime scene, he returned to the precinct.

First on his list was to compile the information he gathered from the bartender at *The Strip* and Martha Jameson to develop a timeline. Both parties witnessed the coming and going of a red sports car and a van–too similar to be a coincidence.

Chapter Thirty-Three

"It's about time you got back," Sam said. "Kirby is screaming for his lawyer, and threatening to sue the department."

"He can do whatever he wants," Aaron said. "They brought in Linda Sanchez's boyfriend, Craig Stewart. I want to talk to him before I see Kirby. Where'd they put him?"

Sam gestured over his left shoulder. "Room two."

"Thanks. Let me know when Kirby's lawyer gets here."

Aaron entered the interrogation room. Craig Stewart sat in a chair, his head down and flexing his fingers. He looked up. He had bushy blond hair and brown eyes, and wore a green polo shirt and tan pants.

"Mr. Stewart, my name is Inspector Randall. Can I get you something to drink?"

Stewart shook his head. "No thanks, but I could use a cigarette. Can I smoke in here?"

"Go ahead."

Stewart took out a pack of cigarettes and a matchbook from his shirt pocket, tapped on the bottom of the pack, and a cigarette dropped to the table. His hands shook visibly when he tried lighting the cigarette. He took a puff and blew smoke into the air.

"Linda kept asking me to quit smoking. I've tried a hundred times. I'd quit for a week then start again. It's tough." He took another puff, and then eyed the cigarette as he rolled it in his fingers. "I guess it doesn't matter now."

"What brand do you smoke?" Aaron asked.

"Winston. I used to smoke Marlboro, but switched a few months ago, hoping Winston wouldn't taste as good, and make it easier to quit. Ridiculous logic, I guess."

"I see," Aaron said, recalling that Marlboro was the brand of cigarette found in the room at the Tremont Inn. "I'm sorry for your loss, Mr. Stewart. How long were you and Ms. Sanchez going together?"

"Next month would have been three years," Stewart said and looked up at Aaron. "Who in the world would want to kill her?"

Aaron nodded, but didn't answer. Instead, he glanced at his watch. It was getting late. Warren Kirby was waiting. The bodies were piling up. He needed answers, and quickly.

"Mr. Stewart, why don't you tell me about the argument you had with your girlfriend?"

Stewart's head jerked up, his eyes wide. "How did you know…" he started, but looked away and nodded. "Her neighbor told you. I know I was a little out of control, but…"

"What started the argument?"

Stewart massaged his forehead. "It had to do with Linda's business trip."

"I understand she flew to San Diego," Aaron said.

"Yes, and that should have tipped me off from the beginning."

"What do you mean?"

"She came home one night and told me her company wanted her to attend a class in San Diego, something about business project organization. Linda even thought it was a little strange, because it came up at the spur of the moment. She said ChemPhen doesn't usually operate that way. She seemed, I don't know, surprised, even a little concerned."

"Did she say why?"

Stewart shook his head. "No. She didn't understand how the class was relevant to her job, but figured she had no choice. She tried not making a big deal of it, said since it was all paid for and she'd never been to San Diego, why not enjoy it, but I could see something was bothering her about the trip. Anyway, the night before she left, we had dinner at Joe's Seafood. We don't normally spend that kind of money, but since this was the first time she was going out of town without me since we'd been together, we figured we'd splurge. Everything at dinner and after went great then, at noon the next day, everything went to hell."

"What happened at noon?"

"I was supposed to drive her to the airport at four o'clock for her six o'clock flight. We wanted to have lunch before she left. Just as I was ready to leave the house, I got a phone call from some guy."

"Who?"

"I don't know, I never found out."

"What did he say?"

Stewart crushed his cigarette into the ashtray and looked up at Aaron. His eyes were welled with tears. He rubbed his eyes and shook his head. "Three years down the drain."

"What did the man say?" Aaron repeated.

Stewart sighed and sat back in the chair, trying to compose himself. "He asked me whether I was concerned Linda was going to San Diego, and whether I asked her why she was going. I asked him who he was, and why it was any of his business. He didn't say, but then asked me how I thought Linda could afford such an expensive car, and what about the necklace she got from her..." Stewart looked down and swallowed, "...lover. I said she had no lover. He repeated it, told me ask her about the necklace, ask her about the car, ask her why Jared Prescott and she had dinner at Zagat's a couple of week ago."

Aaron sat forward in his chair. "He mentioned Jared Prescott's name?"

Stewart nodded. "Yeah, he did. I cussed at the guy, told him he was full of shit. Right before I hung up, he said to check my text messages."

"And did you?" Aaron asked.

Stewart closed his eyes and nodded. "Yeah."

"What did the text say?"

"No words, just a photo of Linda and Prescott at a restaurant. I don't know whether it was Zagat's or not, but it doesn't matter. There they were, the two of them, having dinner together."

"Were they doing anything besides eating dinner?"

Stewart frowned. "No, but isn't that enough?"

"Did the caller send you any other photographs of the two together?"

"No, what are you getting at?"

"If the caller was suggesting your girlfriend and Prescott were having an affair, a photograph of two people having dinner together doesn't prove anything."

Stewart waved his hands back and forth. "You don't understand. Jared Prescott came on to every young woman in the company. It didn't matter whether they were married, engaged, whatever. Linda couldn't stand guys like that. She would never be in the company of a pig like him." He hesitated and massaged his forehead. "At least that's what I thought."

Aaron sat back. He saw anger burn in Stewart's eyes at the mention of Jared Prescott's name. "So, what did you do after seeing the photograph?"

"I lost it. I drove to Linda's house and told her about the phone call. I showed her the photograph, and asked her about the necklace." Stewart leaned forward and slammed his hands on the table. "Do you know what she told me? She said the dinner with Prescott was business related, but she couldn't talk about it because it was confidential, and knew nothing about a necklace."

"Maybe that was the truth," Aaron said with a shrug.

Stewart bared his teeth and slowly shook his head. "No, she lied to me, Inspector. I know, because I went upstairs and looked through her jewelry collection. Even as I was walking up the stairs, she tried to stop me. I found the necklace, all tucked away in a box in her underwear drawer." Stewart slapped the table and sat back. "Her underwear drawer!"

Aaron pursed his lips. "I'm sorry."

"Yeah, sorry, that's what she said, but told me Jared Prescott didn't give her the necklace, and there was nothing going on with him or anyone else. So, I asked her where she got it and why she was hiding it."

"And?"

"She said she couldn't tell me. I threw the box on the floor and told her to find her own damn way to the airport." Stewart ran his hands through his hair and panted.

Aaron watched Stewart without speaking. It took a few minutes for him to calm down, but the interview was far from over. There were still questions to be answered.

Stewart looked at Aaron and turned up his palms. "I'm sorry, Inspector, I thought I was past the affair."

"It's understandable, but I'll still need to know what happened over the course of the following week."

Stewart nodded, but his head looked like it weighed a ton. "I know. Please, give me a minute."

"Take whatever time you need."

Stewart's hands shook again when he took another cigarette from his pocket and lit it. He took a puff and blew smoke out as though he was taking a breath test. "Okay. At the time, I figured it was over between us, but when I heard Jared Prescott was murdered, I called the hotel Linda was staying at in San Diego and left her a message."

"What was the name of the hotel?" Aaron asked.

Stewart rubbed his forehead in thought. "Uh, the Sheraton Mission Valley. She gave me the number before we had the argument in case I needed to get hold of her."

Aaron nodded. The Sheraton Mission Valley was the same hotel Jared Prescott, or someone on his behalf, made reservations at the night he was murdered. "You didn't try her cell phone first?"

"No. I was still mad. Part of me wanted to leave a message saying, your lover is dead. That's what you get for playing around on me."

"Is that what you said?"

"No, the other part of me hoped we could save our relationship, although given what I knew, it probably wasn't realistic."

"Were you able to talk to her?"

"She called me back the next day and said she already knew about Prescott. Her boss, Harlan Grayson, called and left a message."

"Harlan Grayson," Aaron repeated. *Odd that Grayson didn't appoint one of his subordinates to make that call.* "Did she say she talked to Grayson?"

"No, but she sounded, I don't know, weird, still claiming there was nothing between her and Prescott. She sounded at first like she wanted to discuss what happened between us, but I cut the conversation short. I needed more time to think about it… and us."

"Did you talk to her any more that week?"

"Yeah, the next day, Thursday. This time I left a message on her cell phone and asked her to call me back. I wanted to know if we could talk when she got back into town. I wanted to pick her up at the airport but she got in too early and I couldn't get off work. She never called back, so I figured she was just as angry as I was. Actually, I took it as a sign that maybe she was telling me the truth, and even though she couldn't explain the necklace, maybe there really wasn't anything going on."

"What about the car? Did you ask her where it came from?"

"She's had that car for a number of months. I already knew about it. She said the company gave it to her as a recognition award."

Aaron frowned. "ChemPhen gives their employees brand new cars as awards?"

Stewart shrugged. "It's a big company. They can afford it. I'm sure they write it off as an expense."

Aaron pursed his lips. "Still seems a little over the top to me. Did she ever call you back?"

Stewart narrowed his eyes and nodded. "Oh, yeah, did she *ever*. She took a cab from the airport after she got back in town. When she got home, she called and read me the riot act. Apparently, there was damage to her car. She accused me of taking a baseball bat to her fender, and why did I have to break the lock on the garage door? The next thing I know, we're in the middle of another argument, only this time it seemed strange."

"How do you mean, strange?" Aaron asked.

"I can't explain it, but for some reason, I wasn't angry with her. I actually felt guilty because somewhere in the back of my mind I couldn't help thinking she was telling the truth. I guess she had time to think about it and maybe was disappointed I didn't trust her, despite all the so-called evidence."

"So, you never touched her car, never went to her house and took it out for a drive?" Aaron asked.

Stewart's head jerked back. "No, of course not. Why would I? Besides, I don't have a key to her car. Why would you ask that?"

"Ms. Sanchez's neighbor swore she saw you a few hours the day after you two had the argument. Someone dropped you off in a white van, you took the car out for a couple of hours, then brought it back and left in the same white van."

"That's ridiculous. Why would her neighbor say such a thing?"

"She said she knew it was you because you wore a Kangol cap."

Stewart managed to laugh despite the situation. "I stopped wearing that cap months ago. Linda said it looked ridiculous, especially since I always wore it backwards."

"I see. Can you account for your whereabouts on Sunday night?" Aaron asked.

"I was at home, watching TV, still fuming about the argument, and no, I wasn't with anybody."

"What made you come over to the house yesterday?"

"I wasn't going to give up three years without a fight. If I truly believed she was having an affair, I would have let it go, but I wasn't convinced. I decided I'd go over without calling, hoping maybe she'd feel pressured to talk to me."

"And that's when you found her?"

The reality once again set in. Stewart nodded, buried his head in his hands, and sobbed. When he raised his head a minute later, his eyes were red, his cheeks soaked with tears. "I knocked on the door, but she didn't answer, so I checked the garage. Her car was still there, so I used my key to open the door." He closed his eyes and shook his head. "She was just lying there. I'll never get that image out of my mind for as long as I live."

"Mr. Stewart, I'd like to check your cell phone records, and see if we can track down the number of the man who called you."

Stewart reached into his pocket and took out his cell phone. "I'll give it to you right now. I kept it on my recent calls log." He punched numbers into his phone. "It's 832-223-1000."

Aaron wrote down the number. "Thank you."

"Listen," Stewart said, wiping his face with his hands. "It's been a damn long day. I'd like to go home and try to get some sleep."

He studied Stewart for a few moments. "I'll get someone to drive you home, but leave your address and phone number."

Stewart got up from the chair and moved toward the door.

"I'm sorry about Ms. Sanchez," Aaron said.

All Stewart could muster was a weak 'thank you' as he left the room.

Chapter Thirty-Four

Aaron walked over to Sam's desk after Stewart left the precinct, and gave him the number from Stewart's phone. "Sam, see if you can trace that number. I suspect it's a disposable, but it's worth a shot."

"So, what do you think about the boyfriend?" Sam asked.

"I don't think he's guilty of anything," Aaron replied. "I pushed him pretty hard, considering the circumstances. He's pretty broken up, and although he doesn't have an alibi for last week, there are just too many strange things that happened before and after Linda Sanchez left for San Diego. I'd also like you to verify that she actually made it to San Diego. She had reservations at the Sheraton Mission Valley Hotel."

"Will do," Sam said.

"Did Kirby's lawyer get here yet?"

"He's been delayed," Sam said. "It could be a couple of hours. Kirby is one unhappy camper at the moment."

"I'll see if I can get him to talk. Sanchez's boyfriend gave me a few interesting tidbits of information. If Kirby has nothing to hide, he might prefer not to wait for an attorney. There is still a lot that doesn't add up, which is nothing new in this case."

***

Kirby was tugging on his watchband when Aaron entered the interrogation room.

"When my lawyer gets here, the first thing I'm going to do is fire him," Kirby said.

Aaron pulled up a chair and sat down. "We can keep you in this room all day. Two hours is a long time to wait and it could be longer. Apparently, your lawyer has more pressing business than to worry about you."

Kirby squeezed his hands until the knuckles turned white. He looked around the room then turned back. "All right, what do you want to know?"

"Do you know a woman by the name of Linda Sanchez?"

"Yes, Linda works for me. Why do you ask?"

"We found her body this morning."

Kirby slumped in the chair. "My God, Linda's dead? What happened?"

"She was murdered. How long did she work for you?"

"Linda has been working for ChemPhen for about five years. Administratively, she reports to me, but for the past three years or so, she's been working on a special project for Mr. Grayson." Kirby's eyes glazed over. "Jesus, why in the world would anyone want to hurt Linda?"

"What kind of special project?"

Kirby shrugged and studied his hands. "I wasn't privy to that information. It was between Mr. Grayson and Linda."

"You mean to tell me she works for you, but you don't know what she does?"

Kirby looked up at Aaron. "Like I said, it was between Mr. Grayson and Linda."

"Have you ever met her boyfriend, Craig Stewart?"

"No, Linda wasn't much for socializing after work hours. I think she came to only one Christmas party."

"She drove a Nissan 350Z, a car I'm guessing worth over thirty grand. Was she a good employee?"

Kirby looked at Aaron as though he asked him to jump out of a plane without a parachute. "She was ambitious and a hard worker, always on time. I don't understand, Inspector. I thought you brought me in here to talk about my gambling debt. Now you tell me Linda Sanchez was murdered and want to know about her car. What the hell is going on here? Is this some kind of a game?"

"I don't play games, Mr. Kirby, and we'll get to your gambling debt in a minute, but first, I want to know about the car. Her boyfriend said the company gave it to her as a recognition award. Is that true?"

Kirby laughed aloud.

"Something funny, Mr. Kirby?"

"A brand new car as a recognition award? I don't know where her boyfriend got that idea. ChemPhen values their employees more than most, but they're not apt to give away brand new cars, not even to their executives. Where did he get that idea?"

"He said Linda Sanchez told him."

"Then she was pulling his leg or flat out lying," Kirby said. "Anyway, why so much interest in her car? Shouldn't you be trying to find her killer?"

"Trust me, I *will* find her killer, but an eyewitness placed her car at the Tremont Inn the night Jared Prescott was murdered." That was pure speculation at this point, but Kirby didn't need to know that.

"I still don't see what this has to do with me."

Aaron stared into Kirby's eyes for a few moments, then got up and stood against the wall. "Fair enough, then let's talk about your gambling debt. It was paid in full within a few days after Prescott's murder. I have an eyewitness testifying Vic Bryant met with two men at a night club that same night, and handed over a briefcase." Again, speculation, but Aaron wanted to hear Kirby's explanation.

"I'm still not following," Kirby said with a shake of his head.

"We believe the briefcase belonged to Jared Prescott, who we know withdrew one-hundred thousand dollars from his bank account earlier in the day. Have you ever been to a men's club called *The Strip*?"

"No, I haven't, and we've been over this before, Inspector. I told you I don't know who paid off my gambling debt. I'll tell you the same thing next week and next year. I'm tired of getting accused of something I didn't do, and now I get the feeling you're suggesting I was somehow involved in Linda Sanchez's death."

"Who else knows about your gambling debt, and how much you owed Marco?" Aaron asked.

"Nobody. I told you before, I didn't even tell my family."

"Not even Harlan Grayson?"

Kirby frowned. "Grayson? No, he knew I had a gambling problem, but nothing about the loan."

"How much did Grayson know?"

"A few years ago, I approached Mr. Grayson and asked for a raise. I did it around Christmas time, hoping to catch him in a generous mood. I didn't give him any specifics at first, just that I was having financial difficulty."

"At first?"

"Yes. He wanted to know more, so I told him about my gambling problem, but that I was working on quitting, especially since I'd run up such a huge debt. He wouldn't give me a raise, but said the company would pay for counseling."

"Did you take him up on it?"

"No. If I did, I was afraid my family would find out about my problem, so I told him I would get it under control on my own."

"Did you tell him how much you owed or how you got the money?"

"Neither. I didn't want him to know about the loan shark, because I was afraid he might fire me."

"So, other than obviously Johnny Marco, nobody knew how much you owed or who you borrowed the money from?" Aaron asked.

"Nobody, I assure you, Inspector."

"Why didn't you tell me this before when we first discussed the loan?"

Kirby shrugged. "I didn't think my discussion with Mr. Grayson had any relevance."

Aaron nodded. If Eddie Rivers could dig up the sordid details on Kirby's loan, Grayson surely had the resources to get the same information.

"You said Linda Sanchez reported administratively to you. How did she come to work directly for Grayson?" Aaron asked.

"Mr. Grayson took a liking to her and said she had a lot of potential. He said he wanted to groom her for more responsibility in the company."

"Took a liking to her," Aaron said. "Was there suspicion he had more than a professional interest?"

Kirby swallowed and looked around the room as if hoping someone would answer the question for him. "Sure, of course, there were rumors about it, but that's not unusual in a big company. Nobody would ever make accusations or bring it up, because you don't bite the hand that feeds you, especially when it's the hand of someone as powerful as Harlan Grayson."

"Sounds to me like Grayson had everyone running scared," Aaron said. "Doesn't seem like a fun place to work."

Kirby relaxed against the back of the chair and folded his arms. "I'm done talking until my lawyer gets here."

Aaron got up and opened the door to leave, then turned back to Kirby. "Make yourself comfortable."

Aaron updated Sam on the interrogation then told him to release Kirby.

"Do you believe his story?"

Before Aaron could answer, an officer approached, carrying a plastic bag.

"Inspector, we checked out Ms. Sanchez's car, and found this wedged between the console and the driver's seat."

Aaron took the bag and raised it to eye level. Inside was a key attached to a small chain and a piece of plastic labeled 'Tremont Inn 25.'

Sam exhaled. "Well what do you know?"

Aaron handed the bag to Sam. "Sam, get this fingerprinted right away and find out when, where, and who purchased the Nissan 350Z."

"What about the boyfriend? Should I bring him back in?"

"We'll keep tabs on him, but I don't think he's our man," Aaron said.

Chapter Thirty-Five

That evening, when Aaron arrived at his apartment, he recognized the man who called him an hour earlier, saying they needed to talk.

"You're Bryan Dawson," Aaron said. "You used to be an investigative journalist for the Tribune."

"Correct. I've been selling used cars for the past three years."

"What can I do for you, Mr. Dawson?"

Dawson gestured with his arm. "Can we talk inside?"

Aaron opened the door. "Come in. Have a seat."

"Thank you," Dawson said and sat on the sofa.

Aaron sat on the recliner.

"First off," Dawson started, "I wanted to talk to you where there were no ears, and figured your place was as safe as any, although I heard about the attack the other day. It's a tragedy when an officer of the law can't even consider his own home safe."

"We're safe here, so you can talk freely," Aaron assured him. "What's on your mind?"

"I've been following the Prescott case," Dawson said. "I may not be in the newspaper business anymore, but still have my sources. I don't know whether you're familiar with the circumstances of why I'm no longer an investigative journalist."

"Refresh my memory."

"It was a couple of years ago. Do you remember the deaths of two men who worked for ChemPhen Pharmaceuticals?"

Aaron thought for a moment. "Vaguely, although if I remember correctly, one was a homicide, the other was a missing person. I didn't work that case."

"That's correct. The missing person was a process engineer named Paul Delaney. Three days before he disappeared, he was experiencing flu-like symptoms that were getting progressively worse, serious enough to send him to the emergency room at Northwestern Memorial. He never arrived at the ER."

"I remember now. It was a bizarre case."

"That's putting it mildly," Dawson said. "There was a big investigation involving ChemPhen. Delaney was, apparently, working on a big cancer research development project, but the company claimed confidentiality, and couldn't or wouldn't provide details."

"If I recall correctly, ChemPhen was not found to be at fault," Aaron said.

"Harlan Grayson personally handled all the questions from the investigators. He claimed he was the one who told Delaney to go to the ER. I was assigned to cover the investigation. It was my first big assignment. I was young and ambitious, perhaps even a little arrogant, but figured this was a chance to make a name for myself."

"Let me guess," Aaron said. "You ran into a brick wall by the name of Harlan Grayson."

"Right," Dawson said. "Less than two months later, I'm out of the journalism business. Today, I'm a marginally successful used-car salesman. Some name, huh? It would seem freedom of the press applies as long as it doesn't step on the toes of people with money and power."

"This happened a long time ago. Why are you coming to me with this now?"

"Please, bear with me, because Delaney's disappearance was just the tip of the iceberg."

"Okay, you have my attention," Aaron said, intrigued mostly because Harlan Grayson's name was at the core of the discussion.

"During the time I was covering the investigation, I managed to get time with Grayson himself, but the biggest break came from Delaney's brother, Ralph. He said Paul called him and told him about the high-profile project at ChemPhen, which included a promotion and a substantial pay raise. He wanted his brother to come up from Miami to celebrate, even offered to pay for his travel expenses. When his brother arrived in Chicago, it was about that time Paul came down with the flu symptoms."

"Bad timing," Aaron said. "Flu season can be rough in the Midwest."

"Over the counter medication wasn't working, and when Delaney's symptoms worsened, Grayson told him to go to the ER."

"Nice to know Grayson cares about the health of his employees."

"He told me the same thing in so many words. The fact is, Delaney had already scheduled an appointment with his doctor that afternoon for one o'clock."

"What time did Delaney leave for the ER?" Aaron said.

"Just before noon."

"And you believe he could have waited an hour," Aaron said.

Dawson shrugged. "That was my opinion, and I told Grayson."

"What did he say?"

"He claims he talked to Delaney himself and wanted to make sure he was all right. He said a one o'clock appointment means he won't get in until at least two o'clock, and the ER would take care of him a lot quicker."

"That's debatable, although I must admit, I don't disagree with Grayson's logic," Aaron said.

"Paul's brother told me Paul couldn't talk about the project he was working on because it was confidential, supposedly ground-breaking research. The entire staff working on the project was asked to sign confidentiality agreements. There was talk that if their competitors got wind of the project, it could ruin ChemPhen."

"If documents were signed…" Aaron started.

"Yes. I wanted to see those documents, but Grayson said he wouldn't produce them without a warrant, and the police never got that far in their investigation."

"Another brick wall."

"Paul Delaney's planned celebration included two other people, Alex Harris, a friend who also works for ChemPhen, although not part of the project, and Delaney's fiancée, Anne Livingston. He wanted to cancel or delay the party after he got sick, but his brother had already left from Miami. Ralph never got to see his brother. Grayson said he personally called the hospital after he couldn't reach Delaney on his cell phone. This was supposedly a few hours later."

"Grayson himself called to check on an employee with flu symptoms? I find that more than a little curious."

"I thought the same thing," Dawson said, "but Grayson said since he was the one who sent the guy to the hospital, he wanted to make sure he was in good hands. The hospital had no record of admitting Delaney. Grayson said he assumed Delaney felt better and went home to sleep it off. Delaney's fiancée went to his house to check on him after she got off work, because he called her earlier in the day and told her he was going to the ER. He wasn't home and his car was gone. She called the hospital and got the same story, he never checked into the ER, so she called ChemPhen, and Grayson said he'd do everything he could to help her find Delaney."

"I didn't think the old man had it in him," Aaron said.

"Two days later, Anne Livingston filed a missing persons report."

"And I'm guessing Grayson made it clear he would be there to support her," Aaron surmised.

"You got it. That's when the police got involved. Naturally, they talked to Grayson and Delaney's co-workers. All they confirmed was Delaney did indeed have flu symptoms."

"Did anyone follow up on the special project Delaney was working on?"

"That's just it. The police seemed satisfied with Grayson's explanation, and didn't pursue it any further. I mean after all, a guy with flu symptoms going to the ER isn't exactly ground-breaking news. When I started asking questions, I was cut off at the ankles, so never found out what Delaney was working on."

"And they never found Delaney?"

"About a week later, the police located his burned-out car in an area of the city known for heavy drug-dealing and gang activity, but his body was never recovered, so nobody can say one way or another whether the guy is alive or dead."

"I expect it's a cold case by now, and I can verify that, but I'm sensing there's more to the story."

"Much more," Dawson said. "I stayed in contact with Delaney's brother, fiancée, and coworker, to find out what I could about the man. Not surprisingly, they all said Paul had no history of drug use, no ties to gangs, and would never go anywhere near the part of town where they found his car."

"Granted, but I've yet to meet a drug dealer who admitted guilt," Aaron said.

"Point taken," Dawson said, "but the police searched Delaney's desk at work and found no evidence to prove he was involved with drugs. Even Grayson said he couldn't believe Delaney was dealing or using, because if he was, he would know."

"The man does like to be in control of his staff," Aaron said with a shake of his head.

"Personally, I think all Grayson cared about was the name of his precious company getting tarnished with bad press if any of his employees were suspected of dealing drugs."

"A pharmaceuticals company would certainly have access to drugs and a big temptation to someone prone to using or dealing," Aaron said.

"I promised Harris, Livingston, and Delaney's brother I'd do everything I could to find out what happened, but since I was no longer a journalist, I had to tread lightly. Harris said since he worked at ChemPhen, he'd try to talk to Grayson to find out what Paul was working on, although he admitted he probably wouldn't get very far." Dawson paused. "Little did he know that turned out to be a prediction."

"The homicide?" Aaron asked.

"Exactly. About a month later, Harris's body was found in his apartment. His hands were tied behind his back and he was shot in the back of the head, execution-style. Since Delaney was still missing and was good friends with Harris, the police tore apart both men's apartments. Anne Livingston said Delaney had a desktop and a laptop, and was somewhat of a computer geek, but the police didn't find so much as a flash drive."

"Sounds convenient," Aaron said. "Was there anything to suggest Delaney's apartment was ransacked before Harris's body was found?"

"No, and that's when it got ugly. Grayson implied both Delaney and Harris were dealing drugs and probably involved in gang activity. The son-of-a-bitch even suggested Delaney killed Harris and was still alive. He probably sent the police scurrying to see if Delaney was sitting on a beach in Rio sipping martinis."

"Was Harris married or involved with a woman?"

"Not at the time, and the autopsy on him came back clean, although that didn't mean he wasn't dealing. Naturally Grayson cooperated with the investigation, even offered to pay for Harris's funeral expenses, but here's the kicker."

"I can't wait to hear," Aaron said.

"No more than a couple of days into Harris's murder investigation, a known junkie came forward and testified he did business with both Delaney and Harris. Two days later, that junkie was found in an alley, dead from a heroin overdose. Pretty convenient timing, isn't it?"

"*Too* convenient," Aaron agreed. "Did Grayson ever admit talking to Harris?"

"He said Harris never asked him about Delaney, but according to Anne Livingston, Harris told her he talked to Grayson, but got stonewalled."

"One was lying, and I'm betting it wasn't Harris," Aaron said.

"When the subject came up, Grayson blew it off, asking the cops whether they were going to believe him or a known drug dealer. That pretty much closed the issue."

"So far, nothing you've told me can be tied to the Prescott investigation, so I'm not sure what you want me to do. I can't question Grayson on something that happened so long ago, especially on what is likely a cold case."

"You asked me before why I came to you after all this time," Dawson said. "It has to do with the death of Linda Sanchez."

Aaron frowned. "Sanchez? What about her?"

"She called me about three weeks ago, and said she might have a big story for me, but couldn't provide details until she had something more solid. I told her I was no longer in the business, but she said it involved Paul

Delaney and Alex Harris, and something big going on at ChemPhen."

"Why did she call you?"

"She said she got my name from a friend of hers who used to work at ChemPhen."

"Did she say who that friend was?"

"I asked, but she cut the conversation short, said she had to go, but would call me in a few days and let me know more. I never heard from her again. Then I read in the paper she was murdered." Dawson got up and paced the room. "I don't know what you can do with this information, like you said, it's been a couple of years, and frankly, it might not have anything at all to do with Jared Prescott's murder, but with the other killings since then, who knows?"

Aaron rubbed his chin. "I'll consider what you told me, Mr. Dawson, and I don't know what will come out of it, but depending on how far this goes, you could be subpoenaed as a material witness."

"I'll deal with that if and when the time comes. I suspect I'll be accused of wanting to get revenge on Grayson for losing my job, but it doesn't matter. Linda Sanchez called me for a reason, then less than three weeks later, she's murdered in her own home. That's too much of a coincidence in my mind."

Aaron nodded. "No argument there. Thanks for coming to me with this. I expect you'll be hearing from me, and if I were you, I'd watch my back." He stood, and they shook hands.

"Trust me, Inspector, I've been looking over my shoulder for the past three years."

Chapter Thirty-Six

Dr. Taylor called Aaron the next day to provide details on Linda Sanchez's autopsy.

"Cases like these cause me sleepless nights," Dr. Taylor said. "My daughter is the same age as Ms. Sanchez."

"I know what you mean, Wes," Aaron said. "What did you find?"

"The official cause of death was a blow to the back of the head with a blunt object. Contusions on her face were consistent with a brutal beating. Whoever killed her did it in a fit of rage. The time of death was between ten and midnight."

"One other thing, Aaron, the victim's sister flew in from St. Louis and made a positive ID on the body. She said she wanted to talk to the investigator in charge. I gave her your name. She's on her way to the precinct as we speak."

"Thanks, Wes. Give me a call if you find anything else," Aaron said, then hung up the phone.

A few minutes later, an officer appeared in front of Aaron's desk with a woman standing next to him. "Inspector, this is Carla Miller, Linda Sanchez's sister."

Aaron stood and shook the woman's hand. She was five feet eight, attractive with black hair, and green eyes. She wore a white blouse and brown slacks. Her eyes were rimmed with red.

"I'm Inspector Randall. I'm very sorry for your loss, Ms. Miller." He spoke those words what seemed like thousands of times, and each time he sensed they sounded rehearsed and lacked sincerity.

"It's *Mrs.*"

"I'm sorry. I understand you flew in from St. Louis."

"Yes. Linda's boyfriend, Craig called me. My mother and father are flying in from Florida this afternoon. I still can't believe this happened," she said with a shake of her head.

"I know it must be hard," Aaron said, and motioned to a chair. "Please, have a seat. How well do know her boyfriend?"

"Craig is the best thing that ever happened to Linda. They were very much in love. He treated her like a queen. They've been together for a few years and were recently discussing marriage." Miller looked at Aaron with furrowed brow. "You can't possibly think Craig had anything to do with this."

"We don't think so. I'm more interested in a man your sister's neighbor saw at her house that night. She claimed it was Linda's boyfriend, but there are a number of inconsistencies."

"Actually, Inspector, that's why I'm here."

"Oh?"

"Linda loved Craig, but there was someone else in her life. She refused to tell me his name or say much about him other than he was always buying her expensive gifts. She swore she felt nothing for this man and I believed her."

"What kind of expensive gifts?"

"At first it was flowers and candy, but then about six months ago, he bought her a brand new car."

"A red Nissan 350Z," Aaron said.

"That's right. I told Linda it wasn't right to accept the gifts, because it might lead him to believe she cared for him, but more because of her relationship with Craig. Linda knew that, but said there were reasons why she couldn't tell him to stop buying her things."

"Her boyfriend said she got the car as a recognition award, but I have conflicting testimony, and now you're telling me the same. Is it possible this man worked for her company?"

Miller shrugged. "I couldn't say, but suppose it's possible. Last year at Christmas, I came up to Chicago for a visit. She showed me a necklace the man bought her as a Christmas present. He told her he had it custom-made from one of the best jewelers in the city, like he was flaunting his wealth."

Aaron leaned forward, his interest piquing. "Necklace?"

"Yes, why, is that important?"

"It could be. Can you describe it?"

"I can do better than that," Miller said then took out her cell phone and handed it to Aaron. "I have a photo."

The necklace was heart-shaped with a pearl in the middle and diamonds around the border, with a thick gold chain.

"You might not be able to tell from the photo, but it was the most beautiful piece of jewelry I'd ever seen. Personally, I'd be afraid to wear it in public. I couldn't even venture to guess how much it cost, but between this and the new car, this man is obviously rich. I told Linda she needed to give it back to him. She knew keeping the necklace and the car was wrong, but was terrified to return them. I don't know what this man had on her, but it must have been something big. I just wish she had set him straight from the beginning."

"Did your sister ever mention the names Jared Prescott or Warren Kirby?"

"I knew Jared Prescott's name from the news. We even talked about it a little bit, but the other name doesn't sound familiar. Linda didn't talk much about her job, other than to say she was making more money than she ever thought possible. She got a substantial raise a couple of years ago."

"Did your sister say anything about an argument between her and her boyfriend?" Aaron asked.

"Yes, she called me and was very upset, said Craig accused her of having an affair with Jared Prescott. She said there are things going on at her company and her meeting with Mr. Prescott was business, but someone, apparently, took a picture of them at a restaurant. I asked her if Prescott was the man who gave her these expensive gifts, and she said she probably said too much already. She needed to pack for a business trip to San Diego, but promised to call me when she returned. When she got back, she and Craig argued again. She accused him of damaging her car."

Miller glanced at her watch. "Listen, Inspector, I want to thank you for your time, but I need to pick up my parents at the airport."

"Thank you for coming in, Mrs. Miller. You've been a big help, and I promise we'll do everything we can to find the person responsible."

Miller stood and shook Aaron's hand. "Thank you."

Mrs. Miller provided Aaron with a photo of the necklace, in hopes of locating the jeweler.

After Miller left, Aaron worked with Sam to compile a list of thirty-two custom jewelers in the Chicago area organized by geographic location. They each agreed to take eleven from the list. The remaining ten were assigned to another unit.

"Are you giving up on Kirby?" Sam asked.

"Not officially, but based on what Carla Miller told me, there may be someone else involved," Aaron said. "Someone spent a lot of money on Linda Sanchez, and Kirby had a big gambling debt to settle with Johnny Marco, so I doubt he was the one. In any case, I have a strong feeling if we find out who bought the necklace, we'll be closer to the truth, although, there is still the question of the men in the van Vic Bryant met with on the night of Prescott's murder."

Chapter Thirty-Seven

By two-thirty, Aaron had covered eight of the jewelers on the list with no success. Neither Sam nor the other unit had any more success. With only three remaining to ask, he was losing hope until he walked into Jan Dee Custom Jewelers on West Diversey Parkway. The proprietor's name was Dirk Ostrander, a fiftyish man with a narrow gray mustache and friendly smile.

"How may I help you today, sir?"

Aaron produced the picture of the necklace, and Ostrander's eyes flashed immediately with recognition. "Yes, I'm very proud of this piece. It was probably my best work."

"You mean to tell me you made this?" Aaron asked in disbelief.

"I sure did. Would you like me to make one for you?"

Aaron laughed. *That'll be the day.* "No, thank you. I just need to know who purchased the piece."

Ostrander squinted at Aaron. "Excuse me, sir?"

Aaron produced his credentials. "It's a police matter."

Ostrander peered at Aaron's badge and formed an 'o' with his mouth. "I'll have to check my log book." He walked into a room in the back, brought out a sales receipt journal, and opened it. "Here it is. The man's name was Harlan Grayson. I remember him as an older, very distinguished-looking gentleman and…"

"Thank you, sir. Thank you very much." Aaron said, then turned and headed for the door.

"Is Mr. Grayson in any trouble?" Ostrander asked.

"Like I said, it's a police matter. Do you mind telling me how much he paid for the necklace?"

Ostrander looked at his journal. "Fifteen thousand, seven hundred fifty dollars," he said, and raised a finger. "Remember, if you change your mind, I'll be more than happy to make one just like it for you."

"Believe me, you'll be the first one I call," Aaron said with a smile, then left the store. He was looking forward to the opportunity to question Harlan Grayson. This interview would be very different from the previous meetings. Some days it was worth getting up in the morning.

He called Sam from his cell phone on the way back to the precinct to tell him to call off the search for the necklace.

By three-thirty, Aaron updated Vince Sherman on his investigation into Vic Bryant and Linda Sanchez's murder, information gathered from various interviews, and the results of Sam's research efforts, including learning that Linda Sanchez never checked into the Sheraton Mission Valley Hotel in San Diego.

"Vince, I want to bring in Harlan Grayson for questioning. I'd ask for a warrant, but have a feeling my request will fall on deaf ears."

"Yes, a warrant would certainly be out of the question, and what gives you the idea he's involved?"

"I analyzed what Linda Sanchez's neighbor and the bartender at The Strip men's club told me. They both witnessed two men in a white van, and the bartender said the two men handed Linda Sanchez's car over to Vic Bryant. I checked the distance from Linda Sanchez's house to the men's club, and the men's club to Tremont Inn. Add to what Laura Carter told me, the timeline fits."

Sherman frowned. "What timeline?"

"I think the two men stole Linda Sanchez's car and delivered it to Vic Bryant so he could drive it to the Tremont Inn and kill Jared Prescott, then return it so the two men could take it back to Sanchez's house."

Sherman turned up his palms. "Then what you're saying is Vic Bryant truly did kill Jared Prescott."

"Yes, I believe he did, but like I suspected from early in the investigation, he's not the only one involved, certainly not the mastermind. I believe it's a conspiracy, bigger than even *I* realized."

"And you're convinced Harlan Grayson is behind it? What reason would he have to kill his own son-in-law?"

"For starters, he was cheating on his daughter, but I think it goes far beyond that. The Prescott home was fired at, Laura Carter was killed in the park, and Vic Bryant's murder was made to look like a robbery-homicide. Linda Sanchez's boyfriend got a phone call telling him she was having an affair with Prescott right before she was to leave town on a business trip scheduled by ChemPhen at the last minute. A few hours later, after Bryant and the two men in the van were seen doing business together, Jared Prescott is murdered. Sam checked the phone number of the person who called the boyfriend and got nothing. It was likely a disposable, that someone made sure couldn't be traced. What's more, Stewart didn't have a key to Sanchez's car, and there was no evidence of hot wiring, so whoever took it had a key."

"How many people do you think are involved?" Sherman asked.

"Hell, Vince, there could be as many as four or five. Bryan Dawson told me Linda Sanchez called to tell him she had a story regarding something big going on at ChemPhen. It concerned the death and disappearance of two former workers. I've already confirmed Harlan Grayson bought the necklace for Sanchez. Based on what her sister told me, that suggests he probably bought her the car."

Sherman looked out the window and drummed his fingers on his desk. "Harlan Grayson lost two wives, so he had a thing for a younger woman. Maybe the guy was lonely. That doesn't prove he's a killer. And what would ChemPhen be doing that would make a story, and why did Sanchez call Dawson? He's no longer in the business."

"Sanchez said it had something to do with the investigation into the former workers. As far as what ChemPhen is involved in, that's what I'm hoping to find out from Grayson. That's assuming you let me bring him in."

Sherman shook his head. "Did it ever occur to you someone planned all this to implicate Grayson?"

"Frankly, no. How many people would have access to all this information?"

"What about Warren Kirby? You said it yourself. He owed money to a loan shark and a few days after Prescott was killed, the loan is suddenly paid in full."

"Not suddenly, *conveniently,*" Aaron countered. "Forty thousand dollars in an envelope stuck into Johnny Marco's mailbox after Marco's bodyguard gets a call asking for the payoff balance? Kirby made payments in person every month. Why all of a sudden put such a large amount of cash in an envelope instead of deliver it in person? Seems to me a big risk. If the money was stolen…"

"Aaron, that's a weak argument at best and you know it. What about the boyfriend? The neighbor testified she saw him pick up his girlfriend's car on the night in question."

"She never saw his face and her description leaves a lot of room for doubt," Aaron said.

Sherman looked at Aaron long and hard before answering. "I know you won't like to hear this, but this is all circumstantial. Nothing you've told me so far suggests Harlan Grayson is involved."

Aaron's insides caught fire. He gnashed his teeth to calm himself before answering. "Vince, you damn well know if it was someone other than Harlan Grayson, he'd already be sitting in an interrogation room."

"I won't insult your intelligence by denying that, Aaron. Believe me, I know how you feel, but nothing has changed on this subject and its sensitivity. We need something more concrete."

"Unless you want a signed confession complete with photographs and a video tape, this is as concrete as it gets. There was another man in Linda Sanchez's life, and all evidence suggests Harlan Grayson is that man. You *know* I have enough to bring him in."

Sherman sighed heavily. "You've been hoping for something like this ever since you and Grayson first locked horns, Aaron, but don't let your enthusiasm cloud your objectivity. Remember how he reacted when you questioned his daughter and brought in Warren Kirby. Those were nothing compared to this. You're coming straight at him, and he'll take it personal."

"I promise you, Vince, if he's responsible, I don't care how powerful he is or who his friends are, I'll bring him down, and I'll do it legally."

Before Sherman could respond, Sam appeared in the doorway.

"Excuse me, sir. I have information which I think you should both know."

"What is it, Sam?" Aaron said.

"Linda Sanchez's car was purchased at Kelly Nissan in Oak Lawn on the tenth of January this year for thirty-three thousand two hundred dollars. The buyer paid cash."

"Who was the buyer?" Aaron asked.

A tiny grin played at the corner of Sam's mouth. "Harlan Grayson."

Aaron nodded then turned back to Sherman. "Well, Vince?"

Sherman remained stoic for a few moments. "Okay, Aaron, but Grayson is a smart man with friends in high places. If he is somehow involved, and I'm not saying he is, bringing him down won't be easy."

Aaron smiled. "If it was easy, it wouldn't be worth it."

***

Aaron phoned ChemPhen Pharmaceuticals. Harlan Grayson wasn't in his office, and his secretary either didn't know his whereabouts or wasn't telling. Aaron needed to find another source.

Twenty minutes later, he knocked on the door to the Prescott home.

Gordon answered and flashed a smile reeking of insincerity.

How quickly one forgets.

"What can I do for you, Inspector?"

Aaron pushed past Gordon and stood in the foyer. "I need to speak to Mrs. Prescott right away."

"I'm right here, Inspector," she said. Jennifer stood at the top of the staircase wearing a yellow robe. "What is so urgent?"

"We need to speak in private," Aaron said.

"We can go into the study," she said, walking down the stairs.

Aaron followed her into the study. He remained standing while she sat on the sofa.

Aaron brought her up to date on the investigation, including the murders of Laura Carter and Linda Sanchez. When he told her about the gifts her father purchased for Sanchez in an attempt to develop a relationship, her jaw dropped and she laughed.

"If you think my father carried on with a woman half his age, you're out of your mind, Inspector. He has little enough time for a woman his own age, and hasn't even thought about a relationship since the death of my stepmother."

"There was no relationship because Ms. Sanchez felt nothing for your father. Right now, I need to know where he is, nothing more. His secretary said he was out, and didn't, or wouldn't tell me where he was. I want you to call his cell phone and tell him we need to talk… *now*."

Jennifer got up from the sofa. "That's even more ridiculous. First you accuse my father of having an affair, now it sounds as though you're accusing him of murder."

"I need you to make that call right now, Mrs. Prescott."

She folded her arms and shook her head. "My father is no murderer, Mr. Randall."

"It's *Inspector* Randall. Make the call."

Jennifer pressed her lips together and stared down at the floor for a few moments before leaving the room. When she returned, she said, "He's in the lab at ChemPhen." She turned away and headed toward the stairs. "I'll get dressed. I'm going with you."

"You're staying right here. This is police business."

Jennifer glared at Aaron with a look that could cut steel. "He's my father. I have a right."

"You have a beautiful home here with everything you could possibly want. Do you want to give it up for a jail cell?"

Jennifer snorted. "You can't be serious."

"I've never been more serious. Obstructing justice is a serious crime."

"You sure changed your attitude. I used to think you were a decent man."

"I'll be going now," he said. "Remember what I said." He left the house without saying another word.

Chapter Thirty-Eight

A security guard dressed in a brown suit met Aaron at the gate at ChemPhen, and said Mr. Grayson needed to handle an issue at the lab and would be there for at least another hour. He told Aaron he could wait in Grayson's office or he would take him to the lab.

"I need to see him now," Aaron said.

"Follow me then," the guard said.

Aaron followed the guard into the building, through a metal door leading into a small lobby area with a single elevator.

"You look familiar," Aaron said to the guard while waiting for the elevator. "Have we met?"

The guard smiled, showing teeth. "Ever eat at The Bagel restaurant?"

Aaron frowned, and before he could react, the guard pulled his gun and pressed it into Aaron's back.

"Isn't that interesting?" Aaron said. "A Glock. Does Grayson supply his security guards with their weapons or does he pay you enough to buy that on your own?"

"Does it really matter?" the guard said with a shrug.

"Did you kill Eddie Rivers?"

"You ask too many questions, cop. Now, raise your hands, then with your left hand, reach in with two fingers and take out your gun, and hand it to me. *Slowly.*"

"And if I don't?"

The guard brandished his gun. "The cleaning crew will have one hell of a mess to clean off the elevator door, and you'll miss out on a very informative guided tour of Mr. Grayson's lab."

Aaron did as the guard asked. "Who are you?"

"I'm the King of England."

Before Aaron could reply, the elevator door opened, and the guard jammed the gun into Aaron's rib cage. "Get in."

They boarded the elevator, and the guard pushed Aaron against the wall. "Keep your nose against the wall. Don't worry, it's a short ride," the guard said, pressing a button on the panel. The door closed, and the elevator descended.

A few seconds later, the elevator stopped, and the doors opened into a small room. The guard led Aaron to a metal door on the other end. Next to the door was a box with a red and green bulb and a narrow opening.

The guard removed a card from his pocket and slid it down the opening. The light switched from red to green followed by a click.

The guard gestured with the gun. "Open it."

Aaron complied. They entered a large room with several rows of long metal tables, in addition to a number of workstations with computer monitors.

Standing halfway down the center aisle was Harlan Grayson, hands clasped behind his back. He wore khaki pants and a coral polo shirt with an alligator insignia stitched over the left pocket. Next to him stood a man with a thick neck and broad shoulders, wearing a brown suit.

"Welcome, Inspector Randall," Grayson said with a smile, as though he held the winning Powerball ticket. "It must be pretty important to come all the way down here to talk to me. To what do I owe the pleasure of this visit? I'd offer you something to drink, but as you can see," he swept his arm in an arc, "I doubt you'd find anything to your liking."

"This isn't a social call, Grayson. What's going here, and where did you get these two clowns? Thugs 'r us?"

The man in the brown suit stepped forward.

Grayson raised his hand. "That's okay, Karl. Forgive the Inspector's dry sense of humor. Their identity isn't relevant. Now, what's on your mind? My daughter said you had more questions to ask me."

"The fact I was brought down here at gunpoint answers a number of those questions."

"I'm glad to hear that, because you're on my turf now, and if there are any questions to ask, I'll do the asking." Grayson pulled up a chair and sat down.

"Cut the crap, Grayson. We found Linda Sanchez's body. We know you bought her the car and an expensive necklace. By the way, in case you were wondering, she wanted nothing to do with you." Aaron knew insulting Grayson wouldn't help his situation, but he couldn't resist.

Grayson sat back in the chair and tented his index fingers in front of his nose. "You're a smart man, Inspector. I'm interested to hear what you know, or *think* you know."

"You orchestrated everything, planting evidence here and there to send our investigation into different directions, and cast suspicion on different people. It was obvious early on Jared Prescott's murder was a conspiracy. The mark on Prescott's neck and the phone call from the motel to ChemPhen was meant to implicate George Thompson. The phone call to the airport and payoff of his debt implicated Warren Kirby. One of your goons called Sanchez's boyfriend to make him believe she and Prescott were having an affair. We know Bryant killed Prescott, then used Prescott's credit card to make reservations in San Diego the same week Sanchez was there. All that was done to make her boyfriend a suspect in both her and Prescott's murder."

Grayson nodded and smiled at Aaron. "I'm impressed. I'll make a note to send a letter to my good friend the commissioner and recommend you for a citation."

"Save it, Grayson. Your obsession to control the situation is where you made your mistake, and the murder of Linda Sanchez was your biggest. By the way, her boyfriend gave up Marlboro's months ago, and he hasn't worn a Kangol cap for some time."

Grayson furrowed his brow and shrugged.

"That's why Laura Carter was told to smoke a Marlboro, and one of your goons wore a Kangol cap the night he stole Sanchez's car."

"Well, I *am* a busy man, Inspector," Grayson said. "I can't watch everyone twenty-four hours a day. Jared *did* make lots of enemies. It wasn't difficult to point fingers."

"Laura Carter was given specific instructions for renting the room that night," Aaron said. "I already know why you told her to smoke the Marlboro, but why room number twenty-five, with the name and address she used? With your twisted and obsessive mind, I have to believe there was a reason."

Grayson's smile would make a Cheshire cat turn green with envy. "I served in the twenty-fifth infantry in Vietnam. The address number, two-twenty-one, was the month and date my first wife died. Pleasant Creek Drive is the street in Miami where my wife grew up. As to the name, Nancy Edmunds, the 'N' stood for nine, the 'E' for eleven. As I told you, my second wife died on nine-eleven." Grayson turned up his hands. "Frankly, Inspector, I'm disappointed you weren't able to figure that out."

Aaron frowned. "So that's how you honor the deaths of your two wives, by using the information to play games with people's lives? Your head is farther up your ass than I thought."

Aaron thought he detected a flinch, but Grayson recovered and shrugged. "All part of the game."

"Game? Is that what you call this? What the hell is so damned important you needed to snuff out the lives of five people? I can't believe it's just because your son-in-law was unfaithful. What about the shooting at your daughter's home? Do you even care she might have been hurt or killed?"

"My men are well-trained. Jennifer was not in harm's way, and don't be so dramatic. It was a rubber bullet."

"A rubber bullet that required stitches in your bodyguard's leg that might have easily taken out an eye."

"Walker is tough, like all the security men working for me. He'll bounce back. That was an insurance policy. We figured sooner or later, you would investigate Vic Bryant. I didn't know what Jared told him at the motel that night, but couldn't take the chance he knew enough to implicate the company. It was too much of a risk keeping him alive. We knew eventually he needed to be eliminated. We were banking that Bryant's death put this investigation to rest," he said and wagged his finger, "but you just wouldn't let it go."

"So that's why you hired your goons to come to my apartment and plant the earring."

"Unfortunately, the best laid plans don't take incompetence into account," Grayson said.

"What if Bryant didn't agree to kill Prescott?"

"Plan A, B, C, or Z, there's always a way to accomplish our goals."

"Why did you have Laura Carter killed?"

"She was another loose end. We kept tabs on her, and knew about the meeting at the park. We didn't know what she knew or saw that night, but couldn't take any chances."

"Did Vic Bryant kill her?"

"No, but his sniper training during his brief stint in the Army proved to be a very useful piece of information."

"Your shooter had an opportunity to take me out that night. Why didn't he?"

The bodyguard named Karl spoke up. "That would have been fine with me," he said, stroking his jaw. "You pack a decent punch for a city cop."

Aaron narrowed his eyes. "So it was you in my apartment that night. Just so you know, I expect restitution for the damage to my coffee table."

Karl gave a noncommittal shrug. "Bryant was already dead when I ripped the earring out of his ear."

"Yeah, except you're too stupid to know your left from your right."

Karl narrowed his eyes and grit his teeth, but didn't reply.

Aaron turned back to Grayson. "Bryant called your daughter's house that night from the Tremont. I wonder what she'd say if she knew you made her a suspect."

"Jennifer had no involvement in what happened. I knew I could protect her in any case."

"What puzzles me is why you didn't include Tim Lombardi in your plans." Aaron said.

Grayson frowned. "Who is …" he started.

Aaron managed a smile, despite the situation. "Ah, I see. The all-knowing Harlan Grayson isn't so all-knowing after all. Your daughter was having an affair with Lombardi. Odd you know all about the people working for you, but can't keep tabs on your own daughter."

Aaron felt pleased he'd hit a nerve. Grayson's eyes blazed fire for a moment before he looked beyond Aaron and nodded. Aaron's pleasure was short-lived, as the guard standing behind him jabbed the butt of his gun into his lower back. Aaron winced and bent over, holding his back. When he stood erect, Grayson was smirking.

"It's not a good idea to cross paths with me, Inspector. I don't blame my daughter for an affair. Jared played around on her, why should she be deprived?"

"An eye for an eye. Like father, like daughter. I still don't know why you hired Bryant to kill Jared Prescott, and what did Linda Sanchez do to deserve what you did to her?"

Grayson studied his fingernails. "A few minutes ago, you were right when you said it wasn't as simple as Jared being unfaithful to my daughter. It wasn't, and unfortunately, Linda got caught in the middle of it. I hoped to spare her, but she started asking questions, and Jared started digging into places he didn't belong. The truth is, Inspector, you've stumbled onto something way out of your league."

"I'm sure you're dying to tell me," Aaron said.

Grayson stood up from the chair, walked over and leaned against a table, folding his arms in front of his chest. "Do you know what it's like to lose a loved one to terrorism?"

"We've covered this already, ad nauseam," Aaron said, then took a moment to assess the situation. The bodyguards stood too far apart, and any attempt to turn the tables would be certain suicide. His only option was to keep Grayson talking to buy time, although unfortunately, he wasn't expecting backup, so he was on his own.

"Jared was nosing around," Grayson said. "I knew if he found out, he'd threaten to expose us and the project, but not for any noble cause. He wanted control of the company. All he needed to do was wait two years or so and I would have given him the company. I despised him for his impatience and greed, but in the end, it was for the best. He didn't deserve my daughter."

"So you figured eliminating him would solve two problems."

"We're in a war, Inspector. Casualties are inevitable."

"You've been watching too much television."

"Jared got in the way of something bigger than he was, Inspector. He should never have stuck his nose where it didn't belong. I couldn't let that happen, so I hired Vic

Bryant to arrange a meeting with Jared at the motel. He promised Jared key information on the project in exchange for one hundred thousand dollars. Jared didn't know he was dealing with Bryant. I needed Bryant, he needed the money, and their sordid history made him the perfect candidate. Using Linda's car was part of the plan. People were more likely to remember a red sports car than the person driving it. Once Bryant killed Jared and got the money, he delivered it to my men. He kept fifty-grand, the other half paid Kirby's debt. I wasn't about to use my own money."

"Buying someone to do your dirty work doesn't surprise me," Aaron said, "but why didn't you just have one of your goons kill Jared? Why go to all the trouble to implicate other people?"

"My *goons*, as you put it, had no motive. Vic Bryant did, and I'm smart enough to know even the best planned crime leaves incriminating evidence. Besides, as you know by now, I like challenges."

"For all of your planning and scheming, and efforts to throw suspicion somewhere else, I'm here because you screwed up. Screwed up, *big time*."

"I admire your courage and resolve, Inspector. Few people in your situation could retain a sense of humor. You would have done well working for me. But don't get cocky, because you're not going anywhere."

"If that's a threat, I'm sure even *you're* smart enough to know what killing a cop means. I don't care who you are, who you know, or how much power you think you have, people know I'm here. Killing me won't stop whatever you're planning. There will be others. So what exactly is this project, and why do you keep on saying we and us?"

"The project? Yes, the project," Grayson said. "Losing my second wife on nine-eleven provided a new perspective on life and the way I viewed it." His eyes flared. "I felt hatred toward those people I never thought possible."

"By those people I assume you mean Middle Easterners?"

Grayson shook his head. "I'm not that narrow-minded, Inspector. Watch the news. Read the newspapers. Terrorism is a global problem. It's a virus. After nine-eleven, I grieved as all Americans grieved, but once I came to terms with the tragedy of my wife's death, I decided to do something about it."

"A noble ambition," Aaron said with sarcasm, "but the U.S. military has been fighting wars in the Middle East for years without resolution."

"I agree, and I'm afraid that will continue for some time, so decided to attack terrorism on a more national level, make a statement closer to home. I'm sure you're aware of what is going on in Mexico. It's as close to home as we get. Tens of thousands of innocent Americans have been slaughtered by the Mexican drug cartels."

"You've left a lot of dead bodies in your wake, all based on nothing more than revenge."

"Not revenge, Inspector, *justice*. We're going to make things right in a country where the leadership is too afraid to take it to the next level, and do what is necessary to ensure the safety of its citizens."

"Call it what you want, this is about retaliation for the death of your wife on nine-eleven. That wasn't the Mexican drug cartel. Why don't you go after the real perpetrators?"

"As much as we'd like to, we don't have the resources, not to mention the complexity due to logistics. We knew striking closer to home would have tangible and immediate benefits. Granted, the plan is risky and has potential for civilian casualties, but what war doesn't?"

"Like Paul Delaney and Alex Harris," Aaron said. His expectation of getting a reaction from Grayson met with disappointment.

"Yes, that was unfortunate, but Delaney was doomed because he was infected. We couldn't risk an autopsy. Harris wanted answers and pushed too hard. You'd be amazed at how easy it is to plant evidence, even on someone with no criminal history."

"Money solves all problems, doesn't it, Grayson?"

Grayson shrugged. "Once I commit to a cause, I follow through until it succeeds."

"Or fails," Aaron said.

Grayson squinted at Aaron. "Our project is too close to fruition for anyone to stop us now."

"You said Delaney was infected," Aaron said. "Infected how, and is that what this project is all about?"

Grayson smiled. "Your questions are beginning to bore me, but since you won't be around for long, I see no reason to leave you in the dark." He looked toward his left at a partially opened door. "Nathan, do you have anything to add?"

Senator Nathan Caldwell entered the room. He was heavyset with a round face, receding hairline, and tan complexion. He wore dark blue Dockers slacks and a white polo shirt.

He motioned to Karl, who came over. The Senator whispered into his ear. Karl nodded and walked to the elevator.

"Where is he going?" Grayson asked.

Senator Caldwell held up a hand. "He'll be back, Harlan," he said and turned to Aaron. "I heard a lot about you, Inspector. It's a shame to meet under such unfortunate circumstances."

"You're a lot porkier than you look on TV," Aaron said. "What's your involvement in this?"

"You're right, Harlan, he does have an interesting sense of humor. Suffice it to say, I have a vested interest in the project. With Harlan's help, we'll be able to provide our Mexican allies with appropriate aid in their war against the drug cartels."

"What do you mean by *appropriate aid*?"

Caldwell turned to Grayson. "Harlan, your company's research and development made this all possible. Why don't you explain it to our friend? I think the Inspector's tenacity and resolve earns him the right to an explanation. Besides, like you said, he's not going anywhere."

"Of course, Nathan," Grayson replied, and turned to Aaron. "With my company's resources and technology, along with Nathan's political influence, we have the means and resources to make a real difference."

"What resources and technology are you talking about?" Aaron asked. His time was running out, so keeping Grayson talking was the only way to delay the inevitable. Given the size of the man's ego, that wouldn't be difficult.

"Chemical weapons research and development has come a long way. Today we have the capability to limit the range of the effects of chemical weapons over a concentrated area so unintentional loss of life is minimal."

"Minimal, but not eliminated," Aaron said.

"It's unfortunate, but war does carry a certain degree of risk. I've seen it and fought in it. Watching innocent people lose their lives is never easy."

"Collateral damage, huh, Grayson?"

"That depends on your perspective."

Aaron turned to the Senator. "I don't care what he says. Grayson's motivation is pure revenge. I still don't get why you are involved. Is this part of your campaign to lower taxes, provide shelter for the homeless, and illegally produce chemical weapons to eliminate the enemy?"

"The American people will come around," the Senator said. "Drastic measures are required when nothing else is working. Besides, we've taken all necessary precautions to ensure this cannot be tied to us in case it backfires."

Aaron turned to Grayson. "You've manufactured chemical weapons for genocide, and it doesn't matter who the intended target is. You've become a terrorist and allowed your thirst for revenge twist you into believing you're a patriot." To Caldwell he said, "Your plan is falling apart, Senator. Do you think my superiors aren't privy to what I've uncovered? Eliminating me won't change the outcome."

"I covered all the bases, Inspector."

"If you covered all the bases, I wouldn't be here," Aaron said.

"Call it dumb luck, people that can't follow instructions, big mouths, loose ends, but it doesn't matter," Grayson said. "Any evidence will be buried with you. That's why Linda needed to be eliminated. She was hired to handle the paperwork. Manufacturing chemical weapons under the radar required a lot of time and patience. The raw materials must be obtained in small quantities. Nathan's experience working Homeland Security allowed us to bypass security checks. Linda was getting suspicious, then Jared got into the act and pressed me for information.

"So, there *are* more people involved?" Aaron asked.

"We kept the staff on the project to a minimum," Grayson said. "They knew only that they were working on a top secret government project and were paid very well."

"You must understand, Inspector, this project is simply the beginning," Senator Caldwell added. "Once the Mexican drug cartels are crippled, the nation will realize President Kelsing's stand on terrorism is too passive."

"This is nothing more than political greed," Aaron said. "Even if you succeed with your plan, what do you expect will happen? The nation will impeach President Kelsing and put you in the White House? You both are out of your minds." He turned back to Grayson. "What about Eddie Rivers? Just another casualty of war?"

Grayson hunched his shoulders as if eliminating a human life was no more dramatic than taking out the garbage. "He was snooping into Warren's affairs. His death was meant to send your investigation in another direction."

"Eddie was a good friend of mine."

"That is a shame," Grayson said with a smirk.

"Be thankful you have an armed bodyguard, because right now I'd love nothing more than to tear your throat out."

Grayson smiled. "Due process be damned, huh?"

"Yet another one of your mistakes, Grayson," Aaron said, struggling to keep his emotions under control. "Leaving two twenty dollar bills torn in half in his pocket proved it was personal. Your plan had more holes than a golf course."

"Don't make me out to be an evil man, Inspector. I see the big picture. Sacrifices are necessary for the good of the country. That's like blaming the U.S. government for every soldier's death during a war. I must admit, though, I have gained a measure of respect for your dedication. I like your never-say-die attitude. It's something I look for when I hire people to work for me. You have proven to be a worthy adversary."

"Is that why you're spilling your guts? Or is this just another way of inflating your ego?"

"Consider it a farewell gift," Grayson said. "Like I said, Jared didn't deserve my daughter."

"I've talked to your daughter. She's no saint, and I don't think she's any more deserving than he was," Aaron countered, knowing the comment was probably not in his best interests. Aaron saw anger flicker in Grayson's eyes.

"Insulting my daughter won't help your cause," he said with a tight lip.

Aaron shrugged. "According to you, I'm a dead man anyway. I might as well go down fighting."

"Who really paid the ultimate price? Jared made far more enemies than friends while he worked for me, and cheated on my daughter. Vic Bryant was a loser and got what he deserved. As for the other two, one was a snitch with a dim future at best, the other nothing more than a high-class hooker. Linda, well, she disappointed me. She brought it on herself and meddled where she didn't belong. I treated her well, and she didn't appreciate it. You weigh those lives against the lives we'll save in our war against terrorism, and you have to agree it's a small price to pay."

"How are you going to explain a dead cop?" Aaron asked. "Tell the authorities I broke into your lab and you shot me for trespassing?"

Grayson closed one eye and wagged his finger. "That's what I like about you, Inspector. You have good intuition. You're close but it's a little more complex." He waved his arm. "Look around you. This building is old and filled with dangerous chemicals. Sometimes, even the strictness safety standards fail to prevent accidents."

"You're no different than any other criminal with big plans," Aaron said. "What amazes me is the number of mistakes you made."

"I don't make mistakes, Inspector. Whether or not you admit it, you were running around like the proverbial headless chicken."

At that moment, Senator Caldwell's cell phone rang. He listened for a moment, and then said, "Bring them in."

Grayson turned to the Senator. "Bring who in?"

His question was answered when the elevator door opened.

Aaron turned. Jennifer Prescott and Mitchell Walker were led into the room by Karl, his gun trained at their backs.

"Dad, what's going on here?" Jennifer said. "This man came to my house holding a gun. Why did he bring us here?"

Grayson opened his mouth to answer, but Aaron interrupted.

"Go ahead, Daddy. Tell her how you ordered the murder of her husband and four other people. Tell her…"

"Shut up!" Grayson yelled and whirled to look at the Senator. "Nathan, what's going on? My daughter has nothing to do with this." He turned back. "Karl, lower your gun."

For the first time since Aaron met Grayson, he sounded out of control. It was music to Aaron's ears.

The Senator shook his head slowly. "I'm sorry, Harlan, there are just too many loose ends."

"What… you will not dare touch my daughter…"

"Karl, bring them over here next to Harlan," the Senator said.

Karl waved his gun. "You heard the man."

Walker and Jennifer walked over and stood next to Grayson. "Dad, what is he talking about?" Jennifer asked. "This isn't making sense. Talk to me–please." Her voice cracked and Aaron noticed her eyes moisten even from where he stood. Her expression suggested she knew nothing of her father and the Senator's plan.

Grayson turned to the Senator. "Nathan, you can't do this."

"It's too late," the Senator said then nodded to Karl, who pointed his gun at Grayson's chest.

"Nathan, don't," Grayson pleaded. "You need me."

"I'm sorry, Harlan. I can't allow these people to ruin my plans."

"*Your* plans?" Grayson yelled and then shoved Karl against a table and lunged at the Senator. He swung his right arm awkwardly, but the move caught the Senator by surprise. The punch connected on the side of the Senator's face. He pitched backward and fell to the floor.

Karl recovered and fired his gun. The bullet struck Grayson in the side. He reeled for a moment before turning to face Karl, a look of disbelief on his face, then fell to the floor.

"No! Dad!" Jennifer screamed.

This was Aaron's only chance. Karl was focused on Grayson and the Senator. Not taking advantage of the opportunity meant certain death for not only him, but Jennifer Prescott and Walker as well. Another three bodies, four if Grayson died, added to the body count.

But he couldn't do it by himself. He could take one bodyguard but not both. He had only one other possible ally in the room. "Walker!" he yelled.

Fortunately, Walker reacted. He landed a karate chop to Karl's wrist, and the gun clattered to the floor. Walker followed with an elbow to Karl's face, landing flush on the nose. Karl fell backward and landed on the floor, clutching his nose as blood gushed between his fingers.

At the same time Walker engaged Karl, Aaron turned and grabbed the other bodyguard by the shoulders before he could react. As they hit the floor, the force knocked the Glock from the bodyguard's hand.

Aaron landed on top and pushed his left hand against the bodyguard's chest, followed by a right cross to the jaw. The crack was a welcome sound. Aaron reached over and retrieved the Glock. Grabbing the bodyguard's shirt, he turned him over and reached for his handcuffs.

"Consider this the first installment on my coffee table," he said as he cuffed the bodyguard. "You can collect the money from your sorry ass friend, Karl."

He turned. Walker was holding the gun on Karl, lying on the floor, still nursing his broken nose. The Senator lay sprawled motionless on the floor. Grayson was lying on his back next to the Senator.

Jennifer, who had dropped to the floor when the first shot was fired, recovered when she saw the danger was over, and ran to her father. "Dad, are you all right?"

Aaron left Karl on the floor and walked over to Grayson. His eyes fluttered, his breathing was shallow, his face a mask of pain.

With significant effort, he lifted his head and clutched Jennifer's arm. "I'm sorry for everything. I just wanted for you to be happy," he said, laboring to catch his breath.

"Dad, please don't talk," Jennifer said, stroking her father's cheek. "We'll get you some help. You're going to be all right. *We're* going to be all right." She looked up at Aaron, her eyes wet and tears running down her cheeks. "Please, help him."

Aaron called for an ambulance and backup, then inspected the wound on Grayson's back. Blood had soaked his shirt. The odds of him surviving were long. "The ambulance is on its way."

Jennifer gazed into her father's eyes for a few moments before she, too, must have realized her father wouldn't make it. She sat back on the cold cement floor and buried her head in her hands.

Aaron placed a hand on Jennifer's elbow and squeezed it lightly. He saw her in a different light. She was no longer a woman that thumbed her rich nose at society. The events of the past three minutes made all the money, comfort, and social class irrelevant. She now a vulnerable innocent victim of a father that fell far short of his parental responsibility to pursue his own agenda.

Two minutes later, the ambulance arrived, and the paramedics put Grayson on a gurney and hooked him up to an IV. By this time, his eyes were closed; his breathing sporadic and weak.

Jennifer followed the EMT out of the lab and climbed into the back of the ambulance.

Five minutes after the ambulance drove away, Vince Sherman arrived, accompanied by Sam and three backup units. The officers in two of the units cuffed the Senator, put him and the bodyguards into the patrol cars, and took them away.

Aaron and Sherman stood in the middle of the room.

"How did you guys get here so fast?" Aaron asked.

"A neighbor of the Prescott's called the police and said she saw someone taking Mrs. Prescott and another man from her home by force. What happened here, Aaron?"

"Suffice it to say, after reading my report, both you and the commissioner will need a handful of Tylenol and/or a bottle of Scotch."

"That bad?" Sherman asked.

"The killings were part of a much bigger plan, masterminded by Grayson and the Senator."

"You know, Aaron, I wouldn't blame you if you said I told you so."

"Not my style," Aaron replied, then followed Sherman and Sam out the door, while the third unit remained until the crime scene team arrived.

Chapter Thirty-Nine

On Friday, September 9th, Aaron presented his report of the events at Harlan Grayson's lab to Vince Sherman.

Following an extended debrief from Aaron, two FBI agents from Washington assumed custody of Senator Caldwell and the two bodyguards.

Harlan Grayson died on the way to the hospital.

An investigation of Grayson, Senator Caldwell, and ChemPhen, resulted in the interrogation of the members of the lab used to manufacture Sarin gas. A man named Kurt Huber, an alias, was a German scientist heading up the project. He was arrested and interrogated. His real name was Jonas Friedman and he was under investigation with Interpol. Senator Caldwell had used his network to smuggle Friedman out of Germany with all the appropriate identification papers.

Thanks to a recommendation from Vince Sherman and the police commissioner, Bryan Dawson got back his job with the newspaper, complete with a substantial raise, which Dawson called, "pain and suffering back pay."

Aaron returned to his apartment at the end of the day, and tossed his keys on the kitchen table. He was looking forward to the weekend for a much needed and he believed, much-deserved break. He stood in the kitchen staring at the phone and considered for a moment calling Jennifer Prescott. She would have questions, starting with 'why?' Rumors and speculation regarding her father and Senator Caldwell would flow like a waterfall, and the media would be relentless in the months to come. None of what happened was her fault, but she was the only person left to endure the inevitable investigation and publicity. He turned away from the phone, deciding some things are better left alone.

The next morning, Aaron showered and fixed a hearty breakfast of scrambled eggs, sausage, wheat toast, and coffee. He sat down and ate while gazing through the patio window. Clouds covered the sky, and the weatherman had predicted thunderstorms, offering hope for long-awaited relief from the drought. As he downed a forkful of eggs, the buzzer sounded.

He got up and pressed the intercom. "Yes?"

"It's Rachel. Can I come up?"

"Of course," Aaron said. He pressed the buzzer, removed the latch, and opened the door a crack. A minute later, Rachel tapped on the door and entered the apartment. She looked good in a white tank top and blue jogging shorts, smelling of perfume.

"Good morning," Aaron said. "I was just eating breakfast. Care for some eggs and sausage?"

Rachel sniffed the air. "Yes, I smelled it from the hallway, but I already ate, thank you. I will have a cup of coffee though."

Aaron gestured to the kitchen. "Help yourself."

Rachel poured herself a cup of coffee and joined Aaron in the dining room. "Did you see the news? Your case was the leading story. A Senator plotting to supply chemical weapons to Mexico? That's pretty big, not to mention, more than a little scary."

"I just got out of the shower. What did they say?" Aaron asked.

"Shower? How come you didn't wait for me?"

Aaron stopped a forkful of eggs halfway to his mouth and looked at Rachel with raised eyebrows. She had a gleam in her eyes. "Well, if I knew you were coming over…" he started then paused, prompting her to complete the sentence.

"Next time, I'll call ahead and give you a heads up," she said. Before Aaron could answer, she said, "The FBI interrogated the Senator, but so far he's not talking."

"That doesn't surprise me. Politicians can be tight-lipped when they want to be. Too bad they don't take that approach more often. Not much of what they say amounts to a hill of beans. He's probably looking at the death penalty. One thing is for sure, President Kelsing won't need to worry about competition in the next election, at least not from Caldwell."

The phone rang, interrupting the conversation.

"Excuse me," Aaron said, then got up and answered on the third ring.

"Hello? Hi, Vince," he said, then covered the receiver and mouthed the word 'chief' to Rachel. He listened for a few minutes with an occasional 'oh, is that right,' or 'I see,' and then hung up the phone.

"So, what did your boss have to say?"

Aaron returned to the dining room and sat down. "What do you think about that?"

Rachel playfully slapped Aaron on the arm. "Come on, tell me."

"The two bodyguards, Karl Bradford and Roy Tillman, spilled their guts in exchange for a reduced sentence. They confessed to their role in the killings, even where to find the body of Paul Delaney. They said Grayson and the Senator were working with a high-ranking official in the Mexican government to produce the Sarin gas. They planned to deliver it tomorrow." Aaron sipped his coffee and stared straight ahead. "Tomorrow is September eleventh."

"Wow, that's eerie." Rachel breathed.

"Not to Harlan Grayson. He planned everything down to the smallest detail, all for revenge for his second wife's death in the nine-eleven terrorist attacks. You know, the idea wasn't all bad on the surface. Elimination of the drug cartels would do a lot for our nation and Mexico as well, but things got out of hand. It's the same with cop vigilantes. They want justice the courts can't or won't provide, so they take the law into their own hands. Sooner or later, innocent people get caught in the middle."

"Uh-huh," Rachel said.

Aaron looked at Rachel. She had a smug grin on her face. "What do you mean, uh-huh?"

"It sounds to me like you've finally hooked the big fish you've been after for so long. Maybe now you can quit complaining and admit you're good at what you do."

"Funny you should mention that. One of the FBI agents actually asked me if I'd ever consider working for the Bureau. I must admit it is satisfying to know I've done something with potentially far-reaching effects. I guess for now, I'll keep my day job, so I'll need to find something else to complain about."

"I don't doubt that for a second," she said, "but it's okay. I love you just the way you are."

He looked into her eyes and matched her smile, wondering if using the 'L' word was figurative, especially after her comment about the shower.

Rather than sit with a dumb look on his face, he changed the subject. "Speaking of careers, what's going on with Seattle?"

"I turned it down," she said without hesitation. "I'd be too far away from family. I don't know anyone in Seattle, and it would be like starting over. The money would be good, sure, but money isn't the most important thing in the world. There is too much I would miss about Chicago." She looked into Aaron's eyes. "Actually, I'm hoping opportunities here present themselves."

The tone of her voice and the look in her eyes was not lost on Aaron.

"I'm glad," he said, then leaned forward and kissed her long and hard. They embraced before he broke away.

He put his hands on her shoulders and gazed deep into her eyes "What do you say we convene to someplace more comfortable?"

She gestured at the table. "Your eggs are getting cold."

"It's been more than ten seconds. They're already too cold."

Rachel angled her head toward the living room. "I hope you don't mean the sofa. Last time we tried that I tore my favorite blouse."

"I was thinking about the bedroom."

She smiled. "In the interest of safety and saving on clothing expenses, I'll concede."

They got up from the table and walked through the kitchen, arms wrapped tight around each other's waist.

Suddenly, she stopped.

"What's wrong?" he asked, hoping she hadn't changed her mind.

She stepped back, took the phone off the hook, and laid it on the kitchen counter. "Let's make sure we don't have any interruptions this time. With what you accomplished, I'm sure the media is primed to bombard you with interview requests."

Aaron nodded, and they went into the bedroom. He closed the door behind them.

Less than a minute later, thunder cracked in the sky, followed by rain pelting on the windows.

It was a welcome sound to Aaron's ears, and on any other day he would sit at the window and watch the rain, but today his mind was elsewhere.

The End

About Jack Strandburg

Jack Strandburg was born and raised in Cleveland Ohio. He is a degreed professional with a background in Accounting and Information Technology and recently retired after more than 33 years working for a Fortune 500 company. He has been writing since his teenage years.

He self-published an inspirational titled *An Appointment With God: One Ordinary Man's Journey to Faith Through Prayer*, by Trafford Publishing.

His first published novel by Solstice Publishing is *Hustle Henry and the Cue-Ball Kid*, a parody of the movie, *Butch Cassidy and the Sundance Kid*.

His third work, a novella titled *The Monogram Killer*, published by Solstice Publishing, was released in May, 2016.

He is currently working on a short story titled *A Matter of Honor*, writing journals for an upcoming inspirational non-fiction book; and completed 70% of a first draft for a second mystery novel titled *War Zone*.

He is an editor and proofreader for Solstice Publishing.

Jack currently lives with his wife and two grown children, in Sugar Land, Texas. He has three grandchildren.

<u>Social Media</u>:

Website: https://jstrandburg.wordpress.com/

Blog: https://jackstr952.wordpress.com/

Facebook: https://www.facebook.com/jack.strandburg

LinkedIn:
https://www.linkedin.com/in/jack-strandburg-0465a313

Amazon Author Page:
http://www.amazon.com/-/e/B00CM9P9L2

If you enjoyed this story, check out these other Solstice Publishing books by Jack Strandburg:

Hustle Henry and The Cue Ball Kid

Clarence Flannery was luckier than most men his age to discover his life's ambition, particularly in the unpredictable years just following the Civil War. Born with an unmatched skill to play pool, he left his home in Kansas when he turned twenty-six and traveled throughout the Southwestern United States to make his mark as a legendary pool hustler, with every intention of amassing a fortune in the process.

Clarence needed help for both support and protection, and recruited James Skinner as his partner, along with nine other highly-skilled pool players to assist him in his quest. Wanting to be included in the same sentence as Attila the Hun and Alexander the Great, Clarence changed his name to Hustle Henry, Skinner became the Cue-Ball Kid, and the eleven men would go down in history as The Hole-in-the-Table-Bunch, known far and wide for hustling wannabe pool sharks out of their life savings.

All goes to plan and life has a rosy and profitable outlook, but Henry and his men want more than what pool halls and saloons offer, so they decide to challenge the more affluent clientele on a riverboat.

Initially, the venture proves profitable, but the millionaire tycoon and owner of the fleet of riverboats, takes exception, and intends to bring down the Bunch and thrust Henry and The Kid into a life of destitution.

Taking along the Kid's girlfriend, Penelope Henderson, the

Kid and Henry flee to South America – where there will be a final showdown…

Hustle Henry and the Cue-Ball Kid is a fiction work of Western humor with an interesting and amusing cast of characters.

http://bookgoodies.com/a/B00BJ83O5K

The Monogram Killer

When Julia Ballard meets Kelly Nichols, she believed he was the man of her dreams. Julia's best friend has doubts, and her investigation into Nichols's life encourages her suspicions. Despite Jessica's warnings, Julia is convinced he is sincere and cares for her. Nichols is hiding secrets from a legacy he cannot escape, and Julia is the key to a sinister plan. When two homicide detectives combine forces to search for a serial killer, it becomes a race to see who accomplishes their goal first.

http://bookgoodies.com/a/B01G2B7IIC

www.ingramcontent.com/pod-product-compliance
Lightning Source LLC
Chambersburg PA
CBHW072205030726
47501CB00015B/649